A sanctuary

"That's what you've created here, and I will be forever grateful. I have been so alone. Unable to see direction for my life. Not sure if there even is one... When you've loved and lost, you wonder who you are. Whether you can go on. Or even want to."

Brady pondered whether he should continue reading the journal. The words were too emotionally raw. Some other person had come here full of the same thoughts and feelings he had. Unable to help himself, he turned back to the page.

"Regardless of how desolate I feel right now, I have to believe that somewhere out there is someone for me. Someone I can trust. Someone I can love."

Brady stared for the longest time at the signature. Simple. Bare. Exposed. "Nell."

Nell, whoever she was, was more optimistic than he was. God, he hated his blatant, whining self-pity. If Nell had been willing to look for something, why couldn't he?

Absently he realized he was still holding the guest book, his forefinger marking Nell's page. He reread the entry and a crazy idea entered his head. But no crazier than what he'd been doing.

Tomorrow, after he checked out, he would drive to Fayetteville to find Nell.

Dear Reader,

Have you ever experienced a time when all around you others seemed happy, productive and blessed, while you felt burdened by failure, disappointment or loss?

Recently my husband and I had a delightful getaway to a wonderfully hospitable B and B in Jessieville, Arkansas. In each room was a small journal in which previous occupants had recorded impressions of their stay, describing such benefits as reduced stress, renewal of relationships, a redirection of goals—and, of course, special romantic times.

I couldn't help myself. My writer's imagination kicked in. What if (the question with which every story idea begins) someone in the depths of despair were to read such entries? The contrast between the experiences of others and one's own emotional state could be devastating. But…*what if* there was a single entry echoing that same sense of isolation?

Thus was Brady Logan born. A man who has lost almost everything and turned his back on the rest. A man without purpose and direction until he reads that one journal entry that sends him on a quest to find a woman named Nell— who may be the only one capable of understanding why he feels as he does.

It was a pleasure to send the urbane, successful Brady Logan to Fayetteville, Arkansas, a far cry from his Silicon Valley milieu. There he rediscovers the value of simple things and the healing power of new relationships, and, with Nell's help, learns that life offers an abundance of second chances if one can put the past in perspective.

May Nell and Brady affirm your faith in new beginnings!

Laura Abbot

My Name Is Nell
Laura Abbot

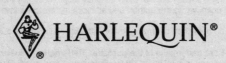

TORONTO • NEW YORK • LONDON
AMSTERDAM • PARIS • SYDNEY • HAMBURG
STOCKHOLM • ATHENS • TOKYO • MILAN • MADRID
PRAGUE • WARSAW • BUDAPEST • AUCKLAND

ISBN 0-373-71162-X

MY NAME IS NELL

Visit us at www.eHarlequin.com

Printed in U.S.A.

For my friend Jackie
with appreciation, affection and admiration

Books by Laura Abbot

HARLEQUIN SUPERROMANCE

Don't miss any of our special offers. Write to us at the
following address for information on our newest releases.

Harlequin Reader Service
U.S.: 3010 Walden Ave., P.O. Box 1325, Buffalo, NY 14269
Canadian: P.O. Box 609, Fort Erie, Ont. L2A 5X3

PROLOGUE

GRIPPING THE STEERING WHEEL of his Escalade, Brady Logan clenched his teeth and focused on the road ahead. The road *away*. He should give a damn. Most men would. But he felt nothing, not even relief.

When he'd made his final tour of the elaborate, expensive, now-empty house in the upscale Silicon Valley community where he, Brooke and their daughter Nicole had made their home, he'd been dry-eyed, detached. After locking the front door for the last time, he'd paused, studying the blinding white-stucco exterior, waiting for any emotion that would make him feel alive. Nothing. Only the familiar numbness.

Now, driving past the sleek four-story headquarters of L&S TechWare, nestled among the lushest landscaping an unlimited budget could provide, he still felt nothing.

Eight months ago he couldn't have imagined picking up like this and walking out. With only ingenious ideas, damn hard work and luck, he and his friend Carl Sutton had built a successful software company, now traded on the Nasdaq. He'd married a beautiful blue-eyed California blonde, purchased the gadget-laden home and cars, hired a live-in housekeeper and yard man and been accepted for membership in clubs so prestigious you didn't inquire about initiation fees, you simply wrote the check—a *large* one. In short, he had "arrived."

The best things, though, money couldn't buy. Brooke had been far more than a trophy wife. She was his other half, full of fun where he was serious, understanding of his long hours and driven work ethic. When he'd thought life couldn't get any better, Nicole had come along and grown into a loving, giggly, remarkably unspoiled preteen who'd won his heart in a way no one else ever had.

Brady gave L&S TechWare one last glance in the rearview mirror, then headed for the Interstate. It didn't matter where he was going. He should care, but he didn't. The important thing was that he *was* going.

Carl had accused him of running away. Hell, maybe he was. As he saw it, though, he had two choices. Stay and slowly, steadily, implode, or get out of Dodge and look for any spark left of the man named Brady Logan.

Here all that remained were sights, sounds, smells and memories—oh, God, the memories—reminding him that in one horrible instant, everything he loved had been wiped from the face of the earth.

Vaporized by one irresponsible drunken son of a bitch, who just happened to be driving a loaded gasoline tanker.

CHAPTER ONE

Late July, seven weeks later
Arkansas

"I DON'T SEE WHY I have to go." Abby slouched in her seat in the airport lounge, kicking at her carry-on bag. Two hanks of straight blond hair hid her features, but Nell Porter could well imagine the surly put-upon look on her thirteen-year-old daughter's face.

"You'll have a good time at your father's," Nell suggested without the faintest trace of conviction in her voice.

"Yeah, sure. Like there's so much to do in stupid Texas."

Nell sighed. This was yet another reprise of the conversation they had once a month when she took Abby to Northwest Arkansas Regional Airport to fly to Dallas for her court-ordered visit with Rick. Abby had no way of knowing how Nell dreaded the gnawing in her stomach every time she had to consign her daughter's care to the airlines—and then to Rick and Clarice, his second wife. In fact, she didn't know which was worse, thinking of her daughter all alone thousands of feet above the ground in these troubled times or picturing her in the manipulative hands of the far-from-maternal Clarice, aka The Other Woman. Even six years later and after professional counseling, bitterness blindsided her, along with those all-too-familiar feelings of unworthiness and betrayal. She stared at her fingers, locked in a death grip, then quite consciously separated her hands and drew a deep breath. That was all behind her. By some miracle, and with the help of family and friends, she'd survived. If only she didn't have to send Abby into the situation…

"Why do you make me go?" Abby's voice was laced with belligerence.

"Honey, we've been over all this. It's not a choice either of us has."

"I hate going. I don't have any friends there."

"What about your dad? He'd be disappointed not to see you."

"Maybe." Looking up finally, Abby tucked a strand of hair behind one bestudded ear. "But he doesn't have a clue what to do with me when I get there. I mean, how many times do I want to go to Six Flags? Besides, I'm missing Tonya's birthday party."

Abby's remarks evoked guilt Nell knew was irrational. As if she could have done any more to influence the custody decision. Or changed the fact Rick was entitled to spend time with their child. Did Abby ever tell her father how she felt about the visits? No. Whenever she was with him, she did a good imitation of the dutiful daughter. Inevitably when she came home, Nell faced the task of picking up the pieces, putting them back together as best she could and then sending Abby on her way the next time. Like now. Abby needed a punching bag, and Nell was handy.

Somehow that insight didn't alleviate the hurt her daughter's petulance generated.

The mechanical drone of a commuter plane drawing up to the gate was accompanied by the disassociated voice of the loudspeaker announcing the arrival of the aircraft Abby would be taking to Dallas. "You need to go through security now," Nell said, rising to her feet.

"I guess." Abby stood, shouldered her bag and trailed Nell all the way to the short line of passengers waiting at the checkpoint.

Nell watched Abby's expression settle into affected pseudo-sophistication, the bored look of the veteran traveler. Yet when she turned and gave Nell a perfunctory hug, her clear gray eyes held not resentment, but misgiving. "Bye, Mom. See ya Sunday night."

"I'll be here," Nell said. She watched Abby pass through the metal detector and pluck her bag from the conveyer belt, then waited to catch a final glimpse of her daughter's rail-thin body as she descended the escalator and vanished from sight.

The empty feeling was always the same. It was enough to drive a person to drink.

But that was out of the question.

STELLA JANES SETTLED in the porch chair next to her daughter, then turned her gaze toward Abby, who stood at the edge of the lawn verging on an elaborate flower bed. "Do you really think that skirt length is appropriate for a middle school child?"

Nell stifled a groan. With too much idle time, her mother overly concerned herself with family. "It's what all the girls are wearing."

Stella continued staring at her granddaughter, who was herding her toddler cousin around the backyard. "I suppose, but that doesn't mean I have to like it."

"Like what?" Nell's statuesque older sister Lily, whose name fit her as well as the chic beige linen slacks and blouse she wore, approached with a tray of lemonade.

"Abby's hem length," Stella said.

Lily paused, then followed her mother's gaze. "I see what you mean."

Nell should be used to it by now, but their united front rankled. Lily and Stella tended to share a similar outlook, usually quite different from hers. They enjoyed what Nell thought of as "girly things" like quilting, home decoration and scrapbooking, while she had always preferred gardening, furniture refinishing and sports. No wonder she had gravitated to her father, finding refuge—and acceptance—in her role as "daddy's girl." There were moments, like this, when she felt like an outsider. As teenagers, her relationship with Lily had been strained, but they had grown closer as adults. Sometimes, in recent years, Lily had even dared to swim against the tide of their mother's wishes. But not often. And not today.

Lily distributed the icy glasses. "When does school start?"

Grateful for the change of subject, Nell let out a breath. "A week from Monday."

"In my day, school never started in August," Stella reminded them. "Always the day after Labor Day."

"It can't come any too soon for me," Nell said. "Abby needs a regular schedule. Time hangs pretty heavy on her hands." When she was at work, Nell worried about her daughter. Aside from helping Lily with little Chase, Abby was at the mercy of friends' mothers thoughtful enough to invite her to their houses. Otherwise she slept late and watched God-knows-what on TV.

Lily sank into the chaise and crossed her feet at the ankles. "At least next week she'll be on vacation with Rick."

"That's supposed to comfort me?"

"Why not? You'll have seven glorious days all to yourself."

"Right. Seven interminable days to worry whether Rick will pay her any attention or, heaven forbid, let Clarice take her shopping like she did last summer." Nell nodded in her daughter's direction. "You think *that* skirt's short? You didn't see the outrageous outfit her charming stepmother selected to complement the salon job she set up for Abby's hair and nails. When she came home, she looked like a prepubescent Britney Spears."

Lily giggled, restoring Nell's good humor. "Clarice always was a piece of work. Poor Abby."

Stella rolled her eyes. "If I live to be a hundred, I'll never understand it."

"It" was the topic her mother avoided. The disgrace of Rick's affair with the "younger woman," the ensuing small-town scandal and the unthinkable divorce, one more way Nell had disappointed her mother's expectations.

"Water under the bridge," Nell mumbled.

"You'll get through the next week all right?" Her mother's anxious eyes signaled her unspoken concern.

Nell clutched her lemonade. Would she forever be under scrutiny? "Yes, Mother. I'll be fine."

She couldn't fault her mother. Not really. She had only herself to blame, but it had taken her a long time—and cost her a great deal of pain—to reach that conclusion.

WHO WAS HE KIDDING ANYWAY? Nothing was better. If anything, it was worse. Brady stared into the murky depths of the thick ceramic mug he cradled between his hands, oblivious to the early morning chatter around him. These Main Street cafés were running together in his mind—each whirling, grease-layered ceiling fan, red leatherette counter stool and kitchen pass-through indistinguishable from the next. Though the spur-and-antler décor in Wyoming differed from this Arkansas country calico, the smell of bacon frying and the cloying cheerfulness of the morning-shift waitress were unsettlingly predictable.

"Decided?" The middle-aged redhead swiped a damp rag across the counter, then extracted a pad and pencil from her apron and eyed him speculatively.

"The special and a large o.j., please."

"Got it," she said and, with economy of motion, refilled his coffee.

Fortunately the adjacent stool was empty. He couldn't have tolerated another desultory conversation highlighted by comments on the weather and the market—cattle, wheat or stock, depending on where he was. Two months. He mentally ticked off the states he'd passed through—Oregon, Idaho, Montana, Wyoming, Nebraska, Missouri and now Arkansas—always avoiding the cities. He needed no reminders of the pressures of suburban affluence, rampant consumerism or commercial success. His frequent phone calls from Carl Sutton took care of that. Regardless of the artifice his business partner employed, underneath, his basic question was always the same: when would Brady get hold of himself and resume his work at L&S TechWare?

Brady didn't have the heart to tell Carl that he rarely thought of the business and gave little consideration even to the next day, much less the interminable future yawning before him. On the other hand, he knew he couldn't continue in his current mode, aimlessly wandering across the country, barely taking in the changing scenery, restlessly moving on after a few days in any one place.

The waitress plunked down a plate laden with eggs, bacon and the biggest biscuit Brady had encountered so far in his travels. "Haven't seen you around. You here for the fishing?"

Mildly curious, Brady looked up. "Fishing?"

"White River trout. We're famous for it."

Why not? "Uh, yeah. Know any good places to stay?"

"Well, there's the resort—"

The mere word *resort* reminded him of California and all that he was fleeing.

"Then there's a B-and-B, if you're into that. Quiet place with all the comforts of home. The Edgewater Inn."

All the comforts of home. Brady doubted it, but the word *home* resonated in a way nothing else had in weeks. "Can you give me directions to the B-and-B?"

"Sure." She pulled a paper napkin from the holder and drew him a rudimentary map.

Later, crossing the bridge over the White River, Brady felt a stirring of interest. He'd done a lot of fly-fishing in Colorado as a kid. Maybe he'd hole up in the Edgewater Inn for a few days, outfit himself and spend time on the river fishing—and making some decisions.

Carl had been right. He couldn't run forever.

"YOU LOOK BEAT," Reggie Pettigrew, the sixty-year-old head librarian, said when Nell reported for work Saturday after taking Abby to the airport.

Setting down the stack of books she'd collected from the outdoor depository, she shot him an I-don't-need-much-of-this look. "Full of compliments this morning, aren't you?"

"Even beat you look good. Big weekend?"

"Reggie, are you trying to get my goat or does it just come naturally? You know I haven't had a big weekend in years. And that's not all bad. They can be highly overrated." She cringed, remembering some of the "big weekends" of her past. "It's Abby. I can't help worrying when she flies to visit her dad."

"Did she give you a hard time again about going?"

"As usual. This time, it's for a week." She began sorting the returned books. "I don't know how I ended up being the bad guy in this arrangement, but she blames me for making her go."

Reggie eyed her over the top of his thick bifocals. "While Prince Charming and his lady love live happily ever after?"

Reggie had a way of seeing straight through her.

"Exactly." She glanced at the wall clock registering 9:59. "But enough about me. The hordes are undoubtedly lined up at the door racing to get to Balzac, Dickens, Faulkner, et al."

"I wish. At least we can count on Clarence Fury and his daily two hours with *The New York Times*."

Nell filled a book cart and made the rounds reshelving. When she'd hit bottom after Rick left her, Reggie had been a godsend hiring her as his assistant. Gradually her role had grown until she was now the children's librarian and coordinator of special adult programs. With the limited library budget, she wasn't able to do as much as she would've liked, but the pre-school story hour was booming and she was having sporadic success with the adult forums she'd initiated in the past year. That reminded her to prepare the flyers for the September forum. A minister from the county hospice board was speaking on death and dying. Not exactly an upper of a topic, but several patrons had expressed an interest.

Automatically reshelving two misplaced volumes, Nell fought the familiar ache in her chest. She bowed her head. It had been nearly seven years. Even so, it was hard for her to believe her father was dead. In the snap of a finger. One day, here. Robust, laughing, vital. The next, gone. Without so much as a fare-you-well.

She straightened and slowly made her way to the main desk. Maybe that was why for so long she'd resisted the death topic for the forum. What if she went to pieces during the discussion? Seemingly her mother and Lily had moved on better than she had after her father's massive heart attack, but there wasn't a day when Nell didn't think of him and miss him.

Like now, with Abby protesting vehemently about her upcoming week with Rick. Her dad would've reassured her that she wasn't the worst mother in the world, that adolescence, too, would pass, that Abby appreciated her more than she was able to let on. Although Nell could spout that kind of self-talk all day, it did nothing to ease the cramping loneliness that fused to her like a second skin.

"Has Hazel Underwood returned that new Patricia Cornwell yet?"

Nell looked up into the scowling face of Minnie Foltz, whose boundless knowledge of murder and mayhem was acquired from the numerous mysteries she devoured.

Nell searched the books lined up on the reserved shelf. "Looks like you're in luck, Minnie."

"Hmphh. I should hope so. I can't figure what takes Hazel so long. That's the *real* mystery."

Nell processed the checkout, acknowledging that at least she'd made one person happy today.

MORNING SUN SILVERED the ripples on the surface of the slow-moving river. Swallows soared and dipped above their mud nests built into the crevices of the facing cliff. Standing thigh-deep in the clear, cold water, Brady pumped his arm, flicking the fly several times before letting it settle upstream from a deep hole. He'd discovered this spot yesterday, pulling in two browns nice enough to keep. Sally, the proprietress and cook at the Edgewater Inn, had been pampering him all week, and last night she'd prepared his fish, which they'd eaten in the kitchen out of sight of the other guests. Somehow the older woman had sensed he was a troubled soul. He'd give her credit. She provided all anyone could ask—good food, soft beds, lazy afternoons in a hammock and splendid fishing.

But it wasn't enough. He wanted to share the place with those he loved. Wanted Brooke nestled beside him in the soft four-poster bed, wanted to hear Nicole's infectious laugh when she caught her first trout, wanted to watch both of them hunched over the chessboard in the inn's living room.

Wading downstream, he reeled in, then cast toward a boulder near the far bank. On either side of the river, the forested hills rose, the deep greens of the trees a contrast to the blue sky. Rounding a bend upstream were three canoes, the occupants grinning and sweating with exertion. Three men and three boys. A father-son outing, maybe. Longing, fierce and potent, stabbed him.

Would anything ever be normal again? How could it be? Not when everywhere he looked were reminders of what he was missing. Not only what he was missing now but, worse by far, what he had bypassed in the name of work when it had been right under his nose.

Too late, he felt the quick tug on his line. He couldn't react fast enough. Asleep at the switch and the big one had gotten away. He barked an ironic "Story of my life." Reeling in, he made his way to shore, removed his waders and gathered his gear.

He'd already been at the Edgewater Inn longer than he'd stayed anywhere. It was time to move on. He couldn't remain here forever, counting on Sally's hospitable and generous nature. Move on where? That was the sixty-four-thousand dollar question.

Because no place had the slightest meaning for him.

Back at the inn, he told Sally he would be leaving in the morning. That final evening he sat on the deck outside his room, his feet up on the railing, watching the sun sink behind the mountain. The occasional cooing of a pair of mourning doves and the soothing sound of the river lapping the rocky shore kept him company. In his hands he held the guest journal Sally had asked him to sign. Each room had one. He opened the paisley cover. The first entry was from 1995, the year Sally had bought the inn. "Wonderful food, wonderful hostess, wonderful place! The slow pace was very therapeutic. Thank you." It was signed "Ron and Shari Huxley, Tulsa, OK."

Brady turned the page. "Oh, Sally, John and I really needed this time away from the children and all our responsibilities. You've created a little piece of heaven here on earth. We can't wait to come back and be spoiled again." This one was signed "Rowena."

Then there was the honeymoon couple who cleverly implied the wedding night had been all anyone could hope for and vowed to return on every anniversary.

Couples. All of them. Made supremely happy by the Edgewater Inn. What could he possibly write? This was a place to be shared, but what was he doing? Nursing his wounds. How did he write about that?

Flicking through the book, he came to one particular entry where the margins were embroidered with small colored pencil drawings of a spruce tree, a dogwood blossom, the rocky cliff above the rushing river, and, at the bottom, a rainbow.

Brady smoothed the page with his hand and began reading.

A sanctuary. That's what you've created here, and I will be forever grateful. I have been so alone. Unable to see a direction for my life. Not sure if there even is one. When you've loved and lost, doubt replaces hope, insecurity replaces confidence and you wonder who you are. Whether you can go on. Or even want to.

Looking up just in time to see the sun drop behind the dark curtain of mountain, Brady pondered whether he should continue reading. The words were too confessional, too emotionally raw—and threatening. Some other individual had come here full of the same thoughts and feelings.

Unable to help himself, he turned back to the graceful handwriting covering the page.

This time of quiet and contemplation has been a great gift, restoring my belief that no matter how severe the storm, rainbows can happen. Regardless of how desolate I feel right now, I have to believe that somewhere out there is someone for me. Someone I can trust. Someone I can love. When I find him, dear Sally, the two of us will come to the Edgewater Inn. Together.

Brady stared for the longest time at the signature. Simple. Bare. Exposed. "Nell."

He stood abruptly and walked to the railing, peering at the grove of pine trees bordering the property. Nell, whoever she was, was more optimistic than he was. As if, like Dorothy, you could click your red-shod heels and suddenly find yourself on the other side of whatever hell you were in.

God, he hated his blatant, whining self-pity. If Nell, desolate and alone, had been willing to look for something better, why couldn't he?

He leaned against a post. This attitude of his was downright depressing. He needed a plan—any plan— and at this point he didn't give much of a damn what it was.

Absently he realized he was still holding the guest book, his forefinger marking Nell's page. He opened it again and squinted in the dim light, just making out the line beneath her signature. "Fayetteville, AR, 1997."

He carried the book back into his room and reread the entry. Several times.

A crazy idea entered his head. But no crazier than what he'd been doing. He needed a purpose. A direction. Short-term, this would work as well as anything.

Tomorrow, after he checked out, he would drive to Fayetteville to find this Nell, a woman who still believed in rainbows.

CHAPTER TWO

TOWERING ABOVE the broad expanse of lawn in front of Old Main, the landmark building of the University of Arkansas campus, were massive oaks and maples, their leaves hanging lifeless in the heat of the late August day. Patches of shade offered only the illusion of coolness. Brady paused, gazing across the sward where members of a fraternity gathered on the porch of their house to welcome a group of rushees. He envied them this carefree time of life. College. What would that have been like?

Once, long ago, he'd assumed that was his destiny. But that was before his mother died and his father hastily remarried. Before he rebelled against his father's unreasonable restrictions and demands. Before he stood up to the old man, told him to take a flying leap and left home. On his own at eighteen. No enlightening classes, fall football weekends, frat parties or eager coeds for him.

All he had in his favor was a knack for computers, a willingness to work his butt off and a cold, simmering rage fueling his ambition.

He headed toward Dickson Street, an off-campus shopping area housing several watering holes. He needed a cool drink. He had thought his plan of starting his search with the university telephone directory was ingenious. The U of A was the town's largest employer, so the odds of finding Nell on campus were better than average. However, after a day hunched over a table in the college library, his eyes were raw from reading endless lists of names. He'd found several Nells. When he'd called, one had turned out to be a secretary in the engineering department suspicious of his motives. Another was a graduate student who knew nothing about any Edgewater Inn. A third, who sounded like Minnie Mouse, asked him what he had in mind, then giggled coquettishly.

The tavern was an oasis in a frustrating day. He settled on a bar stool and ordered a cola. In a nearby booth, three barrel-chested young men were playing a chug-a-lug game. Brady's lip curled. He wanted to knock their pitcher to the floor and demand to know if they were driving. Didn't they understand their stupidity could lead to tragedy? He no longer had any tolerance for overindulgence.

Instead of acting on his instinct, he turned to the bartender and asked if he knew any women named Nell. "That's kind of an old-fashioned name. Most of the chicks these days are Chelseas or Tiffanies, know what I mean?"

Yeah, he did. Besides, he wasn't picturing Nell as a younger woman. More someone his age. Somebody who'd obviously lived through hurt. Then another thought hit him. What if Nell was older, maybe a widow who'd lost her husband after forty years of marriage?

He drained his glass. This was insane. Even if he found his Nell, how could he explain his actions?

She might even accuse him of stalking. What was he hoping to find?

He signaled the bartender for another soda. What would Carl say if he could see him now, sitting in Fayetteville, Arkansas? Everywhere you looked in this town was a depiction of the butt-ugly razorback hog, the beloved mascot of the university. Yet the place had an appealing, slow-paced charm. He grinned sardonically. He had wanted to get away from the Silicon Valley. Well, he had certainly succeeded.

Nursing his drink, he noticed a local newspaper on the seat beside him. He picked it up and scanned the headlines. Zoning issues. School orientation programs. A public library forum. A controversy over pollution of the Illinois River.

As he started to shove it aside, out of the blue he recalled a seemingly vague remark Sally at the Edgewater Inn had made when he'd asked about Nell. "I can't give out personal information about my guests," she'd said. They'd been standing in the living room at the time, where one entire wall was lined with books. "Say," she'd added, gesturing to the shelves as if changing the subject, "do you like to read? I do. Libraries have always been favorite places of mine. How about you?"

At the time he'd mumbled something about not having much time for reading. He remembered being irritated that she hadn't given him any information about Nell. Now, though, he wondered. Maybe she had and he'd been too dense to realize it.

He drained his glass, then began reading the article about the library forum. In the final paragraph, he found what he was looking for. "August's forum on Arab-Israeli relations will be moderated by Nell Porter." He checked the date. Tomorrow night.

At last a genuine lead. He could blend into the audience and size up the latest Nell candidate.

He couldn't believe he was thinking like this. What would he say if he ever found *the* Nell? "Hi, I think we have misery in common?" What kind of way was that to impress anybody? Why did he care?

There was another obstacle. Her entry was dated 1997. Six years ago. What made him think time had stood still for Nell?

Despite the harsh light of reason, he felt compelled to follow his search through to its conclusion. He *would* find Nell.

"DID YOU GET Abby off all right for her vacation with her father?"

To free her hands, Nell settled the phone against her shoulder and continued searching through her office file cabinet. "Yes, Mother. As usual, she trudged through security like a condemned prisoner."

"Why can't you say something to Rick? What's the matter with that man anyway?"

"If I knew the answer to that question, I wouldn't be where I am right now." She pulled out a file folder, skimmed the contents, then discarded it. Where was that background information for her introduction for tonight's forum? "As for communicating with Rick about Abby, a cabbage is a more attentive listener. At some point, Abby is going to have to speak up for herself. She's the only one I can think of who might make a dent in his self-absorption.''

''Do you think it's wise to keep sending her, dear?''

''What choice do I have? Her visits are court-mandated. Besides, in his own way, Rick does care about her.''

Her mother's voice modulated into that concerned, faintly judgmental tone Nell had come to dread. ''Are you sure you'll be all right by yourself? It's a whole week alone. Don't you want to come stay with me?''

Rolling her eyes, Nell prayed for patience. ''I'll be fine, Mother. You can count on it. Besides, I need some time at home to clean out closets and get organized for winter.''

''That doesn't sound much like fun.''

Fun? What would that be like? ''I'll take peace and quiet over fun any day.'' She extracted two folders that had become stuck together. There it was. Her introduction. Breathing a sigh of relief, she grabbed up the phone. ''Look, Mom, I've got to go. The forum starts in half an hour.''

''I just wanted to see how you were doing.''

Nell gritted her teeth. How long would it take before her family trusted her again? ''Thanks, I appreciate your concern. I'll call you later in the week.''

With a sigh of relief, she hung up the phone and studied the bios in front of her—one for a local rabbi and another for the head of the Arab Student League. Using a highlighter, she marked the sections she wanted for her introduction.

Yet she was distracted by her mother's interference. Was being treated like a child a price she would always have to pay?

BRADY FOLLOWED a frumpy-looking pair of retirees into the library meeting room and took a seat on the aisle near the back. He looked around wondering which of the librarians was Nell. Two stood at a side table arranging books about the Mid-East. Another was bent over, conferring with one of the men seated beside the podium. When she straightened, smiled around the room and asked for order, Brady's breath caught in his chest. This was no old woman looking for a dapper widower with whom to share her twilight years.

"Good evening and welcome to tonight's forum. My name is Nell Porter and I'll be your moderator this evening...."

Brady tuned out her words. She was a tall, slender woman—midthirties he judged—with short straw-colored hair cut in uneven lengths, a style that complemented the casualness of her high-waisted denim jumper. When she smiled, her eyes narrowed in delighted crinkles. She wore little makeup and he couldn't help noticing her ringless fingers.

"...it's my pleasure to introduce..."

He became aware that a short, bearded gentleman had stepped to the microphone. Brady's eyes, however, were glued on the graceful way Nell Porter sank into her chair, crossing one long leg over the other, smoothing her skirt, then fixing her attention on the speaker.

She was not like Brooke, a sleek blonde made for designer clothes, Porsches and expensive, understated jewelry. Nell had a fresh, wholesome look, although her tousled hairstyle suggested an impish streak. She appeared thoroughly likeable. Comfortable.

He'd made his living by exercising logic. The thought in his head, however, was anything but logical.

He wanted Nell Porter to be his Edgewater Inn Nell.

"YOU'RE *WHERE?*" Carl did not sound pleased.

"Fayetteville. Arkansas."

"Hmm. I'd hoped you were on your way home."

Home. There was that word again. Didn't Carl understand. He no longer had a home. Staring at the anonymous, monochromatic motel room walls, Brady absently brushed a hand through his hair, still damp from his morning shower. "Not yet."

"I don't suppose it would hurry things along if I said we've got a lotta deals poppin' here and we need you."

The familiar clenching of his stomach gave him his answer. "Sorry, Carl, but I'd be no good to you now."

His partner's tone mellowed. "I don't mean to rush you. I know you need time. It's just—"

"When I'm ready, buddy, I'll let you know."

"What are your plans for the moment?"

Brady studied the cover of the local phone book, bearing a picture of a flowering pink dogwood. "It's nice here. I may stick around a while."

"In *Arkansas?*"

"Don't knock it till you've seen it. Natural beauty,

low cost of living, friendly people. A guy could do a whole lot worse.'' Best of all, it was a radical change from the merry-go-round California lifestyle.

He really should feel guilty about the company, but, ironically, that was the one thing about which he had no guilt. It would survive.

He wasn't so sure about himself. Two or three times a week he woke from a dead sleep drenched in sweat, the odor of diesel fuel clogging his nostrils, his heartbeat in the danger zone—and two names echoing in his consciousness.

His friends had recommended all kinds of therapists and treatments—a regular LaLa Land smorgasbord of palliatives.

Screw that. He'd find his own way. Picking up his billfold and keys, he headed for the door. Today was a day for exploring the area—and stopping by the library. He allowed himself a brief smile of anticipation. Maybe Ms. Porter could help him research area B-and-B's, particularly those along the White River.

NELL PARKED HER CAR near the square and hit her early-morning meeting at the church before heading on to work. The sun had already burned off the dew, and the temperature reading on the bank stood at eighty-five degrees and it wasn't even ten. Another scorcher. The cool of the library would be welcome.

After exchanging greetings with Reggie and the rest of the staff, she had just enough time to circle the chairs in the children's area before the toddlers and their mothers began arriving for story-time. As usual Rodney Fraim's mother could hardly control him. At every chance, he slipped out of her arms and began playing peekaboo from behind the stacks. Most of the rest, however, sat on the carpet, legs crossed, only occasionally fidgeting. Today's book was Katharine Holabird's *Alexander and the Dragon.* Halfway through the story, Nell noticed a tall, dark-haired man quietly observing the children. He looked harmless enough, but you could never be too careful. He pulled out a chair and sat at a table where he continued watching them. He seemed more pensive than menacing, an amused smile softening his strong features when one of the youngsters reacted with laughter to the idea of having a dragon under the bed.

As Nell continued reading and displaying the il-lustrations, she became uncomfortably aware that the man seemed to be studying her rather than the chil-dren. Did she know him? Fighting a breathless sen-sation, she approached the end of the story where Alexander realizes he's no longer afraid of shad-ows—or of his friend the dragon.

A shiver passed through Nell when the man mouthed the lines with her. Why was his expression so sad? Before she could ponder his sudden change, he stood and wandered toward the fiction section.

She shook her head to clear her mind. She must've imagined that fleeting moment of connection with him. She refocused on the boys and girls and com-pleted the story. As she'd anticipated, it gave rise to a lively discussion of what and who lived in the bed-rooms of her tiny listeners.

After helping all the children select and check out their take-home books, she straightened the area and turned toward her office. The good-looking man sat in one of the easy chairs near the main desk, an open book in his lap. But his dark brown eyes followed her. Enough of this. She was uncomfortable with his attention, even though a frisson of something like pleasure took her by surprise.

She crossed to him. "Excuse me, sir, but do I know you?"

He closed his book—which she couldn't help noticing was a Grisham legal thriller—and raised his eyes, a slow smile creating a devilish dimple in his left cheek. "No. I'm Brady Logan." With athletic grace, he rose to his feet and now looked down on her. "I was at the forum last night, so, in a manner of speaking, I know you. Nell Porter, right?"

She clasped her cold hands in front of her. "Yes." She scrambled for words. "Did you enjoy it?"

His eyes narrowed. "Discussion of conflict and violence is more painful than enjoyable." He paused before going on. "I vastly preferred this morning's activities."

"You're obviously familiar with *Alexander and the Dragon.*"

She detected a momentary steeling of his features. He offered no explanation but simply said, "Yes."

She couldn't seem to tear herself away, but there was little more to be said. Steering from the personal, she grasped for the professional. "Is there something I can help you with?"

"As a matter of fact, yes. I'm new to the area and am interested in doing some fly-fishing, maybe locating a nice place along the White River to stay. Have any suggestions?"

Brady Logan didn't strike her as someone so clueless about how to use a library, but then you never knew. "There are a couple of popular resorts near Flippin, or you might consider—"

"I'm more a B-and-B kinda guy."

"Well, in that case—" his eyes found hers, as if he anticipated her next words "—you might try the Edgewater Inn." More to escape his scrutiny than anything, she made her way to the travel section. "Here." She pulled out a directory of Arkansas bed-and-breakfasts. "You can read all about it."

He took the book, thumbing through it until he found the listing and an accompanying photograph. "This looks nice."

"It is." Then she found herself telling him all about her stay there.

"Sounds peaceful," he finally said.

"Very." A poignant memory came to her of cathartic tears shed on a lazy September afternoon rocking on a wooden porch swing overlooking the blue river.

He took her by the arm, then as if realizing he'd overstepped his bounds, he released his grip. "Thanks, Nell Porter. You've been most helpful."

She found it hard to swallow. "I'm glad."

Reggie Pettigrew bustled up alongside them. "Nell, your daughter's on the phone."

A strange look—wistfulness? sadness?—shadowed Brady's face before he seemed to reassemble his features. He nodded his understanding.

"Excuse me," she said, then started for her office.

"Nell?"

She turned around. He smiled, then winked. "Beware of dragons."

On the way to her office, she couldn't explain the tingly feeling short-circuiting her body. She had the strangest sense that he'd been waiting for her. Any number of other librarians could have helped him.

Oddly, instead of making her uncomfortable, the thought filled her with the kind of anticipation she hadn't experienced in years. He was an extremely attractive man.

Any such frivolous thoughts were shattered when she picked up the phone. "Mom." Abby's voice was a harsh whisper. "I hate it here. Do I hafta stay?"

THAT AFTERNOON Brady explored the secluded neighborhoods clinging to the sides of the steep hills rimming Fayetteville, drove north on I-540, astonished at the amount of commercial development, then ended up at a marina on Beaver Lake, where moored boats of all kinds rocked with the gentle swells. As a businessman, he recognized he'd stumbled into an investor's paradise in this burgeoning northwest corner of Arkansas. He left his car and walked across the boardwalk to the marina office where he rented a small pontoon boat for a couple of hours.

Slowly edging past the buoys, he pushed the throttle forward and skimmed over the clear water, practically deserted except for a few die-hard fishermen. If this lake were in California, it would be wall-to-wall boats no matter what the day of the week or time of day. When he reached the middle of a secluded cove, he cut the motor—aware of the peaceful quality of the sudden silence.

Finally he let his thoughts return to Nell. He had been ill-prepared for her effect on him. She was a natural with the children and there was a kind of discomfiting synchronicity in her having selected *Alexander and the Dragon* to read. Nicole's favorite bedtime story. He glanced skyward, willing away the involuntary spasm of grief.

He forced himself to think about Nell again. When she'd approached him in the library, she had seemed skittish, her hands primly folded in front of her, her gray eyes wary. Her nose, dusted lightly with freckles, and her bare red-polished toes contributed to her overall sense of vulnerability. Yet she'd dared to confront him. Admittedly his observation of her had been rather obvious. *When you've loved and lost, doubt replaces hope, insecurity replaces confidence and you wonder who you are.*

The boat bobbed in the wake of a passing jet ski. Was she still all by herself? He knew now she had a daughter. Despite her ringless fingers, was there a Mr. Porter?

He devoutly hoped not.

Since Brooke and Nicole had died, he had been unable to connect with anybody—not his friends, his neighbors or his colleagues. He thought of himself as a wraith. Improbable as it seemed, though, he wanted to connect with Nell Porter.

Switching on the key, he started the motor and made his way back across the lake. By the time he reached the dock, he'd arrived at a decision.

Tomorrow he would look for rental property in Fayetteville. He was staying. And Nell was the reason.

NELL WAS REDECORATING the bulletin board in the children's area with a back-to-school motif when she became aware of a presence behind her. She finished tacking up the book cover she was working on, then turned. Hands in his pockets, Brady Logan stood there smiling a killer smile, then shrugged as if in self-defense. "I'm back."

"Not the proverbial bad penny, I hope," she said, attempting a nonchalance she was far from feeling.

"No. I have a reason for being here."

She needed something to occupy her hands. Selecting another cover from the stack on the table, she said, "Anything I can help you with?"

"I certainly hope so. I'd like you to have lunch with me."

She'd been fully prepared to direct him to the library's fishing collection or to locate the latest issue of *Field and Stream,* but *lunch?* The thought filled her with mild panic. No man had asked her to lunch in a very long time and certainly no one who made her hormones react in such an unseemly fashion. "I beg your pardon?"

He nodded his head. "You heard me right. Lunch. You know, where two people look at a menu, order and have polite conversation while they eat."

Smiling tentatively, she said, "I know what lunch is, but let's face it, I have no idea who you are, really."

"That's why I'm inviting you to lunch—to correct that deficiency." Before she could offer further objections, he went on. "I'm new in town. I'm looking for someone to fill me in on the local scene. I figure a librarian is the perfect resource. This would be completely aboveboard." He drew her to the window. "It's broad daylight, pedestrians are every-where. We could walk to the nearest restaurant, and if you decide I'm a threat, all you have to do is call for help." He touched her lightly on the shoulder. "But I guarantee that won't be necessary."

Nell fought the temptation induced by his honeyed voice and the pressure of his hand on her shoulder. Despite herself, she recalled her reaction to her mother's challenge the other day. Peace and quiet—or fun? This could be fun. On the other hand... "I don't think—"

"Don't think, just say 'yes.' You do have to eat, don't you?"

She made the mistake, then, of looking into his eyes where she found both humor and need. "I—I suppose I could—"

"Great." When he smiled down at her, she couldn't summon a single objection. "I'll wait over in the magazine section."

Then he left her. She studied the book cover in her hand, trying to think what she was doing with it. Flustered, she remembered and picked up a couple of tacks. She shook her head, wondering why in the world she'd agreed to such an improbable invitation. Perhaps the dragon had left the bedroom and now inhabited the library.

As THEY SAUNTERED along Dickson Street toward the restaurant, Brady kept feeding her questions about the town, the university, the local economy. As a native, she provided a wealth of information, but it was hard to concentrate. Her unruly hair shone in the sun, and he found amusing her self-contained way of letting him know this was purely a business appointment.

"I like what I've seen and what I'm hearing. I've decided to stick around a while."

"Oh?"

"This morning I lucked into a furnished condo. A professor leaving on sabbatical had his sub-leasing deal fall through last week. I was in the right place at the right time."

She laughed. "You certainly were. Housing is at a premium this time of year in a university town."

When they reached the brew pub restaurant, he ushered her toward a corner booth. "Hungry?"

"Starving, actually."

"Good." The waiter introduced himself while he set down their water glasses. Brady noticed Nell hadn't looked at her menu. "You already know what you want?"

"I always have the soup-and-sandwich special, but they have great burgers here."

"Okay. That's settled." He signaled the hovering waiter and placed their order. "Now, enough about Fayetteville. Tell me about Nell Porter."

"I have a better idea. You're the stranger I'm having lunch with. What about you?"

He mentally culled the details he could bring himself to share. "I grew up in Colorado. Left home at eighteen and went to work in the software industry in California, then started my own company, which, I'm happy to say, has done extremely well. I was married for fifteen years. One daughter. They, uh…" Damn. His throat was closing down.

"Yes?"

He swallowed, then managed to say, "They were both killed last year in a car accident."

He was unprepared for her hand to cover his, and even less prepared for the jolt of life it sparked. "I'm sorry."

He studied the TV mounted over the bar, then glanced out the window. "Yeah, well, these things happen."

"So what brings you to Arkansas?"

For some reason, he trusted her with the truth. "I couldn't take California any longer. Too much had changed. I've been on the road. Seeing what's out here. Getting a new perspective."

"And?" Her eyes swam with compassion. Why was it welcome from her when it hadn't been from anyone else? *I have been so alone.* Maybe because she knew.

"I like it here. Besides, I needed to stop somewhere. I couldn't go on running." There. He'd said it.

"Brady Logan, whatever it is you're seeking, I hope you find it."

Looking at her, her thin shoulders hunched over the table, her reedlike neck revealing a pronounced pulse beat, he felt a welcome surge of hope. "Me, too." He cleared his throat. "Now it's your turn. Tell me about your daughter. And husband."

Brady noticed a shutter fall over Nell's eyes. Just then the waiter appeared, set down their food and made a show of asking if everything was all right. Brady nodded. After her first tentative spoonful of the steaming soup, Nell answered Brady's question, her attention fixed on her food. "There's no husband.

I've been divorced for six years. My daughter Abby is thirteen and—'' finally she glanced up ''—getting to that stage where parents are a 'drag.' I've been told adolescence is survivable, but I'm not so sure.'' She grinned a wobbly grin.

''You have family here?''

''My father's dead, but my mother still lives here, as do my sister and her family.''

''Are you close?''

''Very, but with all the baggage, too. Since the divorce, my mother and sister are overprotective of me, which I suppose is natural, even though it can be frustrating. But I couldn't have managed without them.''

''You're lucky,'' he said, aware of his faintly bitter tone. He hadn't seen his father or his younger brother since he left home, and so long as the old man was alive, he didn't want to.

''Your ex-husband? Is he still on the scene?''

''He and his new wife live in Dallas. In fact, Abby's visiting them this week.'' Her deliberately neutral tone struck him as odd. She was holding something back. Some hurt.

''Well, since you're alone, what do you say we take in dinner and a movie? Tomorrow night?'' He watched her eyes widen in surprise, then added, ''That is if you think I've passed the test. I'm really quite harmless.'' Well, that wasn't exactly true. She'd be shocked if she knew she was his sole motive for remaining in Fayetteville.

Then she smiled, and the stomach muscles that had been taut since he first saw her this morning relaxed.

"I'd like that." The faint pink of a blush colored her cheeks. "I'd like that very much."

Her pleasure touched a chord, reminding him that he needed to proceed slowly with her. She'd been hurt enough already. And, God knows, so had he.

CHAPTER THREE

NELL HAD RACED HOME from the library, taken a quick shower and now stood in her bra and panties surveying the limited selection in her closet. Dinner and a movie? It wasn't a charity gala, for heaven's sake. Something casual. Nice. She had essentially three choices. One of her unstylish librarian dresses, a two-year-old pair of linen slacks with a matching sweater sporting a small ineradicable stain or a black Mexican fiesta dress she'd bought on a whim for International Month at the library. Wardrobe purchases had been low on her list of priorities, well beneath orthodontia and graduate school tuition.

Glancing at the clock, she stepped into a half slip, then selected the black dress and a pair of onyx and pearl earrings. When the doorbell rang, she slipped into her white sandals, spritzed some cologne in the general direction of her neck, ran a brush quickly through her still-damp hair and only then began to panic. Misgivings echoed in her mind. She didn't even know this man. Why, he could be... She filled in the blank with a number of disturbing possibilities.

All of which dissolved into a faint memory when she opened the door and beheld the flesh-and-blood object of her conjecture. Brady Logan wore crisply pressed khakis and a yellow polo shirt that accented his ruddy tan. His smile made her forget her meager wardrobe and just about everything else. "Hi," he said with a timbre that would melt chocolate. "You look gorgeous."

Perhaps he wasn't a threat after all, simply a man in need of a competent ophthalmologist. At a time like this having fair skin was a definite drawback. "Thank you." Now what? Even Abby possessed more savoir faire.

"I'll let you suggest the restaurant, but we may have to arm wrestle to decide between the new Kate Hudson chick-flick or Brad Pitt's latest."

She picked up her purse, locked the door, then started when he loosely grasped her free hand and led her toward his fancy SUV. "You've given me a tough choice. I love romantic comedies, but what woman can resist Brad Pitt?"

"We can duke that out later. For now, why don't you suggest a restaurant? Something special."

How special? She mentioned a popular chain restaurant and a locally owned bistro and let him choose.

"Let's go for the more intimate. The bistro sounds good."

The more intimate? The mere word rendered her speechless. Fortunately, that wasn't a problem because after he helped her into his Escalade, he filled her in on his further explorations of Fayetteville. At the first major intersection she gave him directions to the restaurant. She wasn't worried about dinner, or even the movie. But afterward… What if? She'd been too busy recovering from the divorce, working on her master's in library science and rearing Abby to worry about dating. After what Rick had done, men weren't subjects she viewed with optimism.

She looked over at Brady, admiring the muscles in his forearms and the way his large hands caressed the steering wheel. What did he expect from her? Was she supposed to invite him in after the movie? Did she even want to? And could she handle her own feelings, which were confusing the daylights out of her? The way they'd met should feel creepy—his coming to the forum, then appearing at the story-time the next day and, if she wasn't mistaken, observing her. Somehow, though, it didn't.

"You know that first morning in the library?"

"Yeah, what about it?"

"I had the distinct impression you were watching me."

"I was." He glanced at her, a grin forming. "You're a very watchable woman, Nell."

Defenseless, she couldn't hold back her smile. "I—I…thank you."

Fun? Oh, yes, but fun shouldn't feel so momentous.

DRIVING NELL HOME from the Cineplex, Brady reflected on how long it had been since he'd had an evening of laughter and companionship. Not since that last weekend when he and Brooke… He quickly censored the thought. Too painful. Yet he couldn't help kicking himself for taking his best friend and mate for granted while he spent twelve to sixteen hour days in pursuit of the American dream—or at least an upwardly mobile male's dream. Why hadn't he spent more time with her and Nicole? Had they known how much he loved them?

"I think that compromise worked well," Nell commented.

"What?" Lost in his thoughts, had he been rude?

"I enjoyed the movie. Believe me, casting my eyes on Mr. Pitt was no hardship."

"I'm glad." She'd scored two major points so far this evening. First, she'd declined wine at the restaurant. Second, he appreciated that she'd willingly given up the romantic comedy at the theater, because he hadn't been sure how much sentiment his unstable emotions could handle.

She grew even more quiet as they neared her neighborhood. When he pulled into her driveway, she cleared her throat and said, "Would you like to come in for coffee?"

He sensed those had been difficult words for her. Was she nervous? Merely being polite? Yet he already dreaded the return to his motel and the loneliness. "I won't stay long," he said by way of reassurance, "but I'd like that."

She settled him in the small added-on family room at the back of the modest one-story house while she bustled in the kitchen. In one corner stood a 1930s pie cabinet, doubling as a TV stand and repository for CD's and books. The sagging sofa was covered in a maroon-and-tan plaid fabric that looked as if it had seen better days. A wooden rocker painted bright blue sat at an angle to the sofa. Propped in the corner were oversize pillows next to a basket holding a colorful assortment of yarns. The combination shouldn't have worked, but instead of looking like a fleamarket display, it had a welcoming, cozy feeling. Brady couldn't help making the comparison to the chrome and leather big-screen viewing room in his house.

"Here you are." Nell set a small tray on the planked coffee table. "I hope you like oatmeal cookies."

"No red-blooded man could refuse," he said, helping himself.

She picked up a mug and took a seat in the rocker. "My husband always liked them."

He studied her, noting her downcast eyes. "Your divorce? Is it amicable?"

"I suppose. It's hard work, though."

"Oh? How's that?"

"My daughter resents having to go to Dallas to visit her father."

Brady said nothing, giving her an opportunity to add whatever she needed to.

"She blames me."

"For what?"

"For all of it. I guess I'm a convenient scapegoat. There was…um…another woman." He noticed her jaw tense. "Abby apparently believes I did something to send her father away. If I had done whatever she thinks I should have, she reasons her father would still be here and she wouldn't have to fly to Dallas monthly." She shrugged. "So you see, it's my fault."

"You know better than that," he said gently.

"I'm willing to accept my share of the responsibility for the breakup of the marriage. It's rarely one-sided, but I don't know how I failed so badly that Rick had to find another woman.''

''Aren't you being hard on yourself? I don't know Rick, but did you ever consider perhaps he has a character flaw?''

She cupped her mug in both hands. ''I felt so stupid. How could I not have seen it coming? What was the matter with me?''

Her misery was evident, yet he felt helpless to address it, not without stepping over the line he'd set for himself. ''Sounds as if you were devastated.''

She nodded. ''Do you have any idea what that does to a woman's self-esteem? I try hard, but it's difficult not to become bitter or vindictive or to poison Abby against her father.''

''One day she'll understand the situation. In the meantime, it's got to be rough on you.'' Pain? No doubt about it, she'd had plenty of firsthand experience.

Smiling sadly, she glanced at him. ''I didn't mean to get into this. It's just so nice to have a little sympathy.''

''I know what you mean.'' But did he? He hadn't been open to any himself. At least not until now.

''Look, I'm sorry. My problems are nothing compared to your loss. I can't imagine how you can carry on.''

''It's been—'' he cursed the gruffness in his voice ''—pure hell.''

''How does a person ever get over something like that?''

''I'm not sure that's possible, but Brooke and Nicole wouldn't want me to give up." He set down his mug. "So I do the best I can, but it isn't easy. Ever."

"It's odd how two lost souls like us happened to get together, isn't it?"

Now was not the time to confess that their meeting had not been a result of chance. "I'm glad I met you, Nell. Talking with you like this makes me feel half-alive again."

"It is nice," she agreed.

Lost in their own thoughts, they sat quietly for several moments. But it wasn't an uncomfortable silence. Quite the contrary. Finally he stood. "I'd better be going. You have to work tomorrow."

Rising to her feet, she said, "And I have an early meeting before work." She walked him to the front door where she paused and, still holding her mug, smiled up at him. "Thank you, Brady. I enjoyed the evening."

"Enough for a repeat?" He wanted more of this comfort of home and companionship and easy affection.

In a nervous gesture, she smoothed the front of her dress. "Yes," she said.

"Would tomorrow night be rushing it?"

"Not at all. In fact, that suits me since Abby will be gone until this weekend."

He wasn't quite sure what she meant. Would Abby's presence be an impediment to their future get-togethers? "How about renting a boat and taking a picnic with us? I'll pick up something at the deli."

"I haven't done anything like that in a long time. It sounds like fun."

Driving back to the motel, he reflected on his temporary sense of well-being. As he had thought on first acquaintance, Nell was an easy woman to be with. One able to honor silence. When she spoke, it was simply and directly. He liked that.

As for that ex-husband of hers, he'd clearly left her feeling diminished. Brady suspected she had no idea what a strong, resilient and lovely woman she was.

TOSSING HER BACKPACK into the overhead bin and taking the window seat, Abby glanced nervously at the passengers still boarding. Weekends were bad enough, but this past seven days with Dad and Clarice had been the pits! She hoped no one sat beside her. She didn't need any well-meaning grown-up playing parent to her. She had enough of those in her life even if she didn't always agree about the "well-meaning" part. Buckling her seat belt, she couldn't avoid looking at the geeky puke-green T-shirt encrusted with a rhinestone palm tree that Clarice had bought for her and insisted she wear home. Never mind it sucked. It had been easier to go along with her than to argue.

A flight attendant checking seat belts walked up and down the aisle, stopping briefly to give Abby a warm smile and the offer of a magazine. She looked like a nice lady, a regular person. She'd prob'ly be a good mother, the kind who baked cookies and was a Girl Scout leader. Not like Clarice who had made Abby go with her to a ritzy country club for a golf lesson. Bor-ing. Not once did anybody ask her if *she'd* like to hit a golf ball. At least she might have been able to. Not like Clarice who whiffed more of-

ten than she connected. Learning the game didn't
seem to matter to her stepmother nearly as much as
showing off her "adorable" new outfit.

On this visit Abby had actually had some time
alone with her father, but that was for lunch at this
fancy-schmancy restaurant where she could hardly
eat for worrying about which fork to use or whether
she'd spill on her dress. She could hardly remember
when her father lived in Fayetteville and a big family
outing was dinner at Applebee's and a movie. Clarice
wouldn't be caught dead in Applebee's.

It was weird how she and her dad didn't have
much to say to one another. He'd asked all the usual
questions about school, the courses she'd be taking,
her friends, at least the ones he could remember.
Along the way he'd use these cutesie names on her—
"Sweet Pea" and "Sugar Lump." Stuff like that.
She'd rather he called her "Spud." That's what
Tonya's father called her on account of how she
would only eat mashed potatoes when she was a
baby. "Spud" had meaning.

When the plane rolled back from the gate, Abby
breathed a sigh of relief. No talkative stranger to ignore. Just her and the clouds. She would never admit
how glad she'd be to get home and see her mother.
She knew Mom worried about her. She really should
try to be nicer—help more around the house, cut out
the complaining and back-talk. But it was hard.

At least she'd escaped Dallas one more time before the ultimate embarrassment. It could happen any
time now. Any place. That was the terrifying part.
Tonya and Allie had already started their periods.
Mom had given her the big talk when she was eleven

and had shown her where the supplies were kept. Lately, like some inflatable doll, she'd felt her body shifting, bloating. She'd even imagined she had cramps.

Okay, so it was all normal, but it couldn't happen in Dallas. Not with Clarice. And no way could she tell Dad. She'd die of embarrassment. Totally.

Please, God, let it be at home. With Mom.

A lump formed in her throat and her eyes stung. She wouldn't cry. That was for babies.

All she wanted was to get back safely and hug her mother.

SUNDAY AFTERNOON after unpacking his bags, Brady surveyed his rented living room. The fusty Victorian look wouldn't have been his choice of décor, but he couldn't argue with furnished—not when all his belongings were in storage in California. There was a part of him that wondered what the hell he was doing settling for any length of time in Fayetteville, Arkansas. Although it was a decision that would make no sense to anyone he knew, it felt right.

Had he simply been ready to stop his running, or was Nell responsible? He liked her. A lot. But he could never again make someone else responsible for his happiness. He stumbled through each day trying to wrap his mind around the reality that he would never see Brooke or Nicole this side of the grave. So what was he really after?

A connection. In the here and now. Some relationship that would remind him he wasn't alone. But what would that look like? And would it be fair to

Nell? She deserved more. A lot more. Right now, though, he was giving all he could.

The evening of their boating excursion, he'd tried to keep things light. The sound of Nell's gentle laughter echoing across the secluded cove they'd found for their picnic and her tales of the characters that frequented the library had made him smile. She told him about her graduate courses at the university and her enjoyment of refinishing furniture. However, she'd reserved most of her enthusiasm for her home, relating how she'd scrimped following the divorce to make the down payment and how she'd done much of the remodeling herself. He doubted any Silicon Valley multi-millionaire took more delight in his surroundings.

He slumped into the brown overstuffed chair smelling faintly of pipe tobacco and picked up the Sunday paper. If he was going to hang around, he needed to fill his time with something productive. Otherwise, Carl would be on his case about getting back to work. An idea had slowly been forming in his brain ever since he'd explored the I-540 corridor.

When he had finished with the business section, he began studying the real estate section. Logic told him he was several years too late, but he had the gut feeling there was still money to be made in this neck of the woods, still a need for venture capital.

And if there was one thing he had a surfeit of, it was money.

"I AM *NOT* wearing this stupid top," Abby said Monday morning.

Nell looked up from the bagel she was smearing

with cream cheese. Abby stood, feet planted, holding out the blouse Nell had ironed the night before as if it were an odious rag. "You asked me to iron it," Nell said, struggling for calm.

"That was yesterday. I just talked with Tonya. Nobody's wearing flowers."

Nell knew how important it was to a junior-high-age girl to appear cool. "Suit yourself but hang that one back in your closet. Also, whatever you wear, I'd appreciate it if your navel was covered."

"Mo-om!"

"You're going to register at school. I doubt your teachers or the principal are keen on exposed body parts."

"Clarice would let me," Abby muttered as she left the room.

Great. Now, suddenly, Clarice was the patron saint of teeny-boppers. Nell knew her daughter was experiencing the mood swings endemic to adolescence, but that didn't make living with her any easier. For a brief moment at the airport, Nell had deluded herself that Abby was glad to see her. She'd even hugged her and uttered the magic words, "I'm so glad to be home."

But that was before Nell asked her to gather her dirty clothes for the wash and before the phone started ringing. Abby had been far more interested in hearing from her friends about all she'd missed during her week in Dallas than in performing any domestic duties. It was so hard to know when to cut her some slack and when to pull in the reins.

While Nell ate her bagel, Abby reappeared, picked up an uncooked Pop-Tart, took a bite, then asked for money. "After enrollment, a bunch of us are gonna eat lunch together."

"And you're promising me that your clothes will be washed by the time I get home?"

"Who cares about the clothes?"

"You do, unless you prefer going naked."

"Okay, okay. You don't need to get on my case."

Oh, really? "Fine. Don't forget to spot-treat the stains."

Abby stood beside her now, one hand held out, palm up. "The money?"

Nell dug in her purse and pulled out a five-dollar bill. "Have a good time. I'll be home around six."

Then, as if the sun had mysteriously come out in the tiny kitchen, Abby smiled. "Thanks, Mom. Love you."

Nell shook her head. There was no predicting her daughter. Up one minute, down the next. How had Stella ever managed with two daughters? More and more frequently these days she appreciated what she and Lily must have put their mother through.

Rinsing off her plate, Nell wondered what Abby would think about Brady. Would she make more of their friendship than was there? Well, that would be her problem. She and Brady were just friends. She enjoyed his company and planned to invite him to a home-cooked meal soon. Maybe as time went on, she'd introduce him to some of her friends. To Lily and her husband Evan. Even to her mother. After all, he knew no one in Fayetteville.

Mental telepathy was working as well as the phone service because just then her mother called. "Hi,

Mom. I only have a minute. I'm on my way to my meeting and work.''

"I won't take much of your time. I just wondered if you enjoyed the film?''

Suddenly the bagel became indigestible. "Film?''

"You know, the Brad Pitt movie. Janelle Davis saw you there.'' Her mother paused to heighten the impact. "With a man.''

"I didn't see her there.''

"Well, she certainly saw you.''

Nell paced to the window, noticing her flower beds needed watering. "Your point?''

"Don't be obtuse, Nell. Who is he?''

"His name is Brady Logan. I met him at the library.''

"At the library? Do you think that's wise taking up with a stranger like that?''

Nell sighed. "I've subjected him to the third degree, and he's checked out. Besides, we're just friends.''

For all her second-guessing, Stella sounded disappointed at that outcome. "I'd rather hoped—''

"*Friends,* Mother. He's not looking for more and neither am I. But I have fun with him.'' There. The concept of fun ought to get her attention.

Stella made a tsking sound. "Just be careful, honey. I don't want anything upsetting you.''

"I'll handle it, Mom. Thank you for your concern.'' Nell had long ago learned that the prudent policy was to keep her mother as happy as possible. "I've got to run. Bye, now.''

Another typical start of a day, Nell thought as she drove downtown. Between Abby and her mother, she already felt like a pinball ratcheting through a maze and it wasn't even eight o'clock.

At least she had one thing going for her, she found a parking spot right in front of the church. She cracked her windows, locked her car and dashed downstairs into the large meeting room just in time to grab a cup of coffee and greet her friends. When the bell in the steeple chimed the hour, Ben Hadley, an elderly gentleman with lively, sparkling eyes who had been a lifesaver for her, opened the meeting, dispensed with a few items of business and then nodded in her direction. She laid her purse on an empty folding chair and made her way to the front of the room. Several people nodded encouragingly to her, and in the back row she noticed two unfamiliar faces. This was by no means the first time she had done this, but it never became any easier. Yet, ironically, it was freeing beyond her capacity to imagine.

She approached the speaker's stand and gripped it for support, emboldened by waves of empathy from those in the audience.

She moistened her lips, then uttered the words that at once condemned and redeemed her. "My name is Nell and I am an alcoholic."

CHAPTER FOUR

NELL SIGHED IN RELIEF after her talk was over. Therapeutic as it was to recall the lessons of the worst times, she always carried away a residue of self-disgust and fear. Sobriety was hardly guaranteed. Instead, it was a daily reprieve. Yet as she left the church, there was a spring in her step, her mood buoyed by the hollow-eyed, yet hopeful expressions on the faces of the two newcomers at the meeting.

Ben Hadley fell in beside her. "Nice job, Nell."

The quiet words of praise filled her with love for her friend, who had been through so much with so many. If anyone lived the Twelve Steps, it was Ben. His humility and selflessness were legendary. "Thank you. I don't know why, but it was especially difficult today."

He kept pace with her. "Any particular reason?"

Nell thought about his question. When she reached her car, she turned to face him. "This may sound funny, but I'm too happy. I…I'm afraid to trust it."

He nodded sagely, then smiled. "It's okay to be happy. You're worth it." He patted her shoulder. "Have a great day."

She sat in the car for several moments. That was one of the hardest lessons—liking herself. Believing she was worthy of approval, acceptance, love. It was so tempting to dwell on the harm she'd done, but the danger with that line of thinking lay in one of the "cures" for negativity. Liquor. Thank God for AA, which had given her the means to face herself and others with forgiveness and love.

Driving to work, she thought about what had made her tell Ben she was happy. She was contented with her job, her home, and, despite the normal ups and downs with Abby and her mother, her relationships. So what was different today? With unflinching honesty, she made herself utter the name. "Brady Logan." She hadn't realized how much she'd missed male companionship, the easy give-and-take of communication, even the sound of a deep voice in her home and the lingering scent of a fragrance decidedly masculine.

Given his situation, friendship was all that he could offer, which suited her fine, because anything else would scare her silly. If they ever moved into intimacy... She cringed. Memory blotted out the sun and in her mind she heard Rick again, flinging his customary accusation. "Can't you loosen up, for God's sake? Or at least try to fake it."

Oh, she'd learned to fake it all right—after several glasses of numbing wine. But it hadn't been enough to save her marriage.

She was obviously no Clarice.

Friend. That sounded just her speed. She hoped Brady never wanted more. If he did, he'd be disappointed. Sex was a thing of the past, and she'd learned there were worse things than doing without a man, particularly a sexually demanding, emotionally abusive one like Rick.

She found a parking place at the library and pulled in, but remained in the car, rendered immobile by a notion that had suddenly surfaced from somewhere in her subconscious. She was kidding herself. The truth? Brady stirred her in a way she'd never experienced and it was exhilarating.

But mostly terrifying.

ABBY'S FIRST WORDS when Nell walked in the house early that evening rocked her. "Grandma told me about your date."

Slowly Nell set down her purse, fighting the tension stiffening her neck. Stella had picked up her granddaughter, and they'd spent the afternoon together. Alike as two peas in a pod, Stella and Abby watched over her with the fierceness of mother eagles. "What date?"

Abby leaned against the kitchen counter, arms folded across her chest. "She said some man took you to a movie."

"Some man did."

"Why didn't I know about it?"

"You were in Dallas."

"So I'm not supposed to know, is that it?"

Nell crossed to the refrigerator and took her time getting out the casserole she'd prepared for dinner. "You make it sound as if I deliberately kept something from you."

"Well, didn't you?"

"It wasn't that big a deal." Nell had no idea whether she sounded convincing. She silently acknowledged her decision not to tell Abby about her outings with Brady and run the risk of upsetting her.

Now, thanks to Stella, she had no choice but to face the issue.

"Who is he?"

"A friend I met at the library."

"Grandma said you need to be careful. That he sorta picked you up."

Nell bit back an unkind retort. "Give me credit for being smarter than that." Yet, what did she really know about Brady Logan? He was a successful businessman and a grieving widower. But beyond that? "He's new in town. We're friends. End of discussion." She preheated the oven. "Now tell me about registration."

Abby eyed her dubiously, aware her mother was changing the subject, then shrugged. "Okay, I guess. Tonya's locker is in the same hall, and we both have Mr. Sanders for English. We had this dumb assembly about the rules. They treat us like babies."

Nell stifled a smile.

"What's his name?"

"Whose name?"

"The man."

Nell put her arm around her daughter, thankful Abby didn't pull away. "Brady Logan," she said in an even voice. "Abby, he's no one you need to be concerned about."

"That's a relief."

Nell turned her daughter so she could look into her eyes. "Honey, things don't stay the same."

"Duh. You think I don't know that? If they did, Dad would still be here."

Nell summoned every ounce of patience. "Someday you will have a boyfriend, go off to college, get

married. And someday it's possible I might have another relationship. Life isn't about standing still. It's
about taking risks. Experiencing the unusual. Meeting new people. If I've learned anything at all, it's
that we must never lose sight of the potential in every
person, in every day. But right now? I'm not looking
for a man, okay?''

Abby looked down. ''Whatever.''

Nell turned back to the casserole, vowing not to
let Abby see the tears of frustration gathering. Behind her, she heard the lid of the cookie jar being
lifted.

''Mom?''

''Yes?''

Abby separated an Oreo and licked the filling off
one wafer before continuing. ''If he ever comes
again, can I meet him?''

''Certainly.''

''He's probably a dweeb, anyway.''

After Abby left the room, Nell slumped over the
counter. She'd had no idea Abby would be so pos-
sessive of her. The last thing she needed was to upset
the family equilibrium. What would she be risking if
she continued her friendship with Brady?

Reflecting on the change in her mood from earlier
in the day, she reached a conclusion. Fate quickly
mocked anyone who claimed to be ''too happy.''

AT NOON ON Wednesday Brady attended his first Rotary meeting since well before the accident. Avoiding
all unnecessary human contact on the road, he'd
never given Rotary a thought, but now it seemed like
a viable way to learn more about the community and

to meet some business leaders. As luck would have it, seated at his table were a local bank president and Buzz Valentine, a commercial realtor. From his off-hand questions, he learned they were both high on the investment potential in the area. This optimism was further advanced by the speaker, who cited regional airport traffic figures in excess of estimated projections.

For a short time there, Brady realized later, he'd actually felt a sizzle of adrenaline at the prospects, proving his business instincts weren't totally dead. After making an appointment with Buzz Valentine for the next day, he decided to spend the rest of the afternoon at the library researching local movers and shakers.

Yeah, Logan.

Okay, and getting a "loneliness fix" from Nell, who had provided him with the only moments of contentment he'd had in many months.

NELL BENT OVER her desk, studying the book list provided by the elementary school reading coordinator, tickled to find several of her favorite titles. She picked up the list and headed for the children's area to pull some books for a shelf display.

"Nell?"

She glanced down and immediately felt her fair skin betray her. "Hi, Brady." She noted the newspapers and business magazines spread on the table around him. "More research?"

"I figure if I'm going to be here awhile, I need to learn all I can about the area economy."

She fingered a magazine cover sporting the well-known face of a nationally prominent entrepreneur headquartered in Northwest Arkansas. "This region isn't the sleepy little byway of yesteryear, thanks to people like him."

Brady cocked an eyebrow. "Hardly. Pretty impressive financials."

Nell fought the mesmerizing sensation produced by gazing into his brown eyes. "Let me know if I can locate anything for you." She held up the lists in her hands. "If you'll excuse me, I have work to do in the children's area."

He stood and started to walk along with her. "Can I help?"

"If you want." Anything was better than having him study her with that unsettling stare. "Here." She handed him the second page of the list. "You could pull some of these titles."

He ran a finger down the page. "*Johnny Tremain* and *The Outsiders*. Wow. I haven't thought of them in years."

"Books have a way of transporting us to the time and place we encountered them, don't they?"

He didn't answer. When she glanced up inquiringly, she was taken aback. Rather than the pleased smile of recognition she expected to see, his jaw had tensed and a frown creased his forehead. Odd.

Finally he said, "I suppose." He laid down a book and turned to gaze out the window. "I try not to think of the past."

He'd said the words more to himself than to her, so she continued pulling volumes in silence. She could understand why the immediate past was difficult for him, but what childhood memories had the books triggered?

She didn't know how long he stood at the window, but when he faced her again, his expression was more relaxed. "You seem to love what you do."

She smiled. "Is it that obvious?"

"Your face lights up when you talk about books. Did you know that?" His voice held a tinge of yearning. "I used to feel that way about my work."

"And now?"

"It seems meaningless. What lasting satisfaction does creating and marketing software provide? You never see the results of your efforts."

"But isn't the challenge of it fulfilling?"

"If you count the reward in dollars and cents."

"You don't?"

He stared over the tops of the shelves. "Not anymore." After an awkward silence, he took a step toward her. "At this point I have more questions than answers, but this much I know. I'm due for a change. Sticking around here for starters."

The intensity of his gaze caused her skin to tingle. "You could do worse."

"Yeah," he said thoughtfully. "There's lots to like. For instance, you're here."

Nell didn't know how to take his remark. Surely he wasn't going to make some life-altering decision based on her. That would be ludicrous. She screwed up her courage. "What's that supposed to mean?"

He gave a crooked smile. "That didn't come out right, did it? What I meant to say is that you've succeeded in helping me think about rejoining the human race."

She hugged two books to her chest, then responded thoughtfully, "Believe me, I know how hard that is to do, but, Brady, it's worth the effort. You have a lot of tomorrows left."

"Tomorrows?" Slowly he shook his head. "Yeah. I like the sound of that." He paused. "Especially from you."

Before Nell could process her reaction to his last words, she sensed the approach of someone and looked beyond Brady. Lily. Her sister's timing was as flawless as her carefully sculpted hairdo and perfectly understated makeup.

"There you are, Nell." Lily sailed into the area. "When I couldn't find you in your office, I thought I'd find you here." With an assessing smile aimed straight at Brady, she said, "And you are—"

"Brady Logan." He extended his hand and shook Lily's.

Lily turned to Nell. "Your friend?"

Lord, now Brady would think she'd been talking about him to her family. "Yes. We met here about a week ago." Nell's voice box didn't seem to be working properly. "This is my sister, Lily Roberts."

Brady nodded acknowledgment.

"The way you were talking, so seriously and all, I figured you weren't just another library patron." Lily indulged in a tinkling laugh that to Nell's ears was replete with sisterly innuendo.

Brady took command. "I am that, too. I'm trying to learn about the Fayetteville area and Nell's been kind enough to assist me."

Lily cocked her head. "In the children's section?"

Nell prayed the floor would swallow her. She

knew her sister. Beyond that flirtatious facade, Lily was determined to pump Brady for information.

Brady gestured toward the library table where he'd been sitting. "It seems I strayed a bit. I volunteered to help Nell."

"How kind," Lily said, ignoring the pleading look Nell was telegraphing her. "I understand you've only been in town a short time."

"That's right."

Lily laid a hand on his arm. "Then you need to get better acquainted, and I have the perfect solution. Evan and I are hosting a barbecue Saturday night for family and some close friends. I dropped by the library to invite Nell, but this is even better. Of course you'll come, too. All our guests will look forward to meeting Nell's new friend."

Nell couldn't be sure, but it sounded as if Lily had put special emphasis on the word *friend.* She couldn't stand by while her sister organized her life. "Lily, Brady may have other plans—"

She didn't get out any more words before she heard Brady say, "Thank you, Lily. I'd like to come."

Lily smiled triumphantly at Nell. "Well, that's settled, then. Six o'clock." Turning to Brady, she sprang her trap. "Since you'll be coming with Nell, she can show you where we live."

"Sounds great." Brady handed Nell his page of the book list. "Guess I'd better get back to my research." Smiling at Lily, he added, "Nice to have met you."

He'd gone only a few steps when Lily grabbed

Nell's arm and purred sexily, "Do many of your customers look like that?"

Nell gritted her teeth. "Do I kill you now or later, sister dear?"

"Kill me? Unless I'm mistaken, which I'm not, I just did you a big favor."

"I'll tell you what I've already told Mother and Abby. Brady and I are just friends."

Lily shot her an incredulous look. "Right."

"It's not like that."

"But it certainly could be." Lily faced her with that trust-me expression that set Nell's nerves on edge. "So you're just friends? Okay. I'll buy that for now."

"Good. He's a grieving widower, Lily. I doubt he's ready for what you have in mind."

"I didn't know. I'm sorry. But still, what's the harm in bringing him to the barbecue?"

Trapped. "Nothing, I guess." She swallowed her trepidations.

Eyeing her up and down, Lily said, "I'll be calling you to set a time to go shopping for your new outfit. You'll want to dazzle him."

Lily quickly back-pedaled toward the door, giving her a ta-ta wave of the fingers. Nell was too angry to move. Hadn't her sister understood a word she'd said?

A new outfit?

She couldn't remember the last time she'd dazzled a man.

And she wasn't about to start now.

WHEN BRADY RETURNED to his condo, the message light on his answering machine was blinking. He kicked off his shoes, padded to the refrigerator for a cold soda, then settled in the overstuffed chair staring at the offending light. It had to be Carl. Some crisis.

He swigged from the can, then rested his head against the back of the chair. He wished he could care. But he didn't. What used to be as important to him as the air he breathed, now affected him not in the least. He'd always heard you weren't supposed to make any major decisions within a year following a spouse's death. But it had been months. Shouldn't he be feeling something about his company? But pride, status, power—none of it meant a thing.

Hell, he'd worked up more energy about the idea slowly forming in his head to develop an upscale conference and resort center on Beaver Lake than he had about any of Carl's importunings. It wasn't about money, although he wasn't so far gone that he didn't want his money to work for him. It was about intangible rewards, permanence. Only with Brooke had he found that.

He closed his eyes and tried to bring her into focus—her long silky hair, her tanned shoulders, but the image kept shifting in his memory. Instead, he pictured the willowy body of Nell Porter topped by her heart-shaped face and big, knowing eyes, her arms cradling books protectively against her breasts.

The damn books. He'd been ill-prepared for the wave of nostalgia that had swept over him. *Johnny Tremain*. He'd suddenly remembered his mother's animated voice reading to him. Remembered lying in bed listening, the words transforming him into a boy in Revolutionary War times. Then, after she closed the book, she tucked the covers around him and kissed him good-night. That was before…

He cursed under his breath. For years he'd pretty much been able to fend off such memories, feeding on his resentment and losing himself in work until forgetfulness became a habit.

What was Nell Porter doing to him anyway? Whatever it was felt way too much like pecking away at his armor. Yet he was drawn to her in ways that made no sense. All he knew was that he felt better when he was around her.

He sat up, drained the soda, punched the Play button on the machine and listened to Carl's edgy voice fill him in on the latest emergency at L&S TechWare.

He should respond. Immediately. Regrettably, that wasn't a priority.

NELL HAD GIVEN IN and gone shopping with Lily. Down deep, she valued her sister's advice. Lily's taste was impeccable. The floral print wraparound skirt and filmy lavender blouse were on sale and, as Lily insisted, were Nell's "colors." Nell had to admit she'd been flattered by the lift of Brady's eyebrows when he picked her up Saturday evening.

Light from the fading sun filtered through the ancient oaks and dappled the manicured lawn as Nell led Brady to the back gate of Lily's house. Stella, Evan's mother and father, and several other couples were already there, clustered around the hors d'oeuvres table set up on the flagstone patio. In a far corner of the yard, Abby corralled Chase. Without consulting Nell, Lily had invited Abby to baby-sit with Chase and spend the night. The obviousness of her maneuver would be amusing if it wasn't so darn uncomfortable. Nell disliked being the focus of Lily's expectations.

"Here's Nell." Her mother broke away from the guests and came toward them, a fixed smile on her face. "And you must be Brady," she said, extending her hand. "I'm Nell's mother, Stella Janes."

"It's nice to meet you," Brady said. "Nell has made me feel most welcome in Arkansas."

"I'm glad to hear my daughter represents the best of Southern hospitality."

"You taught me well," Nell murmured.

Stella tucked her arm through Brady's. "Come meet Lily's husband and the others."

Trailing the pair, Nell sought to unfist her hands, aware of the tension riddling her. This was no big deal, yet she knew her family. They would make something out of nothing. She glanced across the yard and her heart sank. Oblivious to Chase tugging on her shorts, Abby was watching Brady's progress to the patio with narrowed eyes and thinned lips.

Somehow Nell made it through the introductions, ignoring the questioning looks some of the women angled at Brady and her. From the cooler Brady picked out a beer and a soda. "Which would you prefer, Nell?"

Before she could answer, Lily slipped in between them. "My sister doesn't drink."

Nell winced. Would Brady pick up on the point-edness of the remark or was she simply overreacting?

Brady handed Nell the soda, then smiled at the two women. "I don't either, except for an occasional beer."

After Lily excused herself, Brady looked down at Nell, his eyes soft. "I like your family. Nice people."

Nell tore her gaze from him and glanced around. "Yes. They are." Then she noticed Abby sitting in a swing, holding Chase in her lap. The girl's eyes were fixed everywhere but on Nell. "Brady, I'd like you to meet my daughter." She started walking toward Abby, confident Brady was following. "Abby, this is—" When she turned to include him in the introduction, he wasn't right behind her as she'd expected. He had stopped several feet away and his face had gone pale. "—Brady Logan," Nell finished lamely.

As if shaking off a trance, he ran a hand through his hair and approached the swing set. "Hello," he said in a husky voice.

Abby gave him a brief glance, then continued swinging. "'Lo."

Nell stepped forward, took hold of the ropes and brought the swing to a stop. "Brady recently moved here from California," she said in a voice full of a mind-your-manners undertone.

"I know." Abby's stony face had softened not one iota. "Grandma told me."

Nell could only wonder what other tidbits Stella had seen fit to divulge. She turned helplessly to Brady. "And this is Chase, Lily's son," she said running a hand over the toddler's curly hair.

"Hi, Chase."

The boy ducked his head into Abby's shirt. Abby continued to stare at her mother in sullen defiance.

"What grade are you in, Abby?"

Slowly Abby turned to Brady. "Eighth."

Brady's voice sounded strangled. "Hope you enjoy the year."

Nell was missing something. It was as if Brady, usually confident and assured in social situations, had become a tongue-tied adolescent himself.

"Don't you need to mingle or something?" Glaring, Abby nodded in the direction of the adult guests. Her leave-me-alone message was received loud and clear.

"I guess we should. I just wanted you to meet Brady."

"Well, now I have." Abby clutched Chase and stood. Turning to Brady, she mumbled her excuses. "I gotta go feed Chase."

"Glad to have met you," Brady said.

"Yeah." Abby marched past them toward the house.

Abby's rudeness had effectively communicated her displeasure. Nell laid a hand on Brady's arm. "I'm sorry about that. She's usually more pleasant."

Brady shook his head. "Kids. What're you going to do?" He put an arm around her shoulder, a gesture Nell found all too comforting. "I remember."

Nell looked up into eyes haunted with sadness. Then realization struck her. "Oh, Brady, how old was your daughter?"

Brady cleared his throat before answering. "About Abby's age."

"I'm so sorry."

He rested his chin on her head. "Me, too." Then in a soft echo he repeated himself. "Me, too."

There were no words. Brushing a palm across the

front of his starched shirt, Nell lingered in the curve of his embrace before stepping away. "Maybe we should rejoin the party."

He took her by the elbow and led her to a group sitting on the patio. "Brady? Brady Logan?" A prematurely balding man with glasses stood. "What a pleasure. I didn't expect to see you again so soon."

Brady shook the man's hand, then introduced her to Buzz Valentine, who, in turn, presented his wife, Sandy, who made room for her on the glider. Nell knew of Buzz Valentine by reputation. He was a successful commercial realtor and developer, and the couple were very active in the community. While she and Sandy made small talk, Nell couldn't help overhearing Brady and Buzz deep in discussion about various tracts of land. What was going on? How did Brady know Buzz? She drew a quick breath. Maybe Brady *was* serious about staying.

She studied him—earnest, handsome and incredibly virile—and tried to talk sense to herself. These awakenings in her body, involuntary as they were, were embarrassing. And way too powerful. She'd stop them if she could. He'd made his expectations quite clear. Friendship.

Just then he glanced toward her, sending a tender smile meant only for her. Her insides suddenly turned topsy-turvy, and she knew she would have to be careful. Very careful.

He was a sexy, appealing man, and despite all her rationalizations, she had noticed.

Boy, had she noticed!

BRADY WAS GRATEFUL when Nell suggested they be among the first departing guests. Although everyone had been friendly and welcoming, this was more social interaction than he'd had since... Men and women milling in his oversize living room, their expressions set in solemn mourning, their dark garments in stark contrast to the sunny California day flaming beyond the floor-to-ceiling plate glass. Their solicitous murmurs of condolence falling impotently somewhere beyond his consciousness. The palpable air of relief with which they turned from him and hastened to the buffet table. He would forever see the scene in black-and-white shattered by violent splashes of red and yellow behind his pupils, as if grief were being experienced through the lens of an avant-garde cinematographer.

Now, as they approached her house, Nell brought him back to the present moment. "Was this evening difficult for you?"

He eased the car into her drive and shut off the motor, surprised by her insight. "Why do you ask?"

"You've been unusually quiet on the way home."

Sidestepping the necessity of answering, he tried a smile. "Have I been a dull date?"

"Not at all. Everyone, including me, found you quite congenial."

"Congenial enough to invite me in for a while?" He could've escaped, yet he wanted to talk about this evening. All except meeting Abby. He couldn't talk about that. Not yet. Abby's gangly legs, with telltale razor nicks, her half-child, half-woman body, even her braces had wrenched him back to the last time he'd seen Nicole, modeling her new swimsuit for him, her buds of breasts taking him by surprise, her little-girlness metamorphosing into something alien and threatening to a father.

Nell looked up at him questioningly. "You're sure?"

"I'm sure. It's not that late."

Nell dug her house key out of her purse. "Come on then. I'll make us a pot of decaf."

She left Brady in the tiny family room, only the glow of a small table lamp illuminating the space. He put his head back and shut his eyes, letting peace wrap around him like a cocoon. For the first time that evening, he drew a deep breath and let his body relax, appreciating the fact that Nell had not chosen to press him about his reaction to the party.

When she came back, bearing two mugs of coffee, she handed him his, then settled at the other end of the couch. Yet she didn't say anything, just sat, composed, holding the mug between her hands.

Somehow the comfortable silence made it easier for him to begin. "I liked the people I met."

She smiled.

"It's been a while since I've been around so many people in that kind of situation."

"I thought so."

"I—I haven't been ready. For a long time, I couldn't understand how people could laugh freely, seemingly have so few cares. They seemed distant, superficial."

"It's painful, isn't it?"

He set down his mug and looked at her. "You understand."

"Finding yourself alone plunges you into a darkness that can seem never-ending." She, too, set aside her coffee. "When my marriage was falling apart and then my father died so suddenly, I couldn't imagine a world where the sun would shine. Couldn't begin to picture a time when I would have an ordinary day. In fact, the concept of 'ordinary' was utterly foreign to me.''

He stared into her eyes, in which was revealed intimate experience with pain and death. Yet she had found the courage to trust in rainbows. "Do you ever look at people, like at the party, and wonder what they know of suffering?"

"All the time," she said quietly.

"Yet you seem to have been able to go on."

She bit her bottom lip, then nodded. "You will, too."

He moved closer, then without thinking, picked up her hand. "I wouldn't have believed that two weeks ago. But now," he felt his defenses begin to crumble, "I think it may be possible."

"Change is scary, isn't it?"

Was that part of it? Not just grief, but fear of change? "Especially when you can't control the forces that set it in motion."

"Control…ah, yes." She studied him, as if seeking some kind of answer from him. "What is in your control now, Brady?"

It was a big question. One that deserved a thoughtful answer, but at this moment the softness of her skin beneath his fingers and the luminous quality in her eyes suggested what he desperately needed to control was the pounding of his heart. Because, more than anything, he wanted to pull her close, taste her lips, smell her skin. And that surprised him.

He steadied his emotions and answered her. "More than there has been in quite a while. I'm staying here, I'm letting my partner handle the business until I make some decisions about the future.''

''Can you let some of it be beyond your control?''

He moved so that she was in the curve of his arm. How would she react if she knew he'd even orchestrated their meeting? ''How can you already know me so well? I must come across as a controlling kind of guy.''

''You're a man, aren't you?''

He loved the teasing twinkle in her eye. ''Guilty as charged.''

''Well?''

''Seriously? It's hard for me to sit back and let things happen.''

She reached up and caressed his cheek. ''And you couldn't prevent the accident.''

He lowered his head, aware of the dark night lurking outside the circle of lamplight. ''No.''

''That's the hardest part,'' she said. ''Accepting that there are many things beyond our ability to control.''

''Were you born wise?''

''Hardly,'' she said, and he saw the hint of pain in her eyes.

He lifted his hand from her shoulder and toyed with her hair. ''We sure did get serious.''

''And our coffee's probably cold.'' She leaned forward and retrieved her mug, tasted it, then smiled. ''If you hurry, it might still warm your innards.''

He laughed. ''Innards. Now that's the first hillbilly-ism I've heard from you.''

''But probably not the last.'' She batted her eyes and then added, ''You'uns be rat fine, fer a man.''

''Rat?''

"Right," she explained.

They kept the conversation light until it was time for him to leave. In the front hall, he paused. She looked up at him, her big eyes fixed on his, and he couldn't think of a thing to say. The silence was charged with overtones of need...and control. Finally, he remembered himself. "Thank you. I had a great evening."

For the second time that night, she laid her palm on his chest, and he was sure she could feel the rapid beating of his heart. "So did I."

He covered her hand with his and then, before he could censor himself, he leaned forward and kissed her, gently, fleetingly. Not at all like he wanted to. What he wanted was to crush her to him and salve all those places where emotions had rubbed him raw, where healing had never begun. Maybe never would.

Then he was aware only of the softness of her lips beneath his, the hint of a coffee taste in her mouth and a delicious soothing warmth spreading through his body. When he released her, she gazed up at him with a question in her eyes.

Her voice was tremulous. "Friends?"

"Friends," he repeated.

"Good night," she whispered.

Later standing beside his car in the still, late summer evening, listening to tree frogs and the insistent barking of a neighbor's dog, Brady began to wonder. Was it possible simply to remain friends with Nell?

His body was demanding more. Hell, she was no longer pecking at his armor. She had pierced it.

And it was far beyond his control.

CHAPTER FIVE

AFTER LUNCH the next day, Lily and Evan dropped Abby off at home. She muttered a perfunctory "hello" to Nell before bolting to her room and closing her door. Sighing, Nell set aside the sketch book in which she'd been drawing. Friends had told her that the early teens were the worst for girls, and she had no trouble believing it. Rioting hormones had changed her daughter from a tractable, sweet child into a rebellious, insecure adolescent, who had no intention of continuing to share her inner life, at least with her mother.

Yet Nell really needed to address Abby's behavior last night. Regardless of Brady's experience with teenagers, Abby's attitude had been embarrassing. What would it take to convince her Brady posed no threat?

Nell had replayed the kiss at the door repeatedly and had concluded it was nothing more than a casual gesture, friend-to-friend. At least for him. And that was a good thing. She couldn't risk emotional involvement and the potential for falling back into the trap of failure and self-doubt.

She'd experienced plenty of that, thanks to Rick. Over and over she had asked herself where things had gone wrong. Had she been that bad a wife?

They'd met in college, a classic case of opposites attracting. She, the quiet, studious coed, drawn to the gregarious, life-of-the-party frat president. During their courtship, it was as if he drew confidence from her adoration. For her, being at Rick's side meant inclusion into social groups. Besides, his blond good looks reminded her of her father. It had been easy to say "yes" when he'd asked to marry her.

Maybe they should have left Fayetteville early in their marriage, seen something of the world, learned to depend on each other. Perhaps everything had come too easily, been too familiar. Right out of college, Rick took a job with the athletic department of the university. That meant long workdays, travel and weekends full of sporting events. And parties.

When Abby was an infant, Nell had been able to beg off most of those occasions, despite Rick's impatience with her. He couldn't understand why she didn't want to hire a baby-sitter three or more nights a week. Then, as time went on and he was more entrenched in the monied, fast world of big-time donors and alumni, it became more and more terrifying to accompany him.

It was then the drinking first began.

Just one or two to loosen up. When that no longer sufficed, she'd graduated to a quick nip before leaving home. All around her, whether at tailgate parties or testimonial dinners, there was liquor. Soothing, relaxing, *addictive* liquor.

From Abby's room issued the sound of her CD player, turned up high. Nell bit her lip, knowing it wasn't the music that had her on edge, but her memories. Rick had never understood her shyness. He'd married a homebody when he'd wanted a hostess. And a lover. Had she really been that inadequate? All she knew was a day had come when she'd panicked, sure she couldn't be what he needed her to be. Wanted her to be. And she'd self-medicated. Boy, had she ever.

No wonder Abby was concerned about Brady. She'd seen one marriage break up. Abby needed complications no more than Nell did, and she tried in her awkwardly loving way to protect both of them from change. That's why the kiss could mean nothing. Nell absolutely could not—would not—let herself become vulnerable again.

She rose to her feet, determined to reassure Abby. She walked down the hall and knocked on the bedroom door.

"What?" Abby's tone was not welcoming.

"May I come in?"

"I guess."

Abby had thrown her skirt on the floor and lay sprawled on her bed, clad in cutoff jeans and a sleeveless T-shirt, reading a teen magazine, her stuffed animals forming a phalanx around her. With an irritated sigh, she reached over to the bedside table and turned down the volume of the CD player.

"How was your time at Lily's?"

"Okay."

Count on a teenager never to volunteer anything. "Did Chase behave himself?"

"Yeah. He's cute." Abby flipped the page of her magazine.

"About last night—"

"What about it?"

"Could you look at me while we're talking?" The minute the words were out of her mouth, Nell regretted them. Accusations hardly facilitated open communication.

"Sure." Abby made a show of laying her magazine aside, sitting up, tucking her knees to her chest and staring directly at her mother. "Satisfied?"

"Oh, Abby, I'm sorry. I don't mean to come off as a shrew."

Abby quirked her mouth in disbelief.

"I, uh, was disappointed in your manners at the party."

"What about them?"

"You were not very pleasant when I introduced Mr. Logan."

Abby shrugged. "So?"

"He is my friend, and I expected better from you."

"Your *friend?* What kind of friend?" She chewed a hangnail, her sarcasm belied by the fear in her eyes.

"Abby, he's a nice man. Someone I enjoy visiting with. That's all. Why can't you just accept what I'm saying?"

"Get real, Mom."

"What's that supposed to mean?"

"He's interested in you. There. Are you happy?"

Nell stared, dumbfounded at her daughter. "Why would you say a thing like that?"

Abby threw her a disgusted look. "I saw it, Mom. Are you blind? Didn't you see the way he was looking at you? All goo-goo-eyed?"

No words came. Nell felt the heat of a blush coloring her face.

"So quit giving me that 'friend' crap, all right?" And with that, Abby rolled over, picked up the magazine and turned up the CD player.

Heart thudding, Nell slunk out of the room, flabbergasted. She wanted to protest, but she couldn't. Not without lying to her daughter—and herself.

She, too, had seen the look.

"WHADDYA THINK the mystery meat is?" Tonya set down her tray and took the seat Abby had saved for her in the school cafeteria.

"Something that may have been bologna in a former life." Abby moved her fork around her plate. "Disguised with yukky barbecue paste."

"Yummy," Tonya said, patting her bare midriff and puffing out her cheeks as if in preparation to hurl.

The sick, sweet smell of canned corn turned Abby's stomach. "I'm not hungry anyway."

Just then a freckle-faced boy walked by and, using his spoon as a drumstick, thwacked the two girls on the head. "Puh-leeze," Tonya whined to his departing back. "Grow up."

"Boys can be disgusting," Abby said, tearing off a portion of her roll and putting it in her mouth.

"*Some* boys," amended Tonya, casting a meaningful glance at a table near the food line.

Abby looked in the same direction, where a bunch of jocks sat hunched over their trays. "Dream on."

"Abby, quit putting on a big act. I noticed Alan Voyle talking to you at your locker."

Abby didn't feel like discussing him right now, even with her best friend. "So?"

"I think he likes you."

Abby couldn't suppress a thrill of interest. "No way."

"You shoulda seen how he looked at you."

Ordinarily she'd have been ecstatic. Alan was ultra cool, but Tonya had innocently reminded her of what she'd been trying to forget—the way that man had looked at her mother. She shoved away her tray, fighting tears.

Tonya studied her. "You okay?"

Abby stood. "Not really." She picked up her tray and made a beeline for the return counter.

"Wait up!" Tonya was right behind her. "You're acting weird."

"Why not? My whole life is weird."

"C'mon." Tonya grabbed her by the arm, steered her toward a floor-to-ceiling window at the end of a row of lockers and pulled her down on the carpet. Abby rested her chin on her knees and stared outside where hummingbirds flitted to a feeder hanging near the science room and a squirrel scampered across the grass. "Okay. So what's the matter?"

"What would you say if I told you my mother has a boyfriend?" There. She'd said it. Out loud. Abby watched while, as if in slow-motion, her friend's eyes widened.

"No way."

Abby was surprised by the tick of irritation. Like Tonya couldn't imagine her mother being attractive enough or something?

Tonya leaned forward, her face alive with curiosity. "Go on. Tell me. Who is it?"

"This man."

"Well, duh."

"She, er, met him at the library." How romantic did that sound?

"He must be super nerdy."

Abby shook her head. "He's not. He's actually kinda handsome."

"So what's the problem?" Tonya waited, then shook her head as if she had miraculously been given the answer to her own question. "Yeah, I guess they are kinda old."

"It's not that, it's just…weird." Abby felt stupid. What did "weird" communicate? Nothing. But she had no other words for her feelings.

"Why?"

"Mom and I have finally got it all together. We don't need anybody. Especially not him."

Tonya looked puzzled. "Yeah, but wouldn't your mom like a man? I mean, she's not *that* old, I guess."

The locker area was beginning to fill up with students getting their books for their next class. Abby leaned forward and hissed in Tonya's ear, "You don't get it, do you?"

Tonya shrugged. "I guess not."

"My mother doesn't need anybody but me. Somebody else might not understand." She gulped. "He might make everything worse."

Tonya laid a hand on Abby's knee. "Jeez, are you thinking maybe," she faltered, "like maybe your mom would—"

Abby hung her head. "Yeah. What if she liked this guy and he didn't like her? Maybe she'd—" Abby couldn't finish.

"Start drinking again?"

Abby nodded mutely.

"She prob'ly wouldn't."

"Yeah, but if she did—" Abby raised tear-filled eyes to her friend "—I couldn't stand it."

The bell for the next period rang, and both girls jumped. Tonya was the first to stand. "I gotta go. I have a test." She reached down, took Abby's hand and hauled her to her feet. "But we'll talk after school. Promise."

Oblivious to the hurried commotion around her, Abby watched her friend depart, feeling as alone as she had in a long time. She swiped at her eyes. She knew it was childish to suspect her mother would start drinking again. But there must be a reason her grandmother always reminded her to watch out for Nell. Like maybe Grandma thought her mother needed a keeper.

Brady Logan might be an okay guy. But Abby couldn't help thinking he'd end up upsetting her mother. And that would not be good.

When the second bell rang, Abby's stomach plummeted. Now she'd have to walk into math class late. Everyone would be staring at her, noticing her skinny legs, gross braces and stringy hair.

Eighth grade sucked.

Except maybe for Alan Voyle.

NELL DIDN'T HAVE TO GO in for work Monday until mid-afternoon, so following her morning meeting, she went to yoga class, grabbed a quick bite and then returned home to work some more on the pencil sketch she planned to give her mother for Christmas.

No sooner had she put on some soothing music and settled at her desk than the doorbell rang.

When she answered it, there stood Lily in a powder blue shorts outfit with Chase, looking adorable in a pint-size cowboy suit. "Hope you're not busy," Lily said hopefully.

Nell stood aside and held the door open. "Just doing some drawing. Come on in." Nell hunkered beside Chase. "Hey, squirt, got a hug for your auntie?" He reached his chubby arms around her neck and planted a wet kiss on her cheek.

"Bocks," he said.

"Smart kid. You remembered, didn't you?"

Lily looked puzzled. "What?"

"Abby's old blocks." Nell led the way to the family room, where she opened the chest and pulled out a box of brightly colored wooden blocks. Chase sat down and began happily pouring them out onto the floor and then reassembling them in structures meaningful only to him.

Abby turned to her sister. "Coffee? Soda?"

"No, thanks." Lily looked lovingly at Chase. "But I could sure use a strong dose of adult conversation."

Nell laughed as they both sat down on the sofa. "I remember that phase. Believe me, when he's a teenager, you may long for diapers and wall-to-wall toys."

"Ah, the joys of parenthood. Each phase has its own set of challenges, I guess."

"Today I'm tempted to trade you mine for yours," Nell said remembering Abby's freeze-out yesterday.

Lily raised a brow. "Not our sweet Abby?"

"Our 'sweet Abby' and I are having issues."

"Rick and Clarice?"

"She's still not crazy about visiting them in Dallas, but it's more than that. At the same time she wants to assert her independence and shove me away, she watches over my every move."

Lily's expression softened. "Can you blame her?"

Nell considered her sister's question, knowing she meant it kindly, not judgmentally. "No. I put her…you…through some awful times. When I think what could've happened that night—"

"Shh. That's all behind you."

As if it could ever be behind her. Didn't her sister get it? She lived with her mistakes every day. Nell struggled to keep her tone reasonable. "No, Lily, it will never be over and done with, but I try to deal with it in a healthy way. And today I'm worried about Abby. It's as if she thinks she single-handedly has to make sure nothing changes."

Lily leaned over and helped Chase restack the tower he'd toppled. "What are we really talking about?"

"Brady Logan."

Lily's head popped up and she turned to Nell. "That's what Abby's worried about?"

Nell nodded. "Before you start in, I want to be clear here. I don't need Mother's critical take on this right now."

"And you think that's what I'll give you?"

No time like the present, Nell decided. "Do you have any idea how often it feels like the two of you gang up on me?"

Lily bristled. "Now, just a minute—"

Nell hurried on. "I realize you both mean well, but you know what I need most today? Not a mother or a sister, but a friend."

"We 'gang up' on you?" Lily seemed genuinely puzzled.

"Sometimes."

Lily touched Nell's hand. "I'm sorry. I never realized you felt that way. It's just that—" She paused as if considering her response, then gave a nod. "Okay. Today it's friends."

Nell gave her sister a brief hug. "I really want to know what you think about Brady and me. I can't make any mistakes."

"Well, I guess there are two ways of looking at the situation. Brady Logan could be an added complication in your life—"

"Which I certainly don't need."

"Or the best thing that's ever happened to you."

"Lily, it's not like that yet—"

"Your misguided, self-effacing modesty has never been one of your more attractive features. My God, the man's crazy about you."

Nell groaned. "Not you, too."

"What do you mean?"

"That's more or less what Abby said."

"Well, there. That proves it. Surely you see it."

Nell felt trapped. "I…what he needs is a friend."

Lily shot her a skeptical look. "But you're at least thinking about more. You can only use that grieving widower defense so long. Honey, what that man needs is not merely a friend, but a healthy roll in the hay and a woman to love the daylights out of him. Now whether that's a wise idea for you or not—"

Nell's stomach moved into her throat. "That would be a big problem for me."

Lily pulled Chase into her lap. "How long has it been?"

Nell averted her eyes, wishing she could pretend to misunderstand the question.

"Since Rick, huh?"

"Yes."

"And that hardly counts, I imagine."

Nell couldn't let her sister know how close to the mark she'd come with that comment. "Lily, this isn't about sex."

"Oh, I agree. It's not *just* about sex."

Chase stuck his thumb in his mouth and settled against Lily's shoulder, his big brown eyes fastened on Nell. "I don't need a man in my life. In fact, I don't need anything that would rock the boat."

"I can understand why rocking the boat wouldn't be desirable, now that you've gotten your act together. But do you think you can go through life never taking risks?"

"No. It's just—"

"That you're scared."

"Terrified," Nell managed to answer in a small voice.

"Now we're getting somewhere! So you *do* like him." Lily fingered Chase's curls. "Beyond friendship."

"Yes, I think I could."

"And the problem is…"

"He doesn't seem ready for more."

"He's still grieving. Give him time, honey. Maybe he's ready and just doesn't know it yet. Go on."

"Then there's Abby."

"Abby's a kid. She would adapt. Besides, she'll be gone in five years. What then? You don't have to be alone, you know."

"It's not that simple. I've been hurt once by a man. I don't need those problems again."

"I won't pretend I'm not concerned about the potential for Brady to upset your equilibrium. But you deserve a chance for happiness. How many obstacles are you throwing in the path? Do you plan to play it safe your whole life?"

Abby clenched her fingers. "If that's what it takes to stay sober."

Chase had fallen asleep nestled in Lily's arms. Carefully she laid him on the sofa cushion between them. "I am so proud of you, Nell, and I grant you I've never experienced what you have, but I can't believe the price for staying sober has to be the potential for happiness with Brady or someone like him. Abby will come around in time. It's easy to dream up objections, but consider the possible benefits, too. For example, Abby sees Rick so infrequently, and Clarice, well, we don't even need to discuss what kind of adult influence she is. Brady could be good for Abby, and for you."

Lily wasn't saying anything Nell hadn't thought of in the dark of the night lying awake, alone. But it wasn't that easy. Besides there was the tragedy in Brady's life. She suspected his healing would take a long time.

"You're awfully quiet," Lily said when Nell didn't respond. "Maybe the best thing is simply to follow your heart."

Nell smiled wistfully. "Promise?"

Lily reached across her sleeping son and squeezed Nell's hand. "Oh, yes, honey. I promise."

Despite the fact she could be infuriating on occasion, Lily was Nell's best friend. Her concern was evident. In the old bad days, Lily had been there for her, big time. And here she was again. Infusing Nell with support.

"What about Mother? She's as protective of me as Abby is."

"Leave Mom to me. This is one time she and I may not see eye to eye, although I understand the pitfalls she might be concerned about."

Nell thought about Brady—his husky, warm laugh, his comforting hands, his kiss so full of tenderness and promise—and wondered if he could ever be hers.

"I won't kid you. I'm still scared, but it has helped to talk about it. Now, before we change the subject, I'll finish with one last thought." She paused for dramatic effect. "I'm going for it with Brady."

"Great. Just don't dwell in fear. It isn't helpful."

Lily had that right. Fear had led Nell to the depths. She couldn't afford to indulge it again.

Buzz Valentine shifted into low gear and steered his Dodge Ram down the steep, rutted track through the woods. Brady braced his feet and hung on to the passenger handlebar.

"Interesting road," Brady remarked dryly.

"It's an old logging road. Lots of them around."

"Where's the lake from here?"

"Over there." Buzz pointed to his left. "Right

now, you'll have to take my word for it, but you'll be able to see it shortly. If you get interested in this property, you'll have to hike it if you want to explore it all.''

"I'm surprised there's this much land left for sale.''

"Old-timers held on to it after the dam was constructed and the lake filled in the '60s. Now some of their heirs are more interested in selling. That's freed up some parcels. But they won't last long.''

Brady couldn't blame the real estate agent for his not-so-subtle application of pressure. It was prime acreage, thick with dogwoods, pine, oaks, sycamores, scrub cedars. Beautiful striated rock ledges rimmed the road.

"Here we are.'' Buzz abruptly stopped the truck. "We'll walk aways from here so I can show you the spot with the best lake view.'' He fumbled behind the seat and pulled out a can of bug repellant. "Spray your feet and legs.''

Taking the can, Brady raised the question. "Why?''

"Ticks and chiggers, friend. They love me. I don't know whether they're partial to you or not, but, trust me, you don't want to find out.''

Brady stepped out of the truck, liberally sprayed himself, then stepped away and took a deep breath. The air was fresh, and all around him dew-covered vegetation sparkled in the morning sun. Brady realized he hadn't known quiet like this since he'd left Colorado those many years ago. The only sounds were bird-calls, the gentle sigh of a soft breeze through the conifers and his own breathing.

Buzz led the way through the trees until they reached a level piece of ground on a cliff high above the water, glinting blue and silver in the light. "This could be the site of your main lodge."

Brady was thinking the same thing. He could visualize a handsome log structure, nestled in the trees, with full views of the lake, meeting rooms done in rustic styles and colors, a first-class dining room with a deck overhanging the lake. Cabins and lodges scattered along the shoreline. He began pacing off the property, thinking about road easements, septic systems, wells. A lot of groundwork before construction could begin. "Politically, how difficult will it be to get the various permissions I'd need?"

Buzz pushed back his cap and scratched his head. "I won't fool you. There'll be some problems. The main one being getting a permit for a multislip dock from the Army Corps of Engineers. You'll have to have your ducks in a row."

"That's the way it is with anything," Brady said. His mind was racing with possibilities. A chunk of ground like this in California would be untouchable for most. "What are we talking about per acre?"

Buzz gave him a figure. Two million would probably get it. Brady knew he had a lot of homework to do before he committed—canvassing business leaders to see if there would be interest in a resort-conference center, talking with county officials, utility companies, the Corps of Engineers. The list was endless, yet the prospect had engaged his imagination. "If you can get me a plat map, I'd like to walk the land in the next day or two. If I like what I see, I'll consider taking an option on the property."

Buzz held out his hand. "You'd never regret that decision."

Grinning, Brady shook Buzz's hand. "Looks like I'll need to purchase my own bug spray."

On the way home, Buzz stopped at his office to pick up the map. That afternoon, Brady sat at the heavy mahogany dining table in his leased condo. *At least this piece of Victoriana has a function,* he thought, spreading out the map. Then, with a legal pad for notes at his side, he commenced studying and brainstorming. It was nearly dark before he looked up, surprised to notice the failing light.

Checking his watch, he calculated California time and put in a call for Carl. After a few pleasantries, Brady got right to the point. "I may need to sell some company stock."

Carl's reaction was guarded. "What's up?"

Brady briefly outlined the project.

Carl's next words were not encouraging. "Have you slipped a cog, pal? You're telling me you want to build a first-rate conference center and resort in the boonies of ever'lovin' Arkansas? You want a challenge? Fine. Come home and take your pick."

After Brady hung up, he sat for a moment, eyes fixed on the map. Carl didn't get it. There was no "home." Certainly not in California. Could he ever go back? He wasn't sure. That partly depended on Nell.

He groaned. Where had that thought come from? Damn it, they were friends. He stood and paced to the window, where he stared down at the concrete parking lot where two boys were skateboarding.

Hell, he'd been kidding himself. He was interested

in Nell. Her sparkly eyes and fragile, feminine body made him long to pull her into his arms. The truth resounding in his head filled him with something akin to panic. How could this be happening?

He pressed his forehead against the cool windowpane. *Oh, Brooke, I miss you and Nicole so much. What would you want me to do?* Was it disloyal to be thinking about Nell? To feel his body quickening even as he asked the question?

As if he were being sent a sign, the phone rang. When he answered, it was Nell, her voice light, animated and soothing, inviting him to dinner Friday evening.

After he hung up, he became aware he was standing in the middle of this anachronistically decorated bachelor pad, in, yes, "ever'lovin' Arkansas," wearing a sappy grin.

FRIDAY NIGHT Abby stood in the small combination living room-dining room eyeing the drop leaf table set for two. When Nell set a bowl of garden flowers in the center, Abby edged closer, glaring at her mother. "What are you trying to do? Ruin my life?"

Nell took a deep breath, then straightened. "You think I could single-handedly do that?"

Abby shrugged. "Looks like you're trying."

"All because I've invited Mr. Logan to dinner?"

"Mom, we're doing fine." Abby's voice rose in protest. "We don't need him."

"It's dinner, Abby, not a life-long commitment."

Abby's jaw tightened, and all she said was, "Oh, brother."

"You have your friends. I have mine."

Abby thrust an arm in the direction of the table. "When did you get out all this fancy junk? We never eat in here. But nothing's too good for Brady, right?" She made the word "Brady" sound like "cootie."

Rather than rising to the bait, Nell turned to the hutch and got out her crystal salt and pepper shakers. After she placed them on the linen tablecloth, she faced Abby. "What's really bothering you about this?"

She watched while Abby chewed her lip, unwilling to look at her mother.

"I asked you a question."

"What do we know about this Brady guy? Huh? So he's your 'friend' and he's from California. That's not much. What's he doing here anyway?"

"I know he is a man who lost his wife and daughter in a tragic automobile accident and he could use all the friends he can get. You included."

Color flooded Abby's cheeks. "I...I didn't know." She hesitated, as if reflecting on the conversation. "That's really sad, but, jeez, that doesn't mean I have to like him."

"No. You'll have to get to know him on your own. If you give him a chance."

"What if I don't want to?"

"I'd be disappointed in you. But that's your choice."

Abby seemed torn between resentment and acceptance. "It's just I'm afraid that—" A car horn sounded from the driveway. Abby wheeled toward the window.

"Afraid of what?"

"Never mind. I gotta go." Abby hurried toward the door. "That's Tonya's dad to take us to the game. Bye."

Like a wind preceding a storm, Abby blew out of the house, leaving Nell standing, defeated, in the living room, enthusiasm for the evening draining from her.

She knew what Abby was afraid of. The same thing she was.

But she had a choice. Living in fear or following the urgings of her heart.

Nell stepped back and surveyed the table—her good china, silver flatware, starched linens. She rubbed her arms against a shiver of anticipation.

Anything could happen when you followed your heart.

BRADY SHOVED BACK his chair. "Thank you, Nell, that was the best dinner I've had in a long time."

She smiled that crinkly smile he could look at all day. "No cook in your bachelor quarters?"

"Not unless you count the leading purveyors of frozen food." He patted his stomach. "Many more meals like that and I'll have to join a gym."

"I know the feeling. I'm stuffed, too." Nell stood and picked up their empty dessert bowls. He followed her into the kitchen. "You don't need to help."

"I want to." He took the dessert bowls from her, then nodded at the stacked dinner plates. "You load those in the dishwasher while I rinse these."

"Thanks. You're certainly more willing help than Abby."

Brady tensed. When he'd first arrived, Nell had mentioned Abby was at a football game. Since then her name hadn't been uttered. Until now. He didn't have so much trouble with the comparisons he drew between Brooke and Nell. The two were very different. But Abby was another matter. After meeting her and from what Nell had told him about her, Abby was a flesh-and-blood reminder of Nicole and what would never be his—the joy and satisfaction of seeing his daughter grow and mature. Although it wasn't Abby's fault, he wasn't sure he could open himself to the pain of a relationship with her.

"There," Nell said, filling the soap dispenser and switching on the dishwasher. "That's done." She ran her fingers through her short hair, then turned to him with a smile of invitation. "Feel like walking that dinner off?"

"Sure. What do you have in mind?"

"There's a small park down at the foot of the hill. We could make the circuit."

Her neighborhood was in an older section of town, with tree-lined sidewalks and deep front yards. When they stepped outside, the sun rested on the horizon, creating long shadows. The heat of the day had been replaced by moderate temperatures. "This way," Nell said, slipping her hand into his as naturally as if she'd always done so. He liked thinking about how they appeared to the few onlookers out watering their grass or sitting on their front porches. A couple. He was comforted by the feel of her warm hand in his, the way she matched his stride. As if they were totally in sync.

"Fayetteville is a nice town," he said. "Homey."

"I don't know if I could ever live in a big city. I'm a small-town kind of girl."

Brady pictured the traffic on the Bayshore Freeway, the commute to the mountains or the ocean, the acres of designer golf courses and upscale malls. He couldn't see her there. "Nothing wrong with that."

"I guess I sound pretty provincial."

He swung their clasped hands playfully. "City slicker meets country girl?"

She looked up, her mouth curved in a warm smile. "Something like that."

He dropped her hand and put his arm around her waist, tugging her close. "Don't you worry, dear lady, my intentions are honorable."

He'd said it in jest, but it had come out wrong. She kept walking, her pace slowing, the smile fading. Finally, she stopped and faced him. "I didn't know you had any intentions."

He stepped closer, bringing her face inches from his. He could smell the lilac sweetness of her perfume, see the question in her eyes. Energy radiated between them. An emotion—spontaneous and undeniable—filled his chest and he somehow managed to utter the words springing from pure feeling. "Neither did I. Until now."

Her eyes locked on his and he reached for both her hands, clutching them as if they were all that kept him from losing himself again. "Nell, would it be all right with you if...I wanted to be more than friends?"

He could sense her body stiffening, see the doubt clouding her eyes. But then she drew a deep breath, and as if it had cleansed the tension, a gentle expression took the place of doubt. "Yes," she said, and he no longer heard the splatter of the sprinkler system at his back nor the traffic noise. All he knew was that something important had just taken place.

"We could see—" he began.

"No expectations. Slow and easy," she said.

"And no more hurt. I promise."

She withdrew one hand and covered his mouth with two fingers. "No promises. I can't trust them."

He cradled her face in his hands. "If I have anything to do about it, you'll be able to."

Then, and only then, she moved into his embrace, wrapping her arms around his neck. "One day at a time," she whispered, before raising her lips to his.

At last.

CHAPTER SIX

AT THE PARK, Brady led Nell to a bench hidden from the street by a row of crape myrtle bushes. Sitting there, nestled in the curve of his arm, she tried to follow her own advice and live in the moment. To ignore all her nagging doubts, to bask in the warmth and strength emanating from the man beside her, to trust the step they had just taken.

To be happy. Now.

But hanging over her head was the specter of alcoholism and its potential to dash her hopes. She would have to tell Brady at some point, but for tonight? She wanted—in this moment—simply to be.

When Brady broke the silence, Nell thought he must've read her mind because all he said was, "Happy?"

She didn't know how to answer him. "I'm afraid of happy."

"You're a profound woman, Nell Porter." He ran his hand up and down her bare arm. "I know exactly what you mean." He hesitated, before continuing. "I've asked myself over and over how I could deserve happiness after…what happened."

"To your family?"

"Yeah. But tonight, being here with you—" he kissed her forehead "—it seems almost attainable."

"I've thought about it a lot. I'm not sure anyone ever 'deserves' happiness. It just happens. The trick is to recognize it and savor it for however long it lasts. It's certainly not a permanent condition." How well she knew. There was a time in her youthful innocence when she had thought she would always be happy. In that idealized view, her father would always be there, Rick would love her forever, and she would be the perfect daughter, wife, mother.

He caressed her cheek with his forefinger. "That's why tonight is special. Being with you, I almost feel whole again. I never thought I would."

Nell leaned back, finding his words both rewarding and burdensome. "I can't make you whole, Brady. That has to come from somewhere inside of you. Healing takes time."

"So I'm told."

"You don't talk much about your wife and daughter." Nell knew she was running the risk of breaking the spell, but his reticence concerned her. "Would you tell me about them? About the accident?"

He picked up a strand of her hair and rubbed it between his fingers. "They don't have anything to do with you."

She could feel him shutting down, returning to a familiar, dark place. "But they do, Brady, if we're to have any…uh…deeper relationship. They'll always be part of you. Part of us." She felt her courage slipping. "If there is going to be an 'us.'"

Across the park at the lighted basketball court, a group of boys exchanged high fives and along the path in front of them came a lone man smoking a cigarette and walking his dog. Brady waited until he passed with a pleasant "Good evening."

"Brooke was…a golden girl. She came to work for us right out of college. In the Human Resources department. Her smile could light up my day. She was intelligent, energetic, funny. And unbelievably, she liked me."

Nell's ears perked up at "unbelievably." Had he thought so little of himself?

"I was a workaholic, driven to succeed, but she married me anyway. She never complained, at least not in any major way, and tried her best to be supportive. Then Nicole came along. I couldn't believe how lucky we were to have a good life, more money than we could ever need and a perfect daughter." His voice wavered. "Nicole was so darn cute. Bright and pretty. And she thought I was special."

"You are," Nell murmured.

Lost in his reminiscence, Brady didn't seem to hear. "I'll never forgive myself for not paying more attention to them. For letting my need for success get in the way. I told myself I was working for our family, but the truth was, I needed the ego boost."

"You couldn't have known what would happen. At the time, you were doing your best for them."

He laid both arms along the back of the bench, threw his head back, then sighed. "No, I wasn't. That night? The accident?"

When she turned to look at him, his eyes were focused on a faraway, anguished memory. "I was supposed to be with them. If I'd been driving— Aw, shit." He ran a hand through his hair.

She didn't know how to help him. He had assumed

a gigantic burden of guilt. "You couldn't have known."

"Oh, yeah, hindsight's 20/20. It was an accident. It could happen to anybody. Believe me, I've heard all the rationalizations. Hell, I'm just a screw-up. That's the story of my life."

Self-pity didn't become him, but Nell sensed there was more to it. Self-pity was indulgent, but he seemed genuinely wounded, and, if she was any judge, those wounds had origins in a time long before the accident. Out of the shadows, Abby's question, the one Nell had avoided dealing with, surfaced. "What do we know about this Brady guy?" Oh, she knew the kinds of things a résumé would include, but she sensed there was more. That he was a deep man, one with secrets.

Secrets. Again her obligation to tell him hers surfaced. But not now. Not when he had pulled her into his arms and tucked her head beneath his chin. "Sorry about that maudlin display. That's not what tonight's about. This is." He kissed her, and this time his lips moved hungrily, his tongue coupling with hers, and all she could do was bury her fingers in his hair and press her body against his, seeking to infuse him with all the pent-up longing she'd been denying.

And that continued to terrify her.

TONYA'S DAD WAS way cool. He'd taken the carload of their friends to McDonald's after the game and had sat in a booth by himself. Like maybe he wasn't even with them. Then the boys had come and taken the table across from the girls. Out of the corner of her eye, Abby noticed Alan Voyle elbow one of the guys aside so he could sit directly across the aisle from her. Maybe it didn't mean anything, but when it happened, Tonya had nudged her and whispered, "See?"

"How about that game?" Alan asked her between bites of his French fries. "Wasn't Decker awesome?"

Clueless about who Decker was, Abby fumbled for an answer. "Great. I was so nervous when the other team nearly tied us at the end."

"You like football?"

Like football? She'd never given it any thought except that games were fun times with her friends. "Yes, I mean, sure. I don't know a whole lot about it, though. You know, the rules and stuff." She prayed that admission wouldn't kill her chances with him.

Alan swiveled in the booth to face her. That sexy lock of dark hair fell over his forehead and Abby's brain turned to mush. "I could teach you. Sometime. If you want."

Gosh, maybe he did like her. "That'd be great."

"I could ride my bike to your house Sunday. Maybe we could watch an NFL game and I could explain some stuff."

McDonald's was her new favorite place in the world. This booth, special forever. "Sure, that'd be fun."

"Okay, then," he grinned, ignoring his buddies who were trying to get his attention. "About two?"

"Fine." Tonya, who had shamelessly eavesdropped, gripped Abby's knee in excitement, probably a good thing because if she wasn't grounded, she could surely fly.

On the way home in the front seat of Tonya's dad's van, Abby didn't say much, still floating in a romantic haze. Alan Voyle was coming to her house. Unbelievable. Finally she mustered her courage and leaned toward Tonya's dad. "Mr. Larkin, what does 'NFL' mean?"

Mr. Larkin seemed surprised she wanted to talk to him, but she was glad she'd asked, because all the way home he explained to her about the leagues and franchises. Maybe she wouldn't look quite so dumb when Alan came over.

Her euphoria took a nosedive when Mr. Larkin pulled into her driveway—behind that man's car. She checked the clock on the dash. It was after eleven. What was *he* still doing at her mother's?

She should've stayed home. It was icky the way her mother put out the good dishes, wore that fancy dress, sprayed that flowery perfume all over herself. Just dinner, she'd said. Not a lifelong commitment. But what if it was? Her dad had remarried. What if her mom did?

Abby murmured a hurried thank-you to Mr. Larkin and a "Call me," to Tonya before plodding to the front door.

"Abby, is that you?" her mother called.

"Yeah."

"Come tell us about the game." *Us.*

She entered the family room, where her mother and Brady sat on the sofa—close together. She looked at her mother, rosy-cheeked and smiling, then at Brady, handsome in a George Clooney sorta way, yet filling up the room like a sci-fi hulk. Abby caught a whiff of his nauseating woodsy after-shave. The cheeseburger she'd had at McDonald's revolted in her stomach and all she could think to say was, "What's he still doing here?"

An irritated frown erased her mother's smile. "Abby, did you leave your manners at the door?"

"Not really." Abby knew she was going to say too much, but she couldn't help herself. "I just wondered. Dinner was over a while ago, right?"

Brady Logan rose to his feet. "I imagine I feel like an intruder to you."

How did he know that? "Yeah, sorta."

"Abby? How many times do I have to tell you? Brady is my friend, and I didn't raise you to treat people so rudely."

Brady laid a hand on her mother's shoulder. "I don't know that she's as rude as she is truthful."

Abby looked away. First, she didn't want to see him touch her mother, but, second, she didn't know what to make of him. He seemed to understand her better than her mother did. Abby studied the coils of the braided rug beneath her feet. "I'm sorry. I guess I was just surprised."

"Understandable," Brady said, glancing at his watch. "And it is late. I should be going."

Good, Abby breathed.

Her mother shot her a look that clearly said *stay here.* "I'll walk you to the door."

Abby sank onto the arm of the sofa, digging at her cuticles. She could hear whispers, but couldn't make out the words. Then it was silent. For too long. What was he doing? Kissing her mother good-night? Gross. Then the sound of the door shutting.

When her mother came back into the room, she sat down. Abby folded her arms around herself, totally miserable.

"Brady isn't going to go away, Abby, so let's hear it. What's your problem with him? Us?"

"You like him, huh?"

"Yes, I do. But that doesn't have to change anything."

"Change anything? It changes everything. It's embarrassing."

"You mean I'm too old?"

Honest to God, Abby didn't know what she meant, just that everything felt weird. "No, but—"

Her mother's expression softened. "You're afraid. I understand. I am, too."

"You—you are?" That was a new thought.

"I like Brady. A lot. But that doesn't mean anything has to change between you and me."

"But what if…he hurts you?"

"You're asking if I'm strong enough now?"

Abby hung her head. "Yeah." She couldn't stand it if her mother started drinking again.

"The truth? I don't know. I think I am. But how will I ever be sure if I don't try?"

"Sometimes I'm just so scared."

"That it'll happen again?"

Abby nodded, mute.

"Let's not borrow trouble, honey."

"Okay." Abby stood, waved her arms helplessly, then said, "I'm going to bed now."

"I love you."

"I love you, too." She started for her bedroom, then, remembering, paused and said, "Mom, is it okay if Alan Voyle comes over Sunday afternoon?"

Her mother's smile was full of love. "Of course."

Abby couldn't wait to get to her room. She had too many things to think about. Her life was nothing but confusion. And Alan was only one part of it.

MONDAY MORNING Nell sought out Ben Hadley following her AA meeting. "Do you have a minute?"

"For you? Always." He led her to the far corner of the room where several folding chairs were arranged in a semicircle. After they sat down, he lay an age-spotted hand on hers. "Now what can I do for you?"

"I need to talk."

"Then I'm happy to listen."

She smiled. So like Ben. He always had a way of letting her figure out things for herself. "I've met a man."

"And?"

"I think I could fall in love with him."

"And this is bad?"

"There are lots of problems."

"Like?"

Briefly she told him about Brady's wife and daughter and his overwhelming grief. "I don't know if I can take on his problems. Compete with the ghosts."

"You can't do either one, but you *can* be the best, most loving Nell Porter in your power."

Abby looked into Ben's wise eyes, and knew he

spoke the truth. "Then there's Abby. She's not happy about Brady."

"He threatens her safe little world."

"Yes. But it's more than that. She's afraid something will happen, and I'll start to drink again."

"That's always a possibility."

She hadn't wanted to hear him say that. She'd wanted assurance that she was "cured," even though she knew that wasn't possible. "I know," she said quietly, remembering the tailspin she'd gone into after her father's death. "Emotionally, I feel stable, but that's today."

"And tomorrow is always about the 'what ifs,' is that it?"

"I'm afraid, Ben."

"That's natural." He eyed her closely. "Have you told him your history?"

"Not yet. I know I have to, but I've been dragging my feet. Avoiding, I guess."

"It would take a pretty big man to overlook your alcoholism, is that what you're saying?"

She nodded, studying the fingers clenched in her lap.

"Are you worth it?"

She looked up, startled. "What do you mean?"

"Worth his love and approval. It sounds as if you're trying to talk yourself out of exploring a relationship with this man." He hesitated, then went on. "When you said earlier you could fall in love with him, I asked you if that was bad? All you did then was give me a laundry list of impediments. Now, I'm asking you another question. When you're with him, does it *feel* bad?"

She was aware of a sudden calm in the room. While they had been talking, the others had left and his question echoed in the silence. She didn't answer right away, recalling Brady's comforting embrace, his vulnerable heart. "No," she whispered.

"Trust the Twelve Steps. You have so much to give, Nell. If you live in fear of hurt, you'll never fully live."

She stood, then placed a hand on the older man's shoulder. "Thanks, Ben. You've given me lots to think about."

Later at her car, she stopped, took a cleansing breath and looked around. The crisp morning air held the first hint of fall, and a few trees showed early signs of color. Abby's moods, like the leaves, were as changeable as the seasons. Yesterday had been better, thanks to Alan Voyle. Giddy with excitement, Abby hadn't asked her once about Brady. The two teens had huddled in the family room, a football game the focus of their attention. Nell couldn't help overhearing Abby with Alan at the door when he left. "Thanks," she'd said. "I just love football."

Nell smiled at the memory. Since when had her daughter had any interest in football? Maybe Alan was just the distraction Abby needed. Nell hoped so because she would certainly welcome relinquishing the spotlight.

TUESDAY WAS OVERCAST, but the land was green under the pewter skies. Occasional wisps of fog flirted with the treetops. The rocky soil beneath Brady's feet was still damp from an early-morning shower, which had intensified the mossy fragrance of the woods.

Brady shouldered his pack and, holding the folded plat map in one hand, strode through the thick brush toward the shoreline. Bisecting a portion of the property was a steep ravine through which a spring-fed stream trickled. Brady studied the terrain, wondering whether it would be necessary to build a bridge to access the lodge site or whether the route Buzz had taken around the ravine would be more practical.

Yesterday he'd stopped by the local Chamber of Commerce to inquire about conventions, conferences and hotel occupancy figures. He'd been pleased with what he'd heard. He didn't want to tip his hand too soon, but every new piece of data served to make him more optimistic about his vision. Tomorrow he had appointments with representatives of two of the major industries headquartered in northwest Arkansas to get a reading on their conference needs.

He paused to caress the lichen-covered trunk of a towering walnut tree, wondering how long it had stood in this spot. He tried to temper his enthusiasm. Plenty ought to deter him from this undertaking. His lack of experience in the hospitality industry, his obligations in California, the financial risk involved. Yet with every step he took through the undergrowth, he knew this was what he was supposed to be doing.

And all because of what a stranger had written in a B-and-B journal.

He didn't believe in miracles. Not after what had happened to Brooke and Nicole. Yet he had the uncanny sense that Brooke was somehow orchestrating his future.

Listen to yourself. You're talking supernatural bullshit. But how else to explain the improbable string of circumstances that had brought him to Arkansas? And to Nell.

The snap of a twig alerted him, and he turned around. There in a small clearing stood a doe with her fawn. When she raised her head to study him in that instant before she darted off through the trees, her big, soft eyes reminded him of Nell's trusting look just before she'd kissed him Friday evening.

She'd given herself to the kiss freely. And her embrace had been as welcome as a warm shower after a grueling workout. Even as he admitted how deep was his need, he cursed himself. He swung savagely at a limb impeding his way. Could he make a new beginning when he was still riddled with guilt? He certainly didn't deserve a second chance.

But he'd promised Nell. He wouldn't hurt her.

Whether he deserved it or not, for the first time in months, he was no longer alone.

"OH, BRADY, I don't know." Excitement and fear warred in Nell. She clasped the phone in hands suddenly clammy. It was too soon.

"It would just be for two nights. I'd really like the company."

Brady had told her about his tentative plans for developing a conference center on the lake, but she hadn't been prepared for this—an invitation to accompany him to Timberview Lodge and Resort on a lake in Missouri. It was a research trip, he'd said.

Would her mother caution her, concerned with the opinions of outsiders? Would Lily encourage her? And Abby? Dear God, she'd be horrified. Nell shook her head in a liberating kind of defiance. This was her decision and hers alone. Was she prepared to go through life acceding to the wishes of others? The answer was "no."

But all she could picture was a cozy double bed in a faux-rustic cabin, complete with a stone chimney and fireplace.

"Nell? You're not saying anything."

"Uh, Abby goes to Dallas this coming weekend."

"That suits me, providing I can get reservations."

"September shouldn't be a problem." Her quivering body and rampaging imagination were not to be denied. Despite her surfacing insecurities and fears, she was actually encouraging him.

"About the quarters? I'll try to get us a two-bedroom cabin."

Never had the words *two-bedroom* been filled with such music. Yet in the midst of the deep breath she was finally able to draw, there was a hitch of regret. "That sounds perfect. Thank you."

After he told her he'd call back with the particulars, they hung up.

And panic set in.

Surely she hadn't been contemplating…*that.* They weren't ready yet. She wasn't ready. He'd find out what a fraud she was. How useless in bed.

Oh, God. Abby. She'd have to give her a number where she could be reached. There would be questions. Lots of them.

For which she had no answers.

Even for herself.

Then, to her horror, Nell recognized the thirst

claiming her body. For the first time in months, every nerve cried out for a drink. For the soothing opiate of vodka—neat.

STELLA JANES SMOOTHED BACK a lock of hair, then leaned across the table of the tea room where she'd met Nell for lunch. "I must say I don't know what to make of it. Do you really know this man well enough to take off for a…romantic weekend?"

"It's not like that, Mother. It's a business trip."

Her mother raised an eyebrow. "Get real, Nell. I know how the cookie crumbles. Why does he need you if it's business?"

Nell added sugar to her tea, stalling for time, knowing she was evading the issue. When she looked up, her mother's expression was more concerned than judgmental. "I'm rationalizing, aren't I?"

"You said it, dear. Not I."

"Mother, the truth is…I'm interested in him. And I think maybe he likes me, too."

"Well, I certainly hope so. But are you, uh, sure you're ready for—" she waved her fingers airily "—whatever this is?"

Abby's heart was pounding at jackhammer speed. She leveled her gaze, looked straight at her mother and told the truth. "No. But I'm going to find out."

"You've straightened out your life. Your problems are over. Why risk anything?"

"First of all, my problems will never be over. I will always be an alcoholic." She noticed her mother wince at her use of the word. "It is very tempting to remain passive. To let events roll past me. But Brady has come into my life. He's important to me. Of course, I'm afraid. I don't want to upset my life any more than you want to see me do that. I have you and Lily and Abby, but…maybe that's not enough. I've been lonely. Brady fills that empty spot in my heart.''

Stella covered Nell's hand. ''Oh, honey. If I could only guarantee you wouldn't get hurt—''

''You can't, Mom. No one can. This is a step I have to take on my own. Granted, it's unknown territory. And I won't lie. The thought of going with Brady this weekend terrifies me so much that, for the first time lately, I craved a drink. But I can't go through life letting the demon rule me.''

Stella patted Nell's hand, then withdrew it to wipe away the tears gathering in her eyes. ''What about Abby?''

''She won't like the idea of my being with Brady, but I'm the adult here. If I sublimate my needs totally for hers, neither of us gains.''

''I hope it works out, dear.'' Stella sighed. ''You need to talk with Abby.''

Nell couldn't overlook the lines of worry pinching her mother's brow, nor the generosity of her understanding. ''I know. I will.''

''Whatever you do, darling, be happy.''

Nell's throat closed, filled with huskiness. ''I'm trying.'' Yet the thought of that first dizzying leap off the cliff of security made the words tremble on her lips.

ABBY LEANED toward the bathroom mirror—horrified. Yuck. There it was—a zit the size of Colorado. Red and crusty and pus-filled. What else could go wrong? She ticked off the calamities in her life. This was her weekend to go visit her dad and Clarice in stupid Dallas. Never mind Alan had asked her to meet him at the high school game and sit with him. She could've died when she had to tell him she couldn't. He probably thought she was the biggest baby in the world, trotting off to Dallas to see Daddy.

Then, worse even than that, her idiot mother was going to do it. Shack up with that man! The mere thought of it gagged her. Had her mother lost her mind? Didn't she read the magazines, watch "Oprah" or anything? Men like that were after one thing. Sex. Hot and heavy.

Gripping the bathroom counter, Abby shut her eyes, trying desperately not to picture her mother naked—with him—rolling around on satin sheets like in R-rated movies. She didn't care what Mom had tried to tell her in their stupid mother-daughter chat. About a woman's needs. About how she liked Brady and how you couldn't find happiness without taking some risks. That was crazy. She and her mother *were* happy. They didn't need anybody else. Despite the hot tears lurking behind her lids, Abby slowly opened her eyes.

Crap. The zit was still there like a giant neon UGLY sign blinking its horrible message to the world.

Studying it, she felt sick. She couldn't get Tonya's words out of her mind. "I always get these huge zits right before my period."

Her stomach did another flip-flop. *Oh, God, no. Please. Don't let it happen. Not this weekend. Not in Dallas.*

CHAPTER SEVEN

NELL HAD ARRANGED her work schedule so that she could be off by two, pick Abby up at school and deliver her to the airport for her flight. That had left her just enough time to race home, freshen up, throw the last few items in her suitcase before Brady arrived at five. She caught her breath when she saw him. His black golf shirt set off his dark eyes and tanned skin and he exuded pure animal magnetism. She might have backed out there and then except for his broad grin, deepening his dimple, that made her feel special. Tingly. Not at all the way the librarian mother of a thirteen-year-old ought to feel.

"Ready?"

She didn't know if she was reading something into his question, but it was fraught with promise—and danger. "I…I'll be just a minute."

She ducked back into her bedroom, leaned against the closed door and tried to calm her rioting emotions. Was she doing the right thing? There was an awful inevitability to the next few hours, and she knew, whatever happened, it would shift her world. And yet…

She managed a wry chuckle. She wanted this. This whatever-it-was.

She picked up her suitcase, lifted her chin and returned to Brady, a smile masking her insecurities and doubts. "I'm ready."

He took her bag from her, then led her to his SUV. He glanced skyward. "Looks like we have a beautiful evening ahead of us."

Hoping he was, in fact, referring only to the weather, she nodded in agreement. He helped her into the front seat and then they were leaving her house behind. Superstitiously she kept watching it in the passenger side mirror, as if once it was no longer visible, her security would disappear.

Apparently tuning in to her uncertainty, Brady picked up her hand, dwarfed in his, and gave it an encouraging squeeze. "You haven't done this in a while, have you?"

"What?" The word came out staccato.

"Had a weekend away. With a man."

"No." She laughed shakily. "I'm kind of rusty in the dating game."

"I know. Me, too."

Then it hit her. This must be difficult for him, as well. He'd been married a long time. Had clearly loved his wife. Oh, God. She might be his first relationship since Brooke's death, just as he was her first since Rick. She looked up shyly, studying his face. Wondering if he was as nervous as she was. In a gesture of understanding, she caressed the back of his hand with her thumb. "We're a fine pair, aren't we? I guess we'll fumble our way through this together."

"To tell you the truth, I feel like a geeky teenager on a big date with the prom queen."

She blushed. "I've never been confused with a prom queen."

He turned his head, and the look on his face reduced her to a pool of honey. "Then somebody just wasn't looking, because you're beautiful."

Nell hardly knew how to react to the compliment. Rick had called her his "funny face." Lovingly. At first. "Beautiful" was out of her league. "Thank you," she murmured. "You almost make me believe it."

He had a wonderful laugh that rolled up from deep in his chest. "You don't get it, do you? You *are* beautiful." Then he looked at her again, the humor fading from his eyes. "Somebody must've really done a number on you."

Was she that needful? That transparent? "They did. Uh, *he* did," she amended.

"Your husband?"

"I...wasn't what he wanted."

"He was a fool."

"But that's all in the past."

"Yet you haven't forgotten how he made you feel, have you?"

"Not really."

"Well, starting right now, we're going to change that."

"How?"

"For starters, repeat after me, 'I am beautiful.'"

She crossed her arms and sent him a dubious look. "Right."

"No really. C'mon. Try it."

She felt like a fool, but softly she mumbled, "I am beautiful."

Brady gave her a playful knock on the head. "Not like that. With gusto. Like this." He bellowed the phrase, then repeated it. "Join in now. One, two, three…"

And she was doing it. With him. There they were. Two grown-ups driving down the highway hollering, "I am beautiful!"

But that wasn't the most amazing part. No, it was the way he was looking at her.

For the first time ever, she believed it. She felt beautiful.

Best of all, Brady seemed to believe it.

AFTER A LEISURELY DINNER at one of the resort's highly regarded restaurants, they walked along a lighted path toward their cabin. Pausing at a picturesque footbridge crossing a gurgling stream, Brady leaned against the rail and surveyed the scene. Nell could practically hear the wheels turning in his brain. Already he'd taken in quite a bit, commenting at dinner about the check-in procedure, parking situation, signage and layout of the facility.

"I like the space and openness. Guests need to feel they have room to breathe."

Nell nodded. "The landscaping contributes to that sense. Just manicured enough, not overly cultivated, yet colorful. I've never seen such gorgeous mums."

Brady took her arm, then, and they strolled on. Maybe this really was a business trip. Maybe she'd overreacted. Seen more in the invitation than was there. Their cabin, perched right above the lake, was commodious, the comfortable pine furniture and rust and forest-green North Woods fabrics welcoming.

The two bedrooms, each with its own bath, flanked the living room with its vaulted ceiling. A lakeside deck ran the full width of the cabin. If the decor was intended to make the guests feel pampered, it was working.

When they reached the cabin, Brady turned a single lamp on low, then busied himself in the tiny kitchenette. "How about some spiced cider? On the deck?"

Nell retrieved a sweater from her room, then waited for him in the two-person wooden glider. Lights from the other cabins were reflected in the calm water of the cove, and in the sky above, stars were visible. She pushed slowly back and forth, content to rest in the moment. Before anything else happened.

"Here," Brady said, shouldering open the door, "get it while it's hot."

Nell took the warm mug and waited for Brady to join her. Soothed by the cinnamon-clove fragrance of the cider, she basked in the illusion that, for the time being, her real life had vanished and all that mattered was sight, smell and the comfort of Brady's warm body beside her as they rocked to and fro. He said nothing, perhaps, like her, caught up in the spell of the night.

Across the cove, a late fisherman motored past the No Wake buoys toward the marina, but other than that, the placement of the cabin provided seclusion.

Finally Brady broke the silence. "What do you think so far?"

"It's wonderful. I felt as if I was on vacation almost from the moment we arrived."

"I'd like to help others feel that same way. You know, it wasn't until I got to the Ozarks that I experienced any calm on this trip."

"You're not the first to say that. We like to think mystical qualities reside in these hills and waters. Early Native American tribes certainly thought so."

She nursed her cider, the scent and taste conjuring up the vivid foliage and brilliant blue skies of autumn. She felt languid, peaceful, when she supposed she should be tense and expectant.

"How did Abby feel about your coming with me?"

Pop went the balloon of self-delusion. "She wasn't thrilled, as you might expect. It's not you. She'd be the same with any man I dated."

"She worries about you."

Nell shot him an arch look. "Oh, yes."

"I wouldn't hurt you."

"But she doesn't know that." Nell hesitated. "I...we were hurt once. It's made her cautious."

He chuckled sardonically. "I guess that makes three cautious people." He took the empty mug from her hands and set it with his on the deck, then settled his arm around her shoulder. "I like being with you, Nell. You make no demands."

"We're lucky. It feels like starting fresh, doesn't it?"

When his fingers leisurely traced up and down her arm, she found it difficult to focus, lost in the sensations generated by even that smallest of caresses.

He stretched out his jean-clad legs, stopping the motion of the glider. "I have a confession."

"Oh?"

"Before...I couldn't think of Brooke without wanting to howl at the moon. But now?" The hand on her arm stilled. "Oh, hell, this is going to sound stupid."

"Not to me," Nell said quietly.

"It's as if she brought me to you. As if...we're supposed to be here. Together."

Nell turned her face to his. "I feel the same way."

For a breathless moment, neither moved. Then, with a jerk of the glider, he rose, drew her to her feet and enclosed her in a hug that made her forget the stars, the lake, everything but the musky smell and muscled body of the man she wanted—in every way. She had time only to whisper "Brady," before his lips closed over hers in a kiss so deep, so needful she was helpless with longing. Urgings and instincts she had thought dead spiraled through her. She cupped his face, the rough feel of his whiskers beneath her fingers driving her to meet his lips, his tongue, with joyful abandon.

Then, as she slid her arms around his neck, his lips sought her eyes, her temple, and again her mouth. His hands moved restlessly over her back, then clutched her closer, nestling her hips against his erection.

As if jerked from a warm pool into harsh cold, she tensed, a gasp trapped in her throat. He wasn't going to stop.

Then came an equally disturbing thought. She hadn't wanted him to. She refocused on him—his needs, his gentleness, his hands caressing her short hair, his breath smelling faintly of clove. Yes. No. A primal scream ripped at her chest, clawing for expression. Closing her eyes, she fought the olfactory comparison cruelly toying with her mind. Clove. Juniper. Gin. Clove, juniper…oblivion.

She whirled away from Brady, leaning for support on the railing facing the lake, drawing deep breaths of clean night air. He took a hesitant step toward her. "Nell?" The concern in his voice tore at her heart. "Are you all right? Did I do something…wrong?"

When she slowly pivoted, the hurt in his eyes pierced her. "No," she whispered. Laying a hand on his cheek, she prayed for the right words to somehow explain what had to feel to him like rejection, the last thing he needed. "I thought I was ready." Her throat caught. "I want to be."

He took her hand in his and raised it to his lips. "I want you, Nell, but only when you say it's all right."

If she could have changed her mind in that instant, she would have, but before she could act on that impulse, he'd put his arm around her and was leading her inside to the cozy sofa facing the fireplace. After he settled her with a fleece throw around her shoulders, he sat on the hearth, hands clasped between his knees.

"I'm sorry," she murmured.

"No apology needed. I came on too strong."

"No, it's not that. It's just—" she gave a harsh little laugh "—I'm rusty."

"We both are. And we have time." He smiled then, in a way that again made her feel beautiful. Lulled, she was unprepared for his next words. "Tell me what he did to you."

She didn't have to ask whom he meant. Her eyes

filled with tears and all she could do was shake her head.

Then Brady was beside her, cuddling her against him. "Talk to me, Nell. Get it out."

She struggled for the breath trapped in her rib cage. "He…he thought something was wrong with me. I couldn't respond like he wanted."

She felt Brady's jaw clench against her temple, but he said nothing. Just waited.

"He said I was prudish. That I, uh, wasn't woman enough to satisfy a man. Satisfy him." Hot with shame, she buried her face in his shoulder.

He tipped up her chin. "Was it always like that?"

Nell thought about his question. "No, I guess not at first. I don't remember when things got worse. Maybe after Abby came. I tried, but it didn't seem to matter what I did. Whatever it was he wanted, I couldn't give."

"So he found someone else?" Brady's tone was guarded.

"Yes." She lifted a finger to wipe the tear that trickled down her cheek.

"How did that make you feel?"

"Like I was sexless. Worthless. A failure." She couldn't believe she'd said the words aloud, after so many years of having them hurled at her—and believing them.

"That selfish son of a bitch," she heard Brady growl before he took hold of both shoulders and turned her to face him directly. "He was the failure, Nell, and I don't care how long it takes, I intend to prove it to you. What about your needs? How much concern and consideration for you did he exhibit?"

She shrugged helplessly, giving him his answer. "I tried so hard to save the marriage."

He ran his hands over her shoulders and down her arms. "I'm sure you did. You define the word *giving*." He pulled her into his embrace. "Now, let me give to you." He kissed her hair. "What you need right now is a good night's sleep."

Rewrapping her in the throw, he led her to her bedroom, pausing at the door to kiss her again with a tenderness that felt like balm. "Good night, beautiful lady," he said, then quietly closed the door as he left.

Nell leaned, weak-kneed, against the door, her fingers finding the knots in the pine. Brady's kindness and understanding, his self-denial, shook her to the core. She had not known there were men like him. Had never expected she would be given a second chance.

She'd told him. Not everything, but almost everything. She knew she owed him the rest.

She drew the throw even more tightly around herself in a futile effort to thwart the chill racking her. No. Not yet. He would hate her when he learned the truth.

Liquor had not saved her with Rick.

It could ruin her with Brady.

BRADY LAY ON HIS BACK staring at the bedroom ceiling for a good hour after he left Nell at her door. As he'd suspected, that bastard of a husband *had* done a number on her. If he was any judge, she was well out of her marriage. He'd known men like that—in locker rooms, at business meetings—for whom women existed merely as pawns in games of sexual supremacy. A my-dick-is-bigger-than-yours kind of infantilism. What her husband had done to Nell probably bordered on abuse. And she'd bought into his low opinion of her.

Damn it! He socked his pillow, then rolled onto his stomach. Nell had no idea the extent to which she'd turned him on tonight. It had taken every ounce of willpower to send her off to her own bed. Brooke had taught him sensitivity and tenderness went a long way toward satisfying a woman, so he would be patient with Nell. Gritting his teeth, he acknowledged it wouldn't be easy, though. He ached with needs of his own—to feel Nell's warm, naked flesh beneath his, to cup her small, soft breasts in his hands, to fill her until she cried for joy.

The ache in his groin was a powerful signal that after months of merely existing, he was living again and that, in time, his stormy days would pass, replaced by a vibrant rainbow named Nell.

A CLICKING NOISE, like a bird tapping on a window, drew Nell from the fuzzy depths of a dreamless sleep. She snuggled into the covers in an effort to escape wakefulness. *Scritch.* She turned toward the window, then cocked open one eye. *Scritch. Scritch.* Irritated, she rolled out of bed, padded across the floor and parted the drape. In the faint light, she saw that her ''intruder'' was a small twig scraping back and forth against the glass in a strong wind that must've come up overnight.

Returning to her bed, Nell glanced at the clock. Six. Too early to get up. She settled back in bed.

Wide awake. Lying there picturing Brady in the crisp yellow Oxford-cloth shirt he wore to dinner, sleeves rolled up to the elbows and his pressed jeans that hugged his firm thighs, she wondered what would have happened last night if she hadn't suddenly been rocketed into the past. Would they have continued, making their way slowly, or not so slowly, to a bed— reaching for each other eagerly in an effort to release that combination of lust and need propelling them both toward intimacy?

Even as she pictured it, she became aware of a pulsing low in her abdomen, a hardening of her nipples. She closed her eyes, inhaling against the message her body was sending. Now. She could go to him. All she would have to do would be get up from the bed, tiptoe through the living room, then crawl in beside him. And she would do it without liquor to blur her vision and numb her inhibitions.

Scritch. Maybe he was awake, too, waiting, as she was, for the moment they'd been heading toward since they'd first met. Yet she'd undoubtedly hurt him last night with her sudden retreat. He didn't ask for that hurt, didn't need it. On the contrary, what he needed was… Oh, God, Lily had nailed it. He needed the comfort and oblivion of love and sex.

Before she could stop to think, Nell stood, smoothed her cotton-knit gown, wishing it were, instead, a wisp of lacy silk, and walked deliberately out of her room, across the living room, pale in the predawn light, and quietly turning the knob, opened the door to Brady's room.

He lay on his back, one arm flung across the extra pillow. With a thudding heart, she studied his mussed hair and the shadow of his beard, then permitted her eyes to graze over his chest and downward where the flat of his stomach disappeared beneath the sheet and blanket.

She could turn back. Flee to the safety of her room. But a buzzing in her ears and a throbbing of her pulse robbed her of that decision.

Quietly, she drew back the cover and slipped into his bed, her gooseflesh warmed by his body heat. She lay on her side, facing him, listening to him breathe, watching his profile, smiling when he suddenly twitched in his sleep. She wanted him both to remain asleep and to wake up.

She feathered her fingers across his chest, watching with delight when his nipples puckered. Then, daringly, she blew.

Gradually she became aware of a hand on her head. She glanced up. Brady was looking at her with a wondering smile, one brow raised in question.

She nodded, then scooted nearer, raining kisses along his collarbone.

He pulled her close. "Nell, you're sure?" he whispered.

And, amazingly, she was. "I couldn't sleep," she murmured.

"I see." His voice was teasing. "Did you come for a back rub?"

"Not exactly." She moved her lips scant inches from his. "I had something more in mind."

"I'm glad to hear it," he said just before running a hand tantalizingly beneath her gown and pulling her even closer. When he kissed her, she forgot about second thoughts completely. But that was only the beginning.

By the time the sun rose, her gown was pooled on the floor and Brady was doing wonderful things to her—with her—things she'd only ever dreamed about. With his fingers. With his mouth. And with something else—a warm, hard something that filled her with wonder and drew from her a delighted cry that started in her womb and raced through her body, erupting at the same time she convulsed in release—total and blessed.

She hadn't known it could be like this.

Hadn't known there were lovers like him.

Brady braced himself above her, pausing to find her eyes. "I was right earlier."

She smiled lazily. "What do you mean?"

"You are a giver."

She surprised herself by laughing out loud. "If I'd known last night what I know now, I'd have given sooner."

He rolled onto his side, taking her with him. "We have all day," he said tracing her upper lip with a forefinger.

"And another whole night," she murmured, snuggling against him.

It seemed an amazing prospect provided by generous, beneficent gods.

NOT UNTIL they were on the way home Sunday afternoon did Nell permit second thoughts to intrude. In some small corner of her brain she'd known their forty-eight hours together was not the real world, that satiation of the senses was not commitment and that their obligations extended far beyond the two of them. But for these idyllic hours with Brady she would make no apologies, nor harbor any expectations. Looking out the window, she reminded herself firmly, "He's only passing through." She would forever be grateful to him for making her feel beautiful and, even more important, desirable.

He hadn't said much since they'd checked out, but then what was there to say that they hadn't already expressed with their bodies? She couldn't expect a vow of undying love. She told herself it had been a lovely weekend, a mere blip on the screen of her life, but nothing with a future. She chewed her lip. Besides, when she told him she was an alcoholic, what then? A frisson of panic stopped her breath. What if he rejected her? Oh, God, he was more than a blip on the screen. A lot more.

She studied his profile, the little nick of a scar beneath his left eye, the softness of his earlobe in contrast to his bearded cheek. He made her heart sing, her blood roar. And then it struck her. She'd already committed. She never would have gone to his bed if she hadn't.

Suddenly she had so much more to lose and the prospect scared her.

"When does Abby get home?"

Brady's question jolted her back to reality. Abby had been horrified enough that she was going with Brady this weekend. How much more critical would she be if she suspected the depth of her mother's feelings for him? "Her flight arrives at 7:35."

"Would you like me to go to the airport with you?"

"Thanks, but I'm not sure Abby's ready for that."

He nodded. Nell wondered what he was thinking, how he saw himself fitting into their lives. Even if only temporarily. He would surely have to return to his business in California soon. If he pursued the idea for the Beaver Lake resort, he'd have to raise money from backers on the West Coast and would probably have an on-site supervisor for the building project. Oh, he'd fly in and out. They'd see each other periodically.

But she wanted more. She looked out the passenger window, barely registering the trees passing in a blur. Like a miracle Brady had come into her life and there was no hiding from the truth—she was falling in love with him.

Even though—God, Abby's question assaulted her again—she didn't know all that much about him, except that he was tenderness and consideration personified.

She faced the road again, watching the narrow two-lane highway dip around the sharp curves and steep descents. Clasping her fingers tightly in her lap, she forced the question to her lips, praying it sounded casual. "Brady, you still haven't told me much about your growing up, about your family."

He put a reassuring hand on her leg. "Feel as if you've been in bed with a stranger?"

"Not exactly."

"But women always want the complete story, right?"

She smiled. "Guilty, sir."

"There's not much to tell. Born in Colorado, left

home right after high school, worked in California, married Brooke. That's it in a nutshell.''

''You've told me all of that before. Would you mind filling in between the lines?''

''Like?''

''Your family. Tell me about your parents. Do you have any brothers or sisters? What are your favorite childhood memories? How often do you see them and...'' She faltered. He'd removed his hand from her leg at the word *family,* and when she looked up at him, his eyes were steely, his body tense, like a cat sensing danger.

''That's history,'' he said in a flat tone.

''*Your* history,'' she said encouragingly. ''I'm interested.''

He ignored her, negotiating a junction of two highways. She'd obviously said something wrong. But what? Her questions had been innocent. Yet she sensed anything she said now would be a mistake.

After a long pause, he spoke. ''I don't mean to be rude, Nell. Let me put it this way. My first eighteen years are off-limits. I try not to think about them and I sure as hell don't want to talk about them. Okay?''

''But surely your mother, your father—''

''Stop. My mother is dead, and if I never hear my father's name again it will be too soon. Suffice it to say, as far as I'm concerned he's dead, too. They're all dead.''

Nell winced at the raw edge of pain slicing through his words. The gentle man with whom she'd made love was gone, replaced by an angry, unforgiving one whose hurt was palpable. And what did he mean ''they're all dead''? Were there others besides his mother and father? Abby had been right. There was more to know. Brady harbored secrets.

But who was she to talk? She had one, too.

After another few miles, Brady raked his fingers through his hair, then turned to her. "Hell, I apologize for that outburst." He cleared his throat. "There are just some things I don't talk about. Not with you, not with anybody."

"Are the emotions that painful?" She knew she risked a great deal with that question, but whatever the history was, he was expending enormous energy in denial.

His expression remained stoical. "Leave it, Nell." His icy words allowed no argument. A slammed door couldn't have reverberated more decisively in Nell's head.

BRADY THREW the Escalade into gear and bolted away from Nell's house. After her pointed questions, the remainder of the trip home had been strained. Of course she wanted to know about his background. Women always did. He'd been through it once for Brooke, who, like the nurturer she was, had urged him to face his past, until she'd eventually realized she might as well save her breath. He hadn't been ready. Still wasn't. And he sure didn't need to go through the whole pathetic story again.

He shook his head, disgusted with himself. Nell deserved so much better. Hell, she even had a right to expect answers, especially after their weekend. He cared about her. He'd even felt, with her in his arms, that he might be beginning to heal.

But she was asking too much. He would not revisit

Glenwood Springs, nor those agonizing months of watching his mother gasping for every breath. And certainly not his father's betrayal of her memory. God damn him, anyway.

He swerved out of the path of an oncoming vehicle, cursing the driver, the narrow street, the stoplight that suddenly turned red and anyone, anything else he could think of.

Waiting for the light to change, he squeezed his eyes shut against the memory of his final fight with the almighty Dale Logan and the ultimatum that had made his father's choice crystal-clear. And his. Brady had stormed out of the house, leaving behind his father, his younger brother, and the stepmother who was making a mockery of his mother's memory.

The beep of a horn caused him to look up—straight at a green light. He moved forward slowly in a vain attempt to calm down. What had Nell asked? "Are the emotions too painful?"

Painful? They shredded his gut. That's why he never looked back.

What must Nell have thought? Jeez, he couldn't help himself. He'd reacted like the certified jackass he was. *Great goin', Logan. You oughta offer a class. How to ruin a romantic weekend in one easy lesson.*

He'd have to make it up to her somehow. She had been so loving. He'd hardly ever had such a delightful surprise as waking up to find her nestled against him, arousing him even before he'd opened his eyes. She had held nothing back. The wonder on her face when she came spoke volumes. She'd never known, never understood what a passionate woman she was. He couldn't hurt her.

And yet he already had.

Long shadows criss-crossed the parking lot at his condo and the smell of hamburgers on a grill caused his stomach to growl. He picked up his overnight bag and walked slowly toward the building. He had some deep thinking to do this evening. About his project, about exorcising the demons Nell's questions had raised, and about Nell herself and his feelings for her, which were growing more and more powerful.

Reaching his building, he heard a car door slam behind him. He pulled out his pass key and was inserting it in the lock, when he heard footsteps behind him, and then a familiar voice.

"Brady, man, where you been? I about went to sleep in my rental car waiting for you."

Brady whirled around. "Carl?"

His partner spread his arms in a none-other gesture. "I got tired of waiting for you to come home to California. I need to visit with you, boy."

"Problems?"

Carl nodded. "You don't know the half of it." Then he studied Brady, his eyes shrewd, despite the pleasant expression on his face. "Invite me in. Let's crack open a beer." He placed a hand on Brady's shoulder, then dropped his voice. "I'm here to talk some sense into you. What the hell are you still doin' in this burg anyway? You need to come home. You've licked your wounds long enough."

Brady stood aside to let Carl enter. No way was he looking forward to the next few hours. Carl was his oldest, best friend, but he would not like what Brady was going to tell him.

CHAPTER EIGHT

CARL SAT on the arm of the sofa, upholstered in a worn Moroccan-inspired fabric, watching Brady unscrew the lids of the beers. "Who did your decorating? Winston Churchill's mother?"

Brady crossed the thick Persian rug overlaying the institutional-tan carpet and handed Carl his brew. "Straight out of Thomas Hardy's bleakest novel, huh?" He settled in the deep leather chair. "What can I tell you? The owner's an English lit prof."

Carl grinned. "Figures. Doing his best on his meager pay to recreate Victorian England, I guess." He took a swig from his bottle, then stood and walked around the room studying the framed lithographs from old issues of *Punch.*

Drawing circles in the condensation on the glass of his bottle, Brady watched, waiting for Carl to get around to the purpose of his visit.

Finally Carl pulled a wooden desk chair closer to Brady and sat down. Leaning forward, he gestured with his beer. "Logan, what the hell are you doing here?"

"I got a good deal. Helped the old guy out."

"Bull. You could've bought the whole complex. Why settle for this?"

"It was temporary."

"Well, that's a relief. So you're coming home soon?"

"I didn't say that." Brady crossed one leg over his knee. "My plans are still up in the air. More to the point, what are you doing here? Not that I'm not glad to see you, but you kinda sprung this visit on me, buddy."

"I got tired of our one-sided phone conversations. I've been worried about you." Carl stretched, crossing his feet at the ankles. "So cut the b.s. You've had time. We've been more than patient at the office, but we need you now. The new products division has a blockbuster idea that requires development approval and the contract with the Department of Defense is at the refinement stage. We can't dick around much longer on either of these projects. And, partner, that's just the tip of the iceberg. I know you've been through hell, but work could be therapeutic, you know."

Brady had known this day would come. He and Carl had started together in a windowless basement office with nothing but dreams and a couple of computers. Once, their "overnight" success had bred further creativity and satisfaction, but even before Brooke's and Nicole's deaths, he'd felt more and more tethered to beepers and cell phones. Even a pleasure boat in the Pacific Ocean had provided minimal escape.

Brady set his beer on the moisture-ringed surface of the wooden end table. "I'll come back to California soon to help handle the responsibilities you mentioned, but I can't stay." He cleared his throat. "I, uh, may never be able to."

His partner's eyes clouded. "I guess I had to see for myself. You can't come to grips with the accident, move on?"

"I'm better, Carl. Honest. But come to grips with it? No way. Could you? I'll never understand how the trucking company could not know their driver was a drunk or how someone hauling flammable materials could be so reckless. Just my luck," his mouth filled with acid, "that he waited for my family on a day I wasn't driving them."

"Jeez, Logan, you can't blame yourself. Guilt will eat you up."

Brady held up his bottle in a mock toast. "Tell me about it." He stood then and moved to the window. "So, you ask what I'm doing here in Arkansas." A college-age couple walked hand-in-hand along the bike path circling the complex. An older man living across the courtyard was filling his bird feeders and down the street three skinny teenagers were shooting hoops. He turned. "It's Norman Rockwell, county fair, schmaltzy Americana, and I love it."

Carl joined him as he turned again to the window. "Maybe you're right. Maybe you need to get this crazy notion out of your system before you move back."

Brady faced his partner. "What if I never move back?"

"Get a grip, brother. You're scaring me."

"I've made a decision. I'm going ahead with the development project here. I'd like to show you around tomorrow, let you see what I have in mind."

Carl looked dubious.

"Please. It's the first project that's captured my interest in a long time."

Carl clapped an arm around his shoulder. "I guess I can spare a day. But there are a couple of stipulations."

"What?"

"That you agree to come home with me for a week or so to get things straightened out."

Brady felt a sigh rip open his chest cavity. "Okay. What else?"

Carl drained his beer, then grinned wolfishly. "You tell me about her."

"Who?"

"I've known you too long, pal. A business deal might interest you, but it wouldn't keep you in the backwoods this long. So I figure there must be a woman."

Brady looked into the cocksure, laughing face of his friend and felt a sudden overwhelming need to confide in someone. He smiled, a culprit caught in the act. "I'll grab you another brew. Then we'll talk. I *have* met someone."

Before he left the room, though, he paused. "Her name is Nell," he said, letting the melody of the name fill the silence—and quicken his senses.

NELL LOOKED OUT her bedroom window Monday morning and groaned. Here came Lily and her mother, marching determinedly up her front walk. The two of them at once. Why was she off work today of all days? A visit from these two was more than she could handle. Especially after the restless night she'd spent second-guessing herself about

Brady. What had she been thinking? *Brazen hussy.* With an epithet suitable for a nineteenth-century novel, she accused herself. Yet being with him had felt so good. So right.

Running a brush through her hair, she smoothed the sweatshirt over her jeans, drew a deep breath and opened the door. After exchanging greetings, she inquired after her nephew. "Where's Chase?"

"At mother's day out at the church," Lily said, leading the way toward the family room, where she perched on the sofa. Stella sat in a blue-canvas director's chair and Nell took the armchair.

"Well?" Smiling, Lily looked directly at her, her eyes inquisitive.

"You didn't waste much time," Nell said dryly.

Stella bristled. "When you didn't call last night, we were worried. Are you all right?"

Nell dug her fingernails into the upholstery. Why wouldn't she be? They would be shocked if she told them just how "all right" she was. *We spent the weekend more or less in bed. And it was g-r-e-a-t!* She wondered if her mother thought she might have soothed her nerves with the contents of a bottle. "I'm fine. Why wouldn't I be?"

An unfathomable signal passed between Stella and Lily, and Lily fielded the conversational ball she'd been tossed. "It might have been, um, stressful." Her sister, the soul of tact.

"In what way?" Seized by a fit of mischief, Nell decided she wasn't going to make it easy.

Lily had the grace to look away. "Well, you know—"

"What Lily's trying to say," Stella interjected, "is

that you don't know Brady very well, and things might've…gone wrong."

If you only knew. "As a matter of fact, I had a delightful weekend. The lodge was lovely, the food scrumptious. All in all, I had quite a pleasant time."

Lily's shoulders relaxed. "Then you didn't—"

"Drink?" Nell took perverse satisfaction in the way both sets of eyes were riveted on her. "No. I didn't." With those words, she recognized increasing symptoms of anger. She could rationalize all she wanted about how supportive and helpful they'd been, but how long would it take before they got the message? She was sober, damn it! She wasn't going to let them get away with such distrust any longer. "Why would you think I would drink? Have I done anything recently to suggest a relapse?"

"No, but—"

Nell didn't wait for her mother to finish. "Then, for God's sake, why can't you let me be? I'm not nineteen going to my first house party with a boy. I'm thirty-four, and in full possession of my faculties."

Spots of color appeared on Lily's cheeks. "I'm sorry, Nell." She looked contrite.

Sulking, her mother joined in. "I had no idea our concern wasn't welcome."

Nell grimaced. Look where too little sleep and too much worry could get you. Leaning forward, she reached for her mother's hand. "It's not unwelcome—" she paused, wondering how to put it "—it's just sometimes I feel like a specimen under a microscope. I know you're both acting out of love for me, but you need to quit trying to protect me."

Crossing the room, Lily knelt at Nell's feet and took her hands. "I see what you mean. Maybe we do gang up on you. We love you. The last thing we want to do is hurt you."

"I know," Nell murmured.

Lily looked up. "So you had a good time, then?"

Nell included her mother in the smile she pasted on her face. "Yes, I did. A very good time. Brady is a nice man."

Stella let out a sigh. "How is Abby doing with all of this?"

"About as you might expect. It's threatening to her that I could be interested in someone. We've been alone a long time."

"That's only natural, dear. She was just a little girl, but she remembers your drinking. Maybe she's worried about what would happen if this man hurts you. Maybe she can't help expecting the worst."

"Surely she doesn't equate the presence of a man in my life with the temptation to drink?"

Nell crumpled in the face of her mother's implication. She had laid a heavy burden on Abby. Instead of dissipating, had her daughter's concerns only deepened over the years?

She closed her eyes in a vain attempt to erase the picture forming in her brain—Rick's humiliating accusations, the cold, snowy night, the fear in six-year-old Abby's screams, the icy blur that was the road in front of her car, the warmth of the alcohol zinging through her veins. Oh, God, did the struggle ever get easier?

Her stomach knotted, and it was taking every last

iota of will not to head directly for the nearest liquor store. The irony of it. Her mother and sister had come out of concern and love to check on her, and that very act of concern, had sent her mind down that dangerous spiral from which there were few avenues of escape.

"Nell?" Lily squeezed her hands.

"I'm fine. Please, quit worrying. I can handle whatever happens." She trembled with sudden doubt.

Stella stood, then moved closer and placed a hand on Nell's shoulder. "I'm sure you can, darling."

But uncertainty lingered in her voice.

After they left, Nell went outside and tried to calm her ragged emotions by concentrating on the beautiful day as she watered her newly planted chrysanthemums. But no good intentions could keep her mind off Brady. Or off Abby and what would be best for the two of them.

The unwelcome question battered her. Could she really handle whatever happened? She was falling in love with a man scarred by a past he refused to speak about. A man who had warned her he liked the fact she made no demands on him. A man perhaps incapable of commitment.

Yet this same man had awakened her to the knowledge that she could be responsive, desirable. Even beautiful. She smiled wistfully, remembering.

She had been wrong that evening when she'd said being with Brady was like starting fresh. She could never start fresh. Brady had understood about Rick, about her hurt. But would he understand when, at

last, she told him the truth? There would be no way
to prepare him for the words "My name is Nell and
I am an alcoholic."

FIRST THING AFTER he and Carl got back to the condo
after tramping the land Monday, Brady ordered flowers delivered to Nell. Not roses. That was predictable.
No. A bird-of-paradise with a card that read *Like this
flower, you are one-of-a-kind beautiful.*

He and Carl had just time to eat a quick dinner of
Memphis-style barbecued ribs before he took his
partner to the airport, where an insistent Carl had
stood by while Brady purchased his own ticket for a
Thursday flight to San Francisco. He owed Carl that
much. The man had been more than patient. Although the money the company had been making
these past months meant little to Brady, he could no
longer afford to be so cavalier about his responsibilities to L&S TechWare.

When he returned home after sitting at the airport
discussing business with Carl until he had to go
through security, Brady called Buzz Valentine and
asked him to get the paperwork ready for taking out
an option on the Beaver Lake property. Earlier Carl
had asked him if he was sure he knew what he was
doing. Brady had laughed, shocked to discover that,
indeed, he was sure, the first thing about which he
could make that claim since the accident.

Next he called Nell and invited himself over. He
wanted to explain in person about his California trip
and his decision to go ahead with the development.
Her voice rippled with pleasure when she thanked
him for the bird-of-paradise. She suggested he wait

until after nine to visit since she would be helping Abby with a school project until then.

When Brady put down the receiver, he found himself wandering through the condo, a vague sense of dissatisfaction marring an otherwise perfect day. What was bugging him?

He pictured Nell and Abby bent over the dining room table, newspapers, popsicle sticks, glue and pipe cleaners spread over the surface. His gut churned. God, the fort. As if suddenly winded, he sank into a chair. Giggles, smears of brown paint, Nicole's blond head bent, her concentration intense as she formed the stockade fence. Brooke coming into the room with her contribution, a tiny American flag and a colorful cavalry guidon she'd stitched. It was one of those rare nights when Brady was home, when he'd brought a huge grin to Nicole's face by offering to help.

Abby. Sooner or later if he continued his relationship with Nell, he'd have to face his conflicted feelings about her daughter. She was part of Nell, as Nicole had been part of him. Maybe if it weren't for the uncanny resemblance, their being nearly the same age, he could handle it.

He groaned. He wanted Nell. Could maybe even consider commitment. But Abby? She was part of the package and deserved his unconditional affection and acceptance, but he didn't know if he would ever be ready to claim another child as his.

California. He didn't want to go. Wanted to avoid the inevitable onslaught of memories and emotions. God, just when life had seemed, at last, to hold promise, reality was grounding him with a vengeance.

He didn't know how long he sat there lost in thought, but when he looked up it was nearly nine. He ran a hand through his hair. Maybe Nell could restore the elusive peace he'd experienced with her this weekend.

But that was asking a lot of her.

"HE'S HERE AGAIN," Abby hissed into the phone. "You'd think a whole weekend would've been enough."

"That's kinda gross when you think about it," Tonya said.

"What?" Abby rolled over on her bed, then stuffed a fat feather pillow beneath her chest.

"You know. The weekend. I mean, like, uh, do you think they did the big nasty?"

Abby clutched the phone, afraid she might puke. It was bad enough she'd asked herself that question, but to hear it come out of Tonya's mouth was disgusting. "Jeez, Tonya, that's sick."

"Well, ex-scuze me, but think about it for a minute. Why else would they go away for a weekend? Especially one when you were in Dallas?"

Abby didn't want to admit it, but she'd had the same thoughts. "I dunno," she mumbled, then added, "but I don't like it."

"Well, maybe you could go live with your dad."

"Not in my lifetime." Abby knew Tonya was just trying to be helpful, but the idea of being holed up with Clarice for any length of time was something she didn't even want to think about. Besides, maybe her mother wasn't so hot on this guy after spending a weekend with him. But, then, what was he doing here tonight and why had her mother looked so happy? Crap.

"How *was* your weekend?" Tonya asked. "I didn't get a chance at school to hear about it."

"Boring. Like always. The big woo this time was going to a Cowboys' game." Abby wouldn't admit that the only thing that had made the outing bearable was that she could tell Alan about it. And she had. After sixth period. He'd given her this big, sexy smile and told her he thought it was cool she liked football.

"That could be okay, I guess." Tonya hesitated and Abby could hear a GameBoy bleeping in the background on the other end of the line. "Did you get home without a visit from our crimson friend?"

Abby flopped over on her back and stared at the ceiling. "Is something wrong with me, Tonya? I mean practically everyone I know has started."

"What does your mom say?"

"That it's normal for it to vary with different girls. But I guess I'd rather be weird than have it start in Dallas." She cast around for a change of subject. She was tired of looking in the mirror every morning wondering if this was the day. "I told Dad about Brady."

"You *did?* What'd he say?"

"He frowned and asked me if I was all right with that."

"And you said?"

"I lied and told him I was happy Mom had a boyfriend." Abby remembered the skeptical expression on her dad's face. "I think he knew I wasn't telling the truth."

"What are they doing now?"

"Who?"

"Your mom and that guy. Is he still there?"

Abby rolled off the bed, tiptoed to the window, parted the blinds and spotted the Escalade parked in the driveway. "Oh, yeah." She glanced at her alarm clock. "Jeez, it's almost eleven."

"Maybe they're like, you know, in love."

Abby's throat was raw with unshed tears. "Yeah, maybe. Look, Tonya, I still gotta study the vocab words for science. I'll talk to you tomorrow." Before Tonya could say anything further, Abby clicked off the phone.

What was the matter with her? She swiped at her eyes. These days every little thing made her cry.

But Brady Logan was no little thing.

BRADY SHOOK HIS HEAD, baffled about how the conversation could have taken such an unpleasant turn. Up to this point, everything had gone smoothly. He'd shared his excitement with Nell over going ahead with preliminary steps to develop the resort and conference center. Even though she'd gripped his hand more tightly when he explained about returning to California for a few days, she'd understood that it was time he shouldered his responsibilities. He'd reassured her that he would be coming back, that he would be spending most of the next few months right here in Fayetteville. So where had things gone wrong?

One little question, that's where. *Do you always run away from your problems?*

They'd been talking about his "sabbatical" from

work and somehow the conversation had segued, once again, to his distant past. To Colorado. "Why haven't you ever been back?" she'd asked.

So he'd told her he'd left right before his high-school graduation. Nothing about the way his father had betrayed his mother's memory or about that last violent argument. That's when she'd asked the question, accused him of running away from his problems.

All he could do was stare at her. "Is that what you think?"

She sat facing him on the sofa, her feet drawn up beneath her skirt. "I think you're a sensitive, kind man who will never be free until you face your past."

"Who appointed you counselor?" He hated the bitterness lacing every word, but, damn it, she was getting too close.

"Is that how it seems?" She hesitated, studying his expression. "I thought we cared enough to begin sharing with each other. That the weekend meant something—"

"It did!"

"But there is a point, Brady, where you shut down. It's as if you only have part of yourself to give. As if you have erected walls you won't permit anyone to breach."

"I can't talk about it, Nell. You'll just have to understand that. I've spent years trying to move beyond the anger and hurt I experienced. Nothing good could come out of revisiting that time."

"I see."

"You'll have to take me as I am. Like it or not."

He longed to touch her, to reassure her, but he owed her this time of reflection. She sat, self-contained, studying her hands, clasped in her lap. He could hear every beat of his heart, every tick of the wall clock.

At last she looked up. "You've made me very happy," she said huskily, "been tender and gentle with me. And now you're asking me to give you your space." She laid a soft hand on his cheek. "It's the least I can do."

He pulled her into an embrace, then kissed the top of her head. "I'll miss you."

"Me, too, you," she murmured.

"I can't make any promises, yet," he whispered.

"I know."

"I wish I could show you right now how much you mean to me."

"Abby—"

"—wouldn't approve."

She nuzzled his neck. "Are we wicked?"

He chuckled. "I hope so."

Then he kissed her, again and again. Wanting to prolong the moment. Wishing he didn't have to leave. Wondering if he could possibly be falling in love again.

IT WAS A STROKE OF LUCK when Ben Hadley came into the library Tuesday afternoon. Nell had been intending to call him. It was time, past time, to talk with him about the topsy-turvy direction her emotional life was taking and to admit she'd done more thinking about a drink in the past few weeks than she had in many months. She recognized the danger signs and they scared her.

Addictions served to define identity for some, so it was all too easy to cling to them, to nourish them. To excuse one's actions because of them. But if ever there was a time she needed to be responsible for herself and for Abby, it was now.

She approached Ben and asked if he had a few minutes. When he allowed that he did, she ushered him into her office and closed the door.

He took the seat across the desk from her. "Something bothering you, Nell?"

She explained to him how important Brady was becoming to her, even about their weekend and how he'd restored her faith in her femininity. "I don't want to hurt Abby in the process, but—"

"You have needs of your own," he finished for her. "Do you love this man?"

"I think I do, but there's a problem." Then, haltingly, she told him about Brady's resistance to revealing his past and what she perceived to be an unhealed wound.

Ben steepled his hands. "He has to tell you when he's ready. On his timetable."

"But what if he never does?"

Ben smiled, as if he'd seen it all. "He must be carrying a pretty heavy burden. He'll lay it down when it's important enough to him to do so."

"Meanwhile?"

"You go on loving him. As he is. If you can."

Nell recognized the wisdom of his words. After all, she'd asked her family to love her as she was.

And they had, despite the fact that at times their love felt suffocating. She nodded. "I want to."

"Good." Ben made no move to leave, as if he intuited she hadn't finished.

"There's one more thing." She grasped the arms of her chair for support. "I...I haven't told him."

Ben cocked his head in question. "Why is that?"

Her mouth felt dry. "I'm afraid."

"So honesty is only a one-way street?"

"What do you mean?"

"You want his whole story, but you're unwilling to risk yours."

"We both fear rejection, is that it?"

Ben waited, saying nothing, letting the truth sink in. After a moment he said, "And, more than once, you've thought about a drink, haven't you?"

"How did you know?"

"I'm well acquainted with fear, Nell."

"I've resisted."

"I thought so. You know you don't have to go through this alone."

"Thanks to AA, I do know. I'm trying really hard."

Ben's eyes were heavy with the toll of experience. "One minute, one hour, one day."

Nell's palms felt moist on the arms of the chair. "I have to tell him, don't I?"

Ben leaned forward. "You know the answer to that question as well as I do."

"Soon?"

"Now, Nell."

Long after Ben left, Nell sat at her desk arranging and rearranging her pencils and pens, knowing she should have been open with Brady from the beginning. And fighting her fear. She'd had enough rejection and humiliation to last a lifetime. But Brady's judgment mattered more than she'd ever thought possible.

Please, God, let him see who I've become, not who I was.

CHAPTER NINE

IT WAS ONE OF THOSE idyllic California Saturdays travel agents and Chamber of Commerce executives dream about—cloudless skies the soft blue of a baby's blanket, the whisper of a breeze rustling through palm fronds, temperatures in the low 70s. Golf courses smelled greener, tennis balls bounced higher, swimming pools glistened Caribbean-turquoise in the morning sunlight.

Brady hated it.

At every turn was a reminder that years of his life amounted to no more than discarded film on the cutting room floor. He hadn't meant to drive by Nicole's school or the beauty salon where Brooke had her hair done. Nor could he understand how he found himself slowing his rental car in front of their former home, now occupied by strangers, trying to ignore a girl's bicycle lying temporarily abandoned in the yard.

Stone-faced, he rolled on through his old neighborhood. Already the house at the corner had been repainted a different color and, in two yards, grass had been replaced by crushed rock and desert plantings. Hell, why should he expect anything to remain the same when his entire world had been blown apart?

Yet as he drove farther past Starbuck's, streetside

cafés, wine boutiques and other upscale merchandisers, memories of the Arkansas landscape dimmed, the way a vivid dream fades like wisps of fog in the early morning sun. He'd phoned Nell Thursday evening after he got settled at the hotel. Since then, however, he'd realized he wouldn't feel right about calling her again until he dealt with the heartache he experienced everywhere he looked. From the first moment he'd walked into his corner office at L&S TechWare and seen the familiar photographs on his credenza—Nicole at her first horse show, Brooke in a stunning cocktail dress at a charity gala, the three of them, suntanned and grinning, on the deck of their sailboat—he'd known Nell was right. He had run away.

But that knowledge didn't make coming back any easier. He'd gone through the motions with Carl, making decisions, signing documents, nodding his head sagely. He'd exchanged greetings with old friends and colleagues without remembering ten minutes later what he'd said. Today, he'd driven down memory lane with the premeditation of a sadomasochist.

Bottom line? He wanted to run away again.

But he owed more than that to Nell. To Brooke's and Nicole's memory. And to himself.

The funeral was long over. Now he'd arrived at the moment of truth. It was time to bury the dead.

With clear-eyed detachment, he made an abrupt U-turn and headed for the cemetery.

BECAUSE OF THE NUMBERS of older patrons who had wanted to attend the adult forum on death and dying,

Nell had rescheduled it for late Saturday morning when more of them would be able to drive to the library. The speaker had done a sensitive job of anticipating the questions and assuring the audience that death was a natural process.

Nell envied those who had been given the opportunity to say goodbye to their loved ones. She had tortured herself after her father had died so suddenly. Had he known how much she loved and appreciated him? What were her last words to him? She couldn't remember and that missing link plagued her. He'd seemed so jolly at Christmastime that year, making his traditional toasts, greeting everyone with a bear hug, laughing uproariously at Abby's antics. Then, a mere three days later, he was dead.

As the speaker responded to a question about medical directives, Nell found herself reliving the days that followed. Rick had been out of town for a New Year's bowl game. When she'd finally reached him at the team hotel, a woman had answered. In the background, a party was clearly in full swing. Just before Rick picked up the receiver, she heard him give the punch line of an off-color joke, followed by raucous male laughter. No matter how many times she looked back on the next minute, she could never explain what had caused her to ask the question, why she hadn't immediately told him about her father. Instead, her first words were, "Who was that woman?"

"What woman?"

"The one who answered the phone."

"Hey, babe, lay off, will you? We're just having a little fun down here, that's all."

And in that moment, she knew. She didn't know how. It made no sense, but she'd never been surer of anything in her life. When she'd called their travel agent the next morning, any lingering doubt had been removed. Rick had left town with a Clarice Townsend.

"…decide whether you want a Do Not Resuscitate order." The speaker was giving valuable information, but Nell couldn't concentrate.

In a single week she had lost her father and learned of her husband's unfaithfulness. In hindsight, she should have kicked Rick out then, but for Abby's sake, they had tried to salvage the marriage. Or rather she had. Rick gave mere lip service to the effort. Over the long months, his vacant stares, secretive phone calls and late nights "at work" took their toll on her self-esteem. Weary with disillusionment, a sense of abandonment and self-hatred, she sought solace in the soothing depths of a bottle. A little vodka in her orange juice to get her going in the morning, rum in her soda to see her through midday, a pick-me-up to lighten her mood before Abby came home from school, two martinis to get through the awful twilight hours when husbands and fathers traditionally returned home from work, and, of course, a nightcap before bed.

At first she'd made excuses, claiming the stress of her father's death, playing the betrayed wife to the hilt, but after a while she didn't worry about excuses. Her only concern was where she would get the next drink. And the next.

God knows what she'd missed, whom she'd hurt. Poor Abby. She'd lost both father and mother in that cruel time. As long as she lived, Nell knew she could never make up that loss to Abby. All she could do was make each new day a good one.

Nell raised her head when a burst of applause indicated the conclusion of the question and answer period. She made her way through the departing patrons to thank the speaker, then as soon as she gracefully could, headed for home.

It was a gorgeous late September day, mild, but with the hint of a cool breeze. The dogwoods and some oaks already sported their autumn finery. Maybe Abby would want to go for a walk with her.

She entered the house through the kitchen door and immediately spotted the note on the counter. *Gone with Tonya and her mother to the mall. Back about four.* So much for a companionable walk with her daughter. She put a kettle on to boil for a cup of tea and rummaged in the pantry for a can of tuna to make a sandwich.

In the quiet of the house, she could no longer avoid thinking about Brady. He'd called Thursday to tell her of his safe arrival, but it had been a short, unsatisfactory conversation. She'd second-guessed herself ever since Monday night. What on earth had made her accuse him of running away from his problems? It didn't take a professional psychologist to know that act was akin to throwing the gauntlet where a man was concerned. He'd made the boundaries very clear. Why had she crossed them?

When the answer surfaced, she sank down on a kitchen stool. She loved him. She wanted to spend the rest of her life with him. To do that, she needed to know everything about him, just as he needed to know all about her.

The shrill whistle of the teakettle intruded on her thoughts, and she poured water over the tea bag in her cup and slapped some tuna, mayonnaise and lettuce between two bread slices. As she chewed on a bite of sandwich, she wondered for the umpteenth time since yesterday, why she hadn't heard from Brady again. He'd promised to call back. Was she fooling herself? Did California hold a bigger attraction for him than he'd let on?

She was cleaning up the kitchen when the phone rang. Finally. It had to be him. She dashed to the wall phone and picked it up, her voice alive with expectation. "Brady?"

A sardonic laugh she'd know anywhere was the first thing she heard, followed by, "Not hardly, Nell. It's Rick."

"Oh." Why had she done a dumb thing like assuming the caller would be Brady? Was she that far gone?

"Not who you were expecting, I gather."

"No."

"Who is he, Nell?"

"Who?"

"The man Abby told me about."

Glancing out the kitchen window, Nell wasn't at all surprised to see a dark cloud glide past, obscuring the sun. It figured. She fought panic. What had Abby told her father?

"Cat got your tongue? I gather his name is Brady."

Nell willed herself a solid backbone. "Yes. What concern is that of yours?"

"That's rather obvious, isn't it? My 'concern' is Abby. I hope you're being discreet."

That was rich! It was all she could do to bite her tongue. "Abby's welfare is uppermost in my mind, and you can rest assured I'm not doing anything you need to worry about. After all, I am entitled to a social life, aren't I?"

"I want Abby to be happy, and if circumstances there are uncomfortable for her, I'm sure we could agree on other arrangements."

Was the man saying what she thought he was? Nell's blood boiled. He was actually suggesting Abby live with him and Clarice. Gritting her teeth, she carefully made her voice neutral. "We share in common the goal of Abby's happiness. I don't expect either of us to jeopardize that again as we once did."

"Clarice and I will be looking out for her welfare."

Nell blinked away angry tears. "So will I, Rick, so will I."

After she hung up, Nell bolted out of the house, oblivious to the gathering storm clouds. Fury propelled her down the street, through the park and up the steep hill on the other side. When she reached the top of the ridge, she stopped, lungs heaving, gasping for breath.

Dear God, what had Abby told her father?

Worse yet, what was he prepared to do?

THE GRAVES WERE on a slight rise, sheltered by a flowering bougainvillea. A prime spot, the cemetery director had said. At the time, the remark had irritated Brady. Even in death, for materialistic Californians, location mattered. Brady kicked at a tuft of grass. Well, it certainly didn't matter now.

He studied the inscriptions on the headstones—the bare facts, the ineffective hints of who Brooke and Nicole had been. What they had meant to him. He wanted to feel something. In this place, surely, he would find a connection with them.

But the scene was too perfect to have any relevance. Manicured grass, carefully trimmed shrubbery, discreet directional markers sectioning up plots of ground. An elaborate filing system for ghosts that didn't take into consideration the all-too-human imperfections—the mole at the base of Brooke's neck, Nicole's funny, long toes and chipped front tooth.

He knelt, hands on the ground, bracing himself, hoping the sensation of grass and earth beneath his fingers would awaken raw emotion. He needed to feel their presence, damn it.

Nothing. Far in the distance he could hear the hum of traffic on the freeway. Here, aside from the occasional trill of a bird, it was quiet. Too quiet.

Ultimately, with an urgency he couldn't explain, he found himself talking. Telling them about the blur of days following the accident, about selling the house, taking time off from work, leaving California. About his desperate cross-country odyssey, his loneliness, his hopelessness. About the gaping hole surrounded by the bone and tissue that was his body.

He placed a hand on each grave, still slightly rounded beneath his palms, and poured out his anger and grief, not even pausing to wipe away tears he was helpless to control.

After a while he rocked back on his heels, drew a handkerchief from his pocket and blew his nose. From the bell tower, a carillon chimed the haunting notes of "Amazing Grace." Unsummoned, the words came to him from a time long ago when his mother, in her soft, true alto, would sing the hymn to him at bedtime. Yet even as the familiar words formed in his mind, he wondered what could possibly save a wretch like him.

When the final note echoed in the silence, he heard in his heart the answer. Nell.

Then, in a hoarse whisper, he told Brooke and Nicole about Nell. About the chance for a new life with her in Arkansas. "I will always love you, my darlings, but I have a decision to make. To live or merely go through the motions. I didn't look for this to happen, didn't seek it exactly, but I think I'm ready to love again. Please understand."

Slowly he stood, knowing he wouldn't receive a response, yet craving one anyway. He waited, hands in his pockets, reluctant to leave. Avoiding a parting that *he* would initiate this time.

Then, without warning, a strong breeze blew across the open space and pink rose petals from a nearby gravesite settled at the foot of Brooke's and Nicole's markers. Whether it was a sign or not, he couldn't say.

All he knew was that he felt their presence—and their blessing.

Drained of emotion, yet more peaceful than he'd been in months, he nodded in acquiescence.

He would choose life.
And Nell.

ABBY SQUIRMED. The way her mother was looking at her made her feel funny. Like she'd done something wrong, but she didn't know what. "I didn't spend any money at the mall, if that's what you think."

Her mother glanced at the kitchen table where bills were spread out in neat piles as if that explained everything. "I'm not angry, Abby. Just preoccupied." She set down her pen and with a weary sigh said, "Did you have a good time?"

"I guess. Mrs. Larkin treated us to lunch and a movie."

"That was nice of her."

Her mother's worry lines grew more pronounced. Whenever she paid bills, it made Abby nervous. Like maybe they were having financial troubles. Abby nodded at the invoices. "Do we, uh, have enough money?"

"Don't you worry about that. We always make do, don't we?"

Well, yeah, but there sure wasn't a lot extra for stuff like getting a new school wardrobe the way Tonya did every year. "I suppose."

"Do you have a minute?"

Oh great. "I was going to my room to read my book for English."

"This won't take long."

Realizing her escape route had been cut off, Abby settled on one of the kitchen stools. "What?"

"First of all, understand I'm not trying to pry."

Right.

"It's about your last weekend in Texas at your dad's."

"What about it?"

"You're aware, of course, that Brady Logan's friendship is important to me. Can you remember exactly what you told your father about that?"

Crap. She'd known the minute she'd said anything to her dad that she should've kept her mouth shut. He'd acted outraged. Like he was threatened or something. Which was a crock because he had Clarice, so what did he care about Mom? He'd left them, not the other way around.

"All I said was that you were up in Missouri with your boyfriend." Bad answer. Her mother's shoulders drooped like they always did when she was disappointed in Abby. "Did I do something wrong?"

"Telling the truth is never wrong. It's just I wouldn't want you making too big a deal of my relationship with Brady."

"But you like him a lot, right?"

When her mother answered, Abby almost had to look away. The longing in her mother's eyes scared her. "Yes, honey, I do."

"Okay, then." Before her mom could go on about stupid Brady, Abby jumped up and fled, only stopping for breath when she reached the refuge of her room. She was no dummy. She'd seen that look before. In the movies. Or sometimes when Tonya's mother looked at Mr. Larkin.

Cripes. She didn't care what her mother said about Brady Logan. It was clear as anything—she was in love with him. Gross.

TONIGHT COULDN'T come soon enough. All day Tuesday at work, Nell walked on air. Brady had called her early Saturday evening from California. With an openness that caused her heart to soar, he'd explained his experience at the cemetery and assured her he was eager to get back to Arkansas—and to her. With low chuckles and playful innuendo, he'd reminded her that their trip to Missouri was only the beginning. She had stopped short of confiding that her newly awakened body had reminded her more than once since that she missed and needed him. Sometimes, out of the blue, she found herself giggling like a schoolgirl. She'd had no idea lovemaking could be so satisfying or so addictive.

She glanced at the clock over the checkout desk. Three more hours and he'd be home. More than once, Reggie Pettigrew had teased her about her daydreaming. If he only knew.

Finally the minutes crept by and it was time to leave work. Driving home, she pictured Brady deplaning, arriving at his condo, maybe taking a shower. Blushing, she lingered over that image. His body was leaner, firmer than Rick's and, with a single caress, could make hers hum. She wanted tonight to be about reunion and easy affection.

Beneath the surface, though, lay a deeper concern—telling him, as she must, about being a recovering alcoholic. She never wanted him to accuse her of duplicity. So now she must face the consequences of her choices and actions. She would tell him. When the opportunity presented itself.

She just hoped that wasn't tonight. She didn't want anything to spoil his homecoming.

BRADY COULDN'T STOP grinning from the moment he left Northwest Arkansas Regional Airport. The air was rich with a hint of wood fires, and the unending foliage took him by surprise after California. Traffic was so light, compared to the coast, that he shook his head in disbelief. It took him all of thirty minutes and a mere three stoplights to reach his condo. He'd told Nell he'd arrive at her place about eight. That would leave him just enough time for a shower and a quick sandwich.

As he let the hot water pour over his shoulders, he sang lustily, feeling happier than he could remember being in a long time. How could he have guessed that the simple act of reading an entry in a guest journal at an Arkansas bed-and-breakfast would change his life? Nell had given him so much. She was gentle and kind and fun. And just unpredictable enough to keep life interesting. He'd bet his last dollar she had no idea the extent to which she turned him on. Well, time would certainly take care of that little problem.

On the way to Nell's, he made a quick stop to pick up a bouquet of daisies. The choice had been easy. They reminded him of her—dainty, yet perky. A natural, refreshing kind of beauty. When he reached her house, he stood a moment on the front porch studying the seasonal wreath, a circle of grapevines decorated with plump, purple artificial grapes and dried leaves. That simple touch left him misty-eyed with a vision of what he could have with Nell.

Yet even with those thoughts, he was unprepared for the wave of feeling that flooded him when she opened the door, her face glowing with a welcoming smile, her slender body reedlike but appropriately rounded in places his fingers itched to explore. "I missed you," he choked out.

When she laid the flowers on the hall table and walked into his waiting arms, he knew this truly was home. "I thought eight o'clock would never come," she whispered.

He looked beyond her, then back into her eyes.

She read his mind. "She's in her room."

"Good," he said just before leaning closer to capture her sweet, full lips and show her with the power of his kiss just how much he'd missed her. That's all it took before his body reacted. He groaned.

"Oh, my," she breathed when she finally managed to step back. "We could be in trouble."

"Bring it on," he growled.

"I'd love to oblige, but there is Abby to consider. What kind of example would we be setting?" Her eyes were playful, but the boundaries had been made clear. She picked up the daisies and nestled them to her chest. "Thank you," she said, then took his hand and led him into the family room, where a plate of brownies and an insulated carafe were waiting. "I thought you might be hungry after your flight."

No way would he tell her he'd just eaten. "Don't mind if I do," he said, helping himself to a brownie.

She busied herself getting a vase for the daisies, then sat beside him on the sofa and poured two cups of coffee.

He took his coffee from her and grinned. "So all we can do is talk?"

"There's nothing wrong with that. It gives me a chance to tell you you're spoiling me. First the bird-of-paradise, and now daisies. A girl could get used to such treatment.''

He set down his cup and moved closer, wrapping an arm around her. ''I certainly hope so.'' He ran a finger down the slope of her nose. ''You're worth it.''

He couldn't believe it. There was genuine doubt in her eyes, when she faced him. ''You think so?''

''I know so,'' he said, planting a kiss on her forehead.

She relaxed against his arm. ''Tell me about your trip.''

She was a good listener and he found himself elaborating about his disenchantment with the pretentious and competitive lifestyle he'd once cultivated. ''The contrast with Fayetteville is mind-boggling.''

In a careful tone, she said, ''This isn't paradise, Brady.''

''No place is. We make our own heavens and hells.''

She tensed, looked at the ceiling, then finally spoke. ''Brady, maybe now is a good time to tell you—'' But before she could go on, the phone rang, shattering the silence. From her bedroom, Abby hollered, ''I'll get it.''

Nell seemed somehow…relieved by the interruption. ''Cross your fingers that's the new boyfriend calling. She's been agonizing all weekend. There's a school dance this coming Friday and she's dying for him to ask her.''

''And he's all of thirteen, right? Trust me, he's scared spitless to invite her for fear she'll turn him down. Asking a girl for a date is the torture of the damned for a guy that age.''

''And this is the voice of experience speaking?''

''Yes, ma'am.'' Although the scene forming in his mind was hardly as innocent as one from *Happy Days*. Sheryl Clay. He hadn't thought of her in years. A ninth grader with tits that were the talk of the junior high locker room. His eighth-grade teammates had dared him to ask her to a school barn dance and hayride. ''Screw off, runt,'' she'd said in response to his stammered invitation. Just one more in the series of rejections that were the rule rather than the exception when he was growing up.

''Where'd you go just now?'' she asked.

''Nowhere.'' He didn't want to tell her and run the risk of opening the door to his past again. She'd just have to understand. That area was hands-off. It wouldn't do her any good, and it sure as hell wouldn't benefit him.

''Mom?'' Abby burst into the room with a smile that made it clear the kid had screwed up his courage. ''It's Alan. He asked me!'' She shrieked with delight. ''Can I go?'' She went down on one knee. ''Please.''

Nell moved away from Brady and affected mock sternness. ''Before I give my answer, haven't you forgotten something?''

Abby looked confused, then turned to Brady. A light bulb went on. ''Oh, hi, Mr. Logan.''

''It's nice to see you, Abby.'' When he uttered those words, he realized it really *was* nice to see her. That he was enjoying the adolescent drama being played out before his eyes.

Abby wiggled with impatience. "Mom? Can I?"

Nell relented and smiled. "Yes, darling, you may."

"I love you," Abby offered her mother before running down the hall.

"Thank God," Nell breathed. "I wasn't sure how she would handle rejection."

"She's your daughter. She'd have survived." He pulled her closer and played with a lock of her hair. "You know, I just realized something important."

"What's that?"

"When I left California after the accident, I made mental shrines to Brooke and Nicole, not allowing myself to see them as anything other than paragons. Somehow I was able to move beyond Brooke when I met you, but I have to confess Abby was giving me serious difficulty."

"What do you mean?"

"She and Nicole are, uh, were so close in age. Nicole had long blond hair, too. Every time I was with Abby or heard you talk about her, all I could focus on was Nicole. On what I was missing. Being a father was very important to me." He paused to collect his thoughts. "I wasn't totally sure about us, Nell, because I didn't know if I could accept Abby. I knew I needed to, but it wasn't happening."

"And now?"

"Saying goodbye to Nicole and then seeing Abby tonight, so upbeat and excited...I finally realized I can't blame Abby for not being Nicole. And if I shut Abby out, then I lose not only you, but the opportunity to enjoy watching another girl grow up." He could hardly go on. "I don't want to miss out on that. On any of it."

Nell laid a soothing hand on his cheek. "I hope you won't have to."

He nestled her closer. "We're pretty lucky, aren't we?"

"Maybe we have the chance to make our own heaven out of the hells we've been through."

He waited for the pounding of his heart to slow before cupping her face and searching her eyes. "I'm counting on it."

"Brady," she breathed, pulling his head closer and lifting her lips to his.

With the diabolical timing of a twisted film director, the phone rang again. Nell pulled back. "Abby'll get it."

Reluctantly, he moved away. "Guess I'll have to behave. We wouldn't want to be caught in the act."

Nell chuckled. "How does it feel being chaperoned by a thirteen-year-old?"

Before he could answer, true to form, Abby yelled down the hall. "It's for you, Mom. It's your sponsor from AA."

Brady could feel blood eddying in his ears. Surely he hadn't heard Abby right. But the stunned look on Nell's face verified that nothing was wrong with his hearing. "AA?" He stood. There had to be some mistake. Something he was missing. As his gaze homed in on Nell, he was helpless to curb the anger twisting his gut. "What is she talking about?"

Nell turned away to pick up the phone, leaving him alone in the silence of what might well be the second worst moment of his life. "Nell?"

Nell murmured something into the receiver, clicked it off and set it on the coffee table, then faced him, her head bowed. "I was going to tell you."

"Tell me what exactly?"

Threading her fingers together in anguish, she lifted her ravaged eyes. "Brady, I am an alcoholic."

CHAPTER TEN

HIS FACE DRAINED of color and his chest heaving, Brady stared at her, awareness slowly replacing shock. "You've got to be kidding."

Nell summoned her voice somehow. "No, Brady, I'm not."

From his distorted mouth came the ragged parody of a laugh. "Some secret you've been keeping from me." He shook his head in disbelief. "Give me a minute." Then, drawing a shaking hand through his hair, he went to the window where he stood, his back rigid.

Nell had expected him to be surprised and had wondered if he would have trouble accepting her once he knew. But this felt like total rejection. And she had no tools to combat it.

Her forehead beaded with clamminess, and she was afraid she was going to throw up. Swallowing hard, she wiped her damp hands on her slacks, then began speaking, her voice a low monotone. She had no idea whether he would listen, but she had to try. To explain—and confess.

"I know I should have told you sooner. I tried to. Earlier, before Alan called. But it's not the sort of thing you go around announcing to people."

He hadn't moved, except to thrust his balled fists into his pockets.

"For what it's worth, I've been sober for six years."

She could barely hear him mumble, "You want a goddamn prize?"

Her face reddened and her heart pounded double-time. "No, but I wouldn't mind a little understanding."

"That's asking quite a bit."

What had happened to the sensitive, gentle man she'd fallen in love with? This icy stranger was someone she didn't know.

He whirled around. "All right, tell me about it. Tell me how you justify it."

"I don't justify it. Alcoholism can happen to anybody. No one is immune. And it happened to me. It's not something I'm proud of, but it's a fact I live with every day."

"Why?"

Nell recoiled. That one anguished word was as much of a concession to understanding as he was going to make. She wanted to pace, to work out the explanation through movement. But she stayed where she was, rooted in an agony that went beyond any AA testimonial. And so she began—with her history of social drinking, her insecurity, the liquid escape she had sought from her father's death and Rick's unfaithfulness. When she finished, she stared into Brady's implacable eyes. "I'm not asking you to condone what I did, but I'd like to think you could understand. Forgive?" The last word came out tremulously as a question.

He shrugged disgustedly, and in that moment Nell knew they were doomed.

"While you're at it, you may as well tell me the rest."

"The rest?"

"How in some moment of glorious revelation you decided to go to AA."

"Glorious revelation?" She snorted. "I wish. Then I wouldn't have come close to losing Abby."

He stepped toward her, his face even grayer. "What are you talking about?"

"The night Rick delivered the divorce papers, we got into a huge fight. He walked out. Abby overheard us and was semi-hysterical and kept crying 'I want my daddy, I want my daddy.' No amount of vodka numbed her protest, so I decided to take her to Rick and let him see just what a mess he'd made of our lives."

She paused, wishing she didn't have to go on. Brady leaned on the arm of the sofa and waited, his jaw working.

"It was a snowy night. The roads were icy. I...I didn't care." Her voice broke. Clearing her throat, she went on, knowing she had to finish, had to accept every measure of damnation from him. "We got to the car, and I strapped Abby in the back seat. She wouldn't stop howling. I dropped my keys in the snow. How I wish I'd never found them." She stopped, unable to continue.

Brady's eyes were locked on his laced fingers. From down the hall Nell could hear the pinging of pipes. Abby was taking a shower.

"Go on," Brady said like a man condemned to hearing the worst.

"But I did find them, and I started driving toward Clarice's apartment. On these hilly streets, ice is treacherous," she said in grotesque understatement. "I never could remember exactly what happened, which wasn't surprising since I was drunk. I woke up in the hospital." Her eyes moistened with emotion, but she struggled for control. "Abby could've been killed in the accident. Only a matter of inches saved her."

A strangled moan erupted from Brady and he strode again to the window.

Determined to finish, Nell went on. "That's what got my attention. AA saved me."

"How convenient for you."

Shocked, Nell rose to her feet and took a step toward him. She'd never encountered such indifference. "What's that supposed to mean?"

Slowly he faced her, his own cheeks tearstained. He looked devastated, and when he spoke, she had the impression he didn't know or care that she was there.

"That your story has a nice, tidy ending. Happily ever after." He practically choked on bitterness. "Brooke and Nicole weren't so lucky. Their particular drunk driver failed to stop at a highway intersection and he hit them broadside."

"*Their* drunk driver? What do you mean?"

"Just what I said. Don't you get it? The tanker driver had a blood alcohol level well above the limit. Brooke and Nicole weren't as lucky as Abby. As if 'luck' had anything to do with it. People like you and that truck driver never consider anyone else, do you?''

She deserved it—every last ounce of his scorn and fury. Everything he valued in life had been lost because someone else, someone like her, had a consuming thirst that blinded him to anything but his own needs for self-gratification or escape. What could she say? Finally, she heard herself mumble, ''I'm sorry. I'd undo it if I could.''

''You can't, Nell.'' He started for the front door, then hesitated and turned around. ''I'm sorry, too. I thought we had something magical. I guess I'm not as good a judge of character as I thought.''

After he left, emptiness echoed throughout the house. She should've known better than to trust that she'd be given a second chance. Reentering the family room, she looked wildly around, trying to beat back a desperate craving for alcohol. *Brady, Brady, Brady.* She couldn't stop repeating his name or gasping with the painful knowledge of the wound she'd opened up in him tonight. And in herself.

For something, anything, to do except grab her keys, dash to the liquor store and drown the fear lodged in her throat, she picked a daisy from the bouquet Brady had brought her earlier, when things had been happy, promising.

One by one she plucked each petal. ''He loves me, he loves me not, he loves me…''

Finally one last petal remained. Why was she surprised? ''He loves me not.''

She collapsed on the sofa, stifling her wrenching sobs with the overstuffed pillow, knowing she had hurt him beyond repair.

But that didn't mean she'd stopped loving him. She couldn't.

CLUTCHING THE STEERING WHEEL like a lifeline, Brady threaded his way through the light traffic on Fayetteville's main drag. Flashing neon lights were nothing more than a haze in his peripheral vision. *Goddammit, goddammit!* With the flat of his hand, he pounded the wheel. He wanted to kick a wall, drive his fist through a pane of glass, anything to obliterate the pain holding him captive.

He still couldn't believe it. He forced himself to repeat Nell's words over and over in his brain. *I am an alcoholic.*

Before, he'd only wondered if God had a malicious streak, now he knew for sure. Enraged, he shook his fist. "You listening up there? Okay, you win. I cry 'Uncle.'"

Of all the things Nell could have done to destroy him, this was the worst. Had it been only a few hours ago he'd considered her unpredictability interesting?

What an ass he was! Thinking that by reading some sappy entry in a B-and-B journal he could find true love. Happiness. Oh, yeah, happiness. Like there was any such thing.

I am an alcoholic. Why hadn't he seen it coming? She didn't drink, her husband had walked out. All the pieces had been there, but he'd painted her as he'd wanted her to be, as he'd needed her to be. The sweet, fun-loving Nell he thought he knew was merely the projection of his own lonely imagination.

He'd thought he was doing a great thing by loving her, restoring her damaged sense of her desirability.

But what was that all about? Had she been using him? He'd read somewhere that alcoholics could be manipulative. Had she been playing him?

Beneath his anger, he knew he was raving. That he was doing Nell a disservice with such cynicism. But he had no outlet for the force of his anger and disillusionment. For…name it…his desolation.

First Brooke and Nicole. Now Nell and Abby. Lost.

Eventually he became more aware of his surroundings. He was in the old-fashioned town square, symbolic of everything he'd come to love about the town—the slower pace, friendlier people, simpler lifestyle.

But was it all based on an illusion? Wishful thinking? Without Nell, could he be happy here?

He grunted. He couldn't be happy anywhere.

That being the case, what did it matter whether it was California or Arkansas? Neither could be *home*.

It was well after midnight when he finally gave up and returned to his condo. The forlorn, repetitive hoot of an owl accompanied him as he walked from his parking space to his door. The musty smell of stale pipe smoke assailed him when he stepped inside. In the moonlight streaming through the windows, he made out the boxy forms of the antique furniture his landlord prized.

In that moment, he was seized by an intense aversion to the place. What the hell was he doing here? From the Edgewater Inn until tonight, had he been living in a fantasy world? Damn, it was as if he had no grip on who he was anymore.

He flicked on the desk lamp and pushed the Play button on the answering machine.

"Hey, buddy, it's Carl. You should be back in Arkansas by now. Since you've been home to California, maybe Fayetteville won't look so good. I know you. You can't stay away. Lemme know when you're comin' back. Bring your Nell if you want to. She'll love it here."

Your Nell. He couldn't blame Carl. That's how he himself used to think of her, dream of her.

The machine played the second message. "Brady, Buzz Valentine. Good news. The option on the land went through fine, but beyond that, I had a call from one of the company executives you spoke with about the conference center. He not only thinks it's a great idea, but his firm wants to consider investing in it. Looks like you're on your way."

Brady hit Rewind and listened to the chuckling of the tape feeding through the mechanism.

Malicious or not, God had a great sense of humor. Now Brady had two choices for his future.

Neither held any appeal.

In the core of his heart, he knew why.

Neither involved Nell.

OBLIVIOUS TO the late afternoon sun filtering through the giant oak and maple trees, Abby pedaled as hard as she could down the hill, through the park and up Tonya's street. She hadn't risked talking to Tonya at school. Someone might have overheard. But she had to tell somebody. The lump in her throat just kept growing. In algebra, when the teacher called on her, she'd been afraid she'd burst into tears and make a complete fool of herself.

This morning her mother had tried to act like everything was normal. Abby didn't have to be a genius to know it wasn't. Red-rimmed eyes, pale skin, a fake laugh, trembling fingers. In a shaky voice Mom had explained that Brady hadn't known about AA until she'd shouted it down the hall. Well, how was she supposed to know it was still a big, dark secret? Even so, she had tried to apologize, but her mother had waved her hands and said in a broken voice, "Let's not talk about last night. Or about Brady. It wasn't your fault." Then Mom had hugged her and whispered, "It was my responsibility, not yours." But that hadn't made her feel any better.

Abby drew in deep lungfuls of air as she skidded to a stop in the Larkins' driveway. She could kill that Brady Logan!

It took five minutes of chitchat with Tonya's mother before the girls could escape to Tonya's bedroom. Mrs. Larkin had forced a sugar cookie on Abby, but she could hardly choke it down. Now she sat curled up in Tonya's beanbag chair, while her friend settled on the floor, leaning against the footboard of her bed, her legs stretched out in front of her.

"Okay, Abby. What's up?"

Abby hugged her knees to her chest. "Oh, God, Tonya, I'm so scared."

"Scared?"

Abby could feel the soft denim of her jeans beneath her fingers, smell the faint scent of fabric softener. "It's Mom."

"What happened?"

All day she'd been waiting to tell Tonya, but now that the time had come, she had trouble beginning. "It's all my fault."

"What is?"

"Mom and Mr. Logan."

Not unkindly, Tonya said, "Earth to Abby. Come in, please. You're not making any sense."

Abby told Tonya about the phone call from Ben Hadley and how she'd mentioned AA in front of Mr. Logan. About how her mom hadn't told him she was an alcoholic.

"What happened then?"

Abby shrugged. "I don't know exactly."

"So what do you think?"

"They must've talked a while, 'cuz I heard him leave later. I waited for Mom to come to bed, but she never did. At least not before I fell asleep. You shoulda seen her this morning. She looked like somebody with a bad case of the flu."

Tonya scooted forward and crossed her legs. "So whaddya think happened?"

"Nothing good. I think maybe he broke up with her."

"Jeez."

"What if she was in love with him?"

"Do you think she was?"

Abby laid her chin on her knees and considered the question before saying, "Yeah, I'm pretty sure. And I messed it up. Totally."

"It wasn't your fault he didn't know she's an alcoholic. A recovering one," Tonya hastily added.

"She was prob'ly going to tell him."

"Sure."

"She was really unhappy this morning. I'm so afraid, Tonya. What if she starts to drink again?"

"You gotta do something."

Abby felt like she might be sick. "What?"

Tonya raised her hands helplessly. "I dunno. Something to fix it."

Like the answer to a prayer, an idea began to take shape in Abby's head. "Maybe she wouldn't drink if—"

"If what?"

Abby continued, thinking aloud. "If she loves Brady, she needs to get him back. Then she'll be happy. When she's happy, she doesn't drink."

"Yeah, but—"

Abby leaped to her feet and began prowling around the room. "I could, like, find out where he lives and go visit him. Tell him how miserable Mom is. How it was all my fault. How she would've told him herself if only I hadn't opened my big mouth."

"It could work."

She stopped in the middle of the room. "How'll I find out where he lives?"

"I guess you'll have to ask your mom."

Abby felt deflated. She didn't want to watch her mother's reaction when she mentioned Brady Logan to her. "Crap. I guess it's not such a good idea after all."

All the way home on her bike, she felt queasy. She ought to be able, somehow, to make things come out right. She arrived home before her mother and went straight to the trash can to see if there were any empty bottles. None.

She should be relieved. Instead, she felt this tightness like the whole situation was about to get worse.

She went to her room and lay down on her bed. She unbuttoned her jeans, wishing the full feeling would go away, but knowing it wouldn't until she did something.

Okay, what would it hurt? She'd ask her mother about Brady Logan.

NELL CHASTISED HERSELF on the way home from work. She'd been barely functional, and it hadn't escaped Reggie's watchful eye. He'd seemed more concerned than upset, but she couldn't risk disappointing her boss. She loved her job. She'd need it now more than ever. To keep her sane. To keep her from jeopardizing her sobriety.

More than anything, she'd longed to lose herself in an alcoholic blur. To have a few blessed hours when she could forget the anguish and judgment written on Brady's face. To block out the awful knowledge that his family had been killed by a drunk driver. By association, she was as guilty in his mind as if she'd been in the cab of that rig.

As she turned in her driveway, she sucked in a sob. She'd lost Brady, and it was a pain even deeper than Rick's defection, which, if she was honest, had contained an element of relief.

She sat for a moment summoning her acting skills. No way did she want to inflict her disappointment and pain on Abby. But this morning that's exactly what she'd done. Bless the girl's heart. It hadn't been her fault. Ben often called. Abby knew him. It had been a natural thing for Abby to say. Besides, in her heart Nell knew she should have told Brady long ago.

She'd been living in violation of the Twelve Steps. She was back to Step Four—"Make a searching and fearless moral inventory." Bottom line, she'd been both self-indulgent and dishonest. She'd call Ben later tonight, talk about the situation—and about her temptation to drink.

Now, though, she had to face Abby. Reassure her.

She found her daughter in the kitchen in the throes of trying to make spaghetti, her efforts clearly a peacemaking gesture. Boiling water had splattered over the stove top and Nell noted the red trail from the empty can of tomatoes to the pot of simmering sauce. "Hi, honey, have a good day?"

"Not really." Like the countertop, Abby's gray Razorbacks sweatshirt sported splotches of red.

Nell tried a joke. "Was Alan absent?"

Abby threw her a get-real look. "No. He was fine." She ducked her head, stirring the pasta with a vengeance. "I was worried about you. You know, about what I said. I just figured Mr. Logan knew."

Nell moved to the stove and put her arm around Abby's waist. "No, honey, he didn't. But that was a natural assumption. I should have told him long before last night."

"Was he mad?"

"Disappointed." Nell sighed internally. Above all, she didn't want Abby assuming ill-placed guilt. "There was something I didn't know about the accident that killed his wife and daughter. Something that explains why Brady couldn't accept that I am a recovering alcoholic."

Abby moved to the spice rack, as if to avoid prox-
imity to her mother. ''What?'' she asked, reaching
for the oregano.

''The accident that killed his wife and daughter
was caused by a drunk driver.''

Abby clutched the spice jar, her face draining of
color. ''How?''

''The man was driving a loaded gasoline tanker.
He ran a stop sign at a highway intersection and he
broadsided them.'' Nell swallowed several times, the
words assuming even more horrible proportions
when she uttered them herself.

''That's awful!'' Abby's eyes were wide. ''His
daughter, how old was she?''

''About your age.''

Nell watched Abby process the information, the
enormity of it sinking in. Finally, Abby returned to
the stove and sprinkled oregano over the sauce.

Nell struggled onward. ''Brady wasn't prepared
for me to be an alcoholic. Neither of us would have
been as hurt if I'd been honest from the beginning.
So, in a way, you did me a favor last night.'' She
paused, then tilted her daughter's chin so she could
look into her eyes. ''Never for one minute should
you blame yourself. This is my fault, mine alone.''

''I guess.'' Abby tested the pasta, then nudged
Nell aside as she carried the steamer pot to the sink.
Carefully she poured off the water and slid the spaghetti into a bowl. Neither of them said anything until after Abby had added the sauce. Then Abby turned
to face Nell. ''I haven't treated Mr. Logan very well.
I didn't know about how it happened. I think I'd like
to write him, like, a sympathy note or something.''

Overcome with relief and pride in her daughter, Nell smiled. "I think that would be very thoughtful."

"Okay. Could you give me his address, then?"

"Sure." Nell pulled a sheet off the grocery list pad and wrote down the information. Maybe writing Brady would give Abby a sense of closure.

As for herself? She didn't believe anything could ever do that.

SHORTLY AFTER SCHOOL the next afternoon Abby and Tonya met at the picnic pavilion in the park. Abby straddled her bike while Tonya sat on the top of a picnic table. "I can't believe you got his address so easily."

"Me neither. The idea just came to me." Abby couldn't admit to her friend how low she felt about saying she'd write a sympathy note. Her mother had made out like she was some sort of junior saint.

"What are you going to say to him?"

"I dunno. What if he isn't even there?"

"I guess you'll have to keep trying."

The pain in Abby's stomach gripped her. Trying this once was bad enough. She couldn't imagine having to do it again. "Maybe he won't even talk to me."

Tonya tossed her head. "He will. Adults always try harder with kids. Makes 'em feel good."

"You won't tell?"

"Of course not." Abby started to interrupt, but Tonya kept right on. "I know, if your mom calls, I'm supposed to say you're in the bathroom or something, right?"

"Right. She'd kill me if she knew I was going to his apartment."

"But you gotta try."

Abby hunched over the handlebars. "Yeah."

Tonya stood up and put a hand on Abby's shoulder. "Well, go on then. You haven't got all day."

Abby straightened and blew out a breath, wishing the panicky ache would go away. She was afraid. What if she failed? "Okay." Bracing herself on one foot, she put the other on the pedal.

"Call me the minute you get home."

"I will." Then Abby shoved off, hoping she could get this whole ordeal over with in a hurry.

Ten minutes later, she sailed down a hill and coasted into the parking lot of the Devonshire Village condominiums. The third building displayed the number she was looking for. She slid off the bike, set the kickstand and looked around. Her heart sank. His SUV was there. In the parking lot. In a way she'd hoped it wouldn't be. Hoped she wouldn't have to face him.

But then she thought about her mother. She needed to be happy. And if Brady Logan was what it took for that to happen, Abby was prepared to help things along. No matter what had happened since, she couldn't forget the way her mother and Mr. Logan had looked at each other when they thought no one was watching.

Wiping her hands along the sides of her jeans, she tried to ignore the scared feeling she had. *Just do it,* she said under her breath, the slogan providing her with the motivation she needed.

She lifted her fist and knocked on his door, convinced he would be able to hear her heart thudding as well.

When the door opened, he seemed taller than she remembered, wearing a navy T-shirt, gray sweatpants and running shoes. His eyes, like her mother's, were bloodshot and his hair was all rumpled. "Abby?" He stepped back. "What can I do for you?"

"We need to talk," she said, sounding even to herself like a character in some dumb soap opera.

He tried to smile, but she could tell he wasn't quite succeeding. "Okay. Come on in."

He ushered her into a living room with all this weird grandma furniture and these crazy framed drawings all over the wall. It wasn't what she'd pictured at all.

He'd apparently observed her reaction because he said, "Looks like a room straight out of Harry Potter, doesn't it?"

She ran a hand across a sofa upholstered in this scratchy fabric that felt like a buzz cut. "Did you pick it out?" That was as polite as she could think to be.

He chuckled then, a sound that filled her with relief. He wasn't going to be mad. "No way. I'm leasing the apartment from one of the professors at the university."

"It smells funny in here."

"Hard not to notice, isn't it?" He gestured to a chair, and she sat down, perching on the edge of the seat. "Could I get you a soda?"

She needed time to think. "Uh, yes. Thank you. That would be good."

"Root beer okay?"

"Sure."

While he was in the kitchen, she studied the creepy condo, noticing all kinds of blueprints and plans spread out on a big table. Should she talk about his family's accident first? About her mother? She rubbed her stomach, worry sitting there like a barbell.

He was smiling when he came back into the room. "Here," he said, handing her a can of root beer. For himself, he had a mug of coffee. He sat across from her in an ugly recliner. "Does your mother know you're here?"

Abby shook her head. "No."

"Shouldn't she?"

"She might not like why I came."

He cradled his mug between his fingers. "Why is that?"

She stared at the steam rising from his coffee. "Because she says it's not my fault, but it was." This wasn't coming out the way she'd intended. She'd meant to start with how sorry she was about his family, but now they were already into the hard part.

"Spilling the beans, you mean?"

"Yeah." Abby squirmed. "I mean, she was going to tell you. She would have. I know she would. But—" She felt an uncomfortable shift in her abdomen.

"She didn't. I hope you understand how that news hit me."

"Mom told me about the accident." She hurried the next part. "I'm so sorry about your wife and daughter. I guess you have a reason to hate alcoholics, but Mom isn't like that.'' She slurped some root beer, trying to moisten her dry, gritty mouth.

He looked up over the lip of his mug, raised his eyebrows and simply said, ''Really?''

Abby fidgeted, feeling all gooshy inside. ''No, she's not. She's worked so hard to stay sober. She's a wonderful mother and people like her and she's trying so hard never to drink again. And you make her happy. If you're not there, I don't know what'll happen and—'' Abby stopped, her face flushing. Something damp was between her legs. Had she spilled the root beer? Slowly she looked down. Nothing. ''I wanna fix things. Please don't hold AA against her. Please don't leave her. She really, really likes you. A lot.''

She ran out of breath and only then did she fully focus on the realization that she might have wet her pants. How embarrassing!

''Abby, I appreciate your defense of your mother and the courage it took to come see me, but—''

Abby jumped to her feet. '''Scuze me, Mr. Logan. Where's the bathroom?''

He stood. ''Are you all right?''

She crossed her legs in anguish. ''I don't know.''

''There. Down the hall on the right.''

''Sorry, I'll be right back,'' she said, scuttling to the bathroom.

She closed the door quickly, then unbuttoned her jeans and started to sit on the commode. What she saw on her panties majorly grossed her out—and humiliated her. Slowly she sank down. She wouldn't be coming right back. She couldn't. She would be spending the rest of her life right here in this bathroom.

Angry tears coursed down her cheeks. No way! Not here. Not now. What was she supposed to do?

All her mother's lovey-dovey reassurances about becoming a woman were nothing but a crock. She buried her head in her hands.

No way had her period started at Brady Logan's.

CHAPTER ELEVEN

BRADY WAITED, uncomfortably aware that several minutes had passed. He hoped to God nothing was wrong. The poor kid. It took guts to come here and assume the blame for what had gone wrong with his and Nell's relationship. Abby must really be worried about her mother. The urgency in her voice as she appealed to him made him feel like a cad. Yet Nell wasn't the one wronged. He was.

He swallowed the last of his coffee. It was already cool. He glanced at his watch. How long had Abby been in the bathroom anyway? She didn't wear much makeup, so odds were she wasn't spending all this time primping.

Maybe she was sick. He stood and paced around the room. He should probably check on her. Make sure she was all right. He walked down the hall and paused outside the bathroom door, listening. Nothing.

Then he heard a sound, like a muffled giggle—or sob. A sense of impending dread filled him. He rapped on the door. "Abby, are you okay?"

The silence was pregnant. Then in a small voice he heard her say, "No."

"Are you sick? What do you need?" He was in way over his head here. He remembered taking care of Nicole when she was tiny, but as she grew older, Brooke was always the one who dealt with illness.

"I'm not sick."

"Did I say something to upset you?"

"No. Could you, uh, could you call my mother? Ask her to come get me?"

"I could take you home, honey."

"No!" Her reaction was sharp and immediate.

It was then he knew. Girl stuff. He closed his eyes, remembering Brooke's recounting to him her mother-daughter talk with Nicole. Nicole had thought becoming a woman sounded "icky," but she could see it might be worth it if someday you could have a baby. He shut down the memory and spoke encouragingly through the door. "It's all right. I'll call your mother. I'll be right back."

He didn't want to do this. Didn't want to hear Nell's voice again. Didn't want the interaction that must follow. He needed their connection severed cleanly. But like everything else in Abby's life, this wasn't her fault either. He picked up the phone and dialed the familiar number.

Their conversation was mercifully businesslike. Holding his emotions in check, he explained the reason Abby had come on her own to see him. Before Nell had time to react, he went on to tell her he suspected Abby had started her period and that she needed her mother. Nell told him this was Abby's first time and promised to come right over.

He set down the phone, feeling totally at sea. What could he do for Abby? If she were Nicole, what would he have done? Said? Finally he went back

down the hall and hunkered outside the door.
"Abby?"

"Yeah?"

"Your mother's on her way. You're sure you're
all right till she gets here?"

Abby's voice sounded forlorn. "Yes."

He'd never been female, of course, but it was
likely the kid was scared to death. Probably no
amount of sex education could prepare an adolescent
girl for this moment.

"Good. I'm going to stay right here with you until
she comes." When she didn't answer, he started talking, saying anything he could think of to soothe her.
"I believe I know what's happened to you today, and
it's the most natural thing in the world, although I
can imagine it's a bit scary, too. If you were Nicole,
that was my daughter's name," he explained, "I'd
be so proud and yet I'd feel kind of sorry for myself
at the same time because it would mean my girl had
begun to grow up. That's an awesome realization for
a father. We dads think we're the only ones who can
protect and care for our daughters. And next thing
you know, some guy's come along and married our
little girl."

"Could you, I mean would you, tell me about her?
Nicole?"

He rocked back and sat on the floor, his head in
his hands. He had to clear his throat twice before he
could begin. "You remind me of her. She had long
blond hair like yours, but her eyes were brown, like
pancake syrup. She enjoyed swimming and boating.
Best of all, she loved horseback riding." A momentary image stabbed him. Nicole clearing her first

jump in a horse show, the grin that creased her face even as she concentrated on the next barrier.

"Did she have her own horse?"

"Sure did. Belle was a honey of a chestnut mare."

"I've never been horseback riding."

He started to say they'd have to do something about that, then checked himself. He was merely getting Abby through these next few moments. After that, he'd never see her again. "It's a lot of fun. Nicole was just beginning to like boys, too. Do you have a boyfriend?" He knew she did, but figured he needed to get her mind off her problem.

"Kinda."

"What's his name?"

"Alan. He plays football." She hesitated. "I'm going with him to the school dance tomorrow night."

"Well, he must be a bright young man to choose you."

She stammered, "I…I, uh, thanks, Mr. Logan."

"Brady," he corrected. "Are you feeling better?"

"A little. I'm so embarrassed."

"Please don't be. I feel kind of privileged to be here with you. I was robbed of that opportunity with my own daughter. It feels right to be celebrating this milestone with you."

"Really?" Her voice seemed stronger.

"You bet. I like you, Abby. If Nicole had lived and you two had met, I think you would have been friends." He hesitated, debating his next words. "You know, I used to resent you."

"You did?"

"You reminded me so much of Nicole I couldn't stand the pain. But I was wrong. Instead of bad times, you remind me of good times with her and of new things she and I might have shared.''

"I'm glad," she said softly just as he heard a knock on the door.

"I think your mother's here."

"Good."

He had just risen to his feet when he thought he heard her speak again. "Did you say something, Abby?"

"Yes. I've been so scared, but you talking to me really helped. Thanks for understanding."

Hell. His eyes grew filmy. He took a handkerchief out of his pocket and blew his nose. The girl had touched a chord no one had reached since Nicole. Nell should be very proud of her daughter. She was quite a young lady.

He grinned crookedly. Given today's events, that described her exactly.

ARRIVING AT THE CONDO, Nell had greeted Brady with cursory thanks, attended to Abby, then whisked her out to her car. Brady had offered to follow in his SUV with Abby's bicycle.

But he wasn't in any hurry now as he approached Nell's street. He didn't want to be sucked into this family event. Didn't want to endure the torture of looking at Nell with his newly opened eyes. An alcoholic. Worse yet, one who had nearly killed her daughter. Well, he hoped she knew how damn lucky she was.

Something about Abby had touched deeply buried paternal feelings. She'd had her share of loss along the way, too. Considering her parents' divorce, her father's remarriage and Nell's drinking, the kid was actually pretty well adjusted. Helpless to make things right for her today, he'd felt sorry for her and disappointed in himself. She'd been so sincere in her defense of her mother. So vulnerable in her distress and embarrassment. Before she left with Nell, he'd had to fight the impulse to gather the girl in a fatherly embrace. How funny. Now that he could accept Abby, a relationship with Nell had become unthinkable.

He pulled into Nell's driveway. He'd given them a half-hour head start, figuring they needed a little mother-daughter time. He turned off the ignition, went to the back of the vehicle and extricated the bicycle, carrying it into the garage, which Nell had left open, probably for that purpose.

He could leave now. Let it be over. But maybe he owed Nell a further explanation of Abby's visit. He didn't want the girl getting into trouble. Not on his account.

Reluctantly, he strolled to the front door and knocked.

"Come in," Nell said when she answered the door. "I guess we need to talk about this." She started toward the family room.

He trailed behind her, wishing he were anywhere else but here. "How is she?"

She shrugged, then gestured for him to sit on the sofa. "Embarrassed, excited, scared."

He took the indicated seat and watched as she deliberately moved to the other side of the room. Silhouetted against the last light of the setting sun, Nell, perched on the edge of the rocker, sat in shadow.

Her cheekbones stood in sharp relief, accentuating dark smudges under her eyes. She wore a pink boat-necked sweater that revealed her collarbone, rigid beneath her soft, pale skin. Brady was having a hard time remembering what she was to him. "Abby's not in trouble?" he finally asked.

"She was too upset about starting her period at your place, although she said you were very understanding. I decided there would be time later to talk about why she came to see you."

"She feels responsible, Nell."

"What do you mean?"

"She thinks if she hadn't assumed I knew your history, that everything would be all right between us. She was trying to fix our relationship."

Nell rubbed the arms of the rocker with her palms, then sighed, a forlorn sound that stabbed Brady in the gut. "No chance of that, I guess."

He forced himself to think about Brooke and Nicole and the agent of their deaths. "No. How could I ever trust you?"

She looked stricken. "You couldn't unless you could forgive not only me, but others who have wronged you."

He stood. "Well, you can forget that."

She raised her eyes. "How far back does your bitterness go, Brady? Isn't it hard to keep slamming doors on people just because they're human and they've failed you?"

A blood vessel in his temple throbbed. "What's that supposed to mean?"

"There's got to be a reason you won't talk about your upbringing. Your family."

"Look, how many times do I have to tell you? That is none of your business."

"Maybe not. But since it no longer matters what I say, I'd like to suggest you can't control the world, especially one in which other people occasionally make a mistake."

"Mistake? Is that what you call nearly killing your daughter?"

Nell, face aflame, rose to her feet. "Don't you think I relive that horror every day of my life? That I haven't spent years acknowledging that fact and attempting to make amends? At least I don't try going it alone in this world."

"What's that supposed to mean?"

"Brady, believe it or not, you're not in charge. I'm not in charge. There *is* a higher power in our lives. When we accept that reality, troubles don't disappear, but life can become more bearable."

If she wasn't a woman, he'd have decked her. He could remember few times he had been so angry. "How dare you spout that AA crap to me?"

"At this point, I have nothing to lose with you. And what I see is this. You, my friend, are every bit as addicted as I am."

"The hell you say. I'm not the one who solves my problems by swilling down booze like it's water."

She clutched herself around the waist, as if restraining herself within some emotional boundary. "No. You solve problems by running away. First from your home and family in Colorado. Then from California. Now, from me." She moved a step closer, her eyes glittering with tears. "Oh, yes. You're addicted. To anger and resentment and guilt."

She stopped to catch her breath, then went on. "You can make fun of AA if you want to, but living those Twelve Steps has saved me and, pray God, will continue to save me. You know, you just might try them yourself."

"Slim chance of that."

"What's the worst thing that could happen? Would it be so terrible to admit to God and someone else the nature of your wrongs? To ask God to help? To make amends to those you've hurt?" She paused, her tone softening. "To find peace through a spiritual awakening? That's what the Twelve Steps are about, and, trust me, they'll work for you, too."

Brady had stood there throughout her lecture, jaws aching from gritting his teeth in anger and denial. Now he loomed over her. "Are you quite finished?"

"Yes, I believe I am. Except for one thing."

He made a mocking out-with-it gesture. "Well, please give me the benefit of the entire spiel."

She laid one small hand on his chest and looked up at him with brimming eyes. Her whisper was barely audible. "I love you, Brady."

He stared at her, his facial muscles paralyzed. What a cheap shot. "Sorry, Nell, you can lay that on me if you want, but no way am I going to assume that guilt on top of all the others you accuse me of." He moved toward the door. "Tell Abby she's a beautiful young woman." He grasped the doorknob, then let go of it to face her one final time. His tone was steely. "Goodbye, Nell."

At his car, he braced himself against the cool metal of the driver's door and sucked in deep breaths of air. He couldn't believe it. By accusing him was she trying to justify her own actions? And what was that last bit about? *I love you, Brady.*

He seethed. *Too damn bad, lady.*

He climbed in the SUV and started toward home, furious with her and with his stupid eyes that insisted on watering. Lady. He laughed derisively. Oh, yeah. Lady. His rainbow lady, who believed in miracles.

Well, Nell could continue to dwell in fantasy land if she chose, but he was totally out of miracles. Love was nothing more than an illusion. No steps, not twelve or twelve hundred, could fix that.

THE DEFINITIVE CLICK of the door shutting behind Brady reminded Nell of the sound of a cork being pulled from a wine bottle. Leaning her back against the door, she rubbed her face with the palms of her hands. *Please God. Don't let me think like that.* It was bad enough he'd walked out of her life, but why was wine—that deep, rich, mellow palliative—her first thought as an antidote for the hollow ache gnawing at her?

Quaking with an onslaught of emotions, she walked back into the family room and sank onto the sofa, holding a pillow against her chest for comfort. He hadn't blinked an eye when she'd told him she loved him. Why had she thought that would make a difference? Yet it was the truth. And for too long she'd withheld truths from him.

The room, nearly dark now, matched her mood. He would never be able to accept her. Even if she remained sober the rest of her days. He was a hard man.

A hurting man.

Sinking her teeth into her fingers simply to experience a pain she could control, she tried to hold back the flood gathering in her throat. She'd said awful things. Hurtful things.

A sob erupted. Then another. Finally she gave in and let the storm come. Her body shook with the force of her loss.

All she wanted was to love him. He needed love so badly.

But she was an alcoholic.

Like a tide, all the old feelings of worthlessness and despair swept over her. She would never be good enough. Sober enough.

Through her tears, she licked her lips, picturing the outlines of a fine bottle of wine, the contents beckoning her with cobralike charm. She pulled up her legs, gripping her knees, then rocked back and forth. *Don't do it. Don't do it.*

Suddenly she heard Abby's bedroom door open. Nell scrambled in her pocket for a tissue and quickly wiped her eyes.

"Mom? Aren't you late for your meeting?" Abby flipped on the lights.

Nell blinked at the onslaught of brightness. The meeting. The nighttime women's AA group she attended every week. The one she'd also missed last week. She was getting careless. Dizzy with fear, she set the pillow aside and looked up at her daughter. "Yes. I...I thought you might need me tonight."

"Mo-om. I'm okay. It's not that big a deal. Like you said, I'll get used to having periods. Anyway, you know how worried I've been. Like maybe I was a freak or something."

"Oh, honey, you're not a freak."

"It was kinda weird, though, being at Brady's." Amazingly, her face lit up. "He told me to call him that. He's really pretty cool, you know."

Nell didn't trust herself to speak.

"Did you guys get everything fixed up?"

Nell felt as if all the air in her lungs had disappeared in a single whoosh. She patted the seat beside her. "Sit down."

Abby wrinkled her nose questioningly, but sat beside her mother. "I'm not gonna like this, am I?"

"Probably not. For what it's worth, honey, neither do I." She tried to clear the frog in her throat. "I don't think we'll be seeing Brady anymore."

"But I thought if I told him how much you like him and everything…"

"I appreciate what you tried to do. But it was too late. He can't accept the fact that I'm an alcoholic."

Abby glowed with indignation. "But you're not really."

Nell put her arm around her daughter and drew her close. "Oh, but I am, Abby. And you must never forget it. I have a disease, just like people who are victims of high blood pressure or tuberculosis. My body cannot tolerate alcohol. Not even one drink. How Brady chooses to react to that fact is his business."

Nell saw the pain in Abby's eyes. "But, Mom, you love him, don't you?"

Nell kissed the top of her daughter's head. Then after a few moments of silence, she said, "Yes, Abby, I do."

"So what're you gonna do?"

With a finality that turned her to stone, Nell said, "There's nothing I can do."

Straightening so she could look squarely at her mother, Abby said, "You won't start drinking again, will you?"

Nell took a deep breath. "I won't have a drink tonight."

"But that's not good enough. What about the rest of the time?"

"Tonight is as much as I can promise, Abby. You know how it goes. One day at a time."

If Abby only knew how hard it was going to be these next few minutes, hours. This one night. Brady's rejection had left a hole in her heart no amount of liquor could fill.

But the wine remained a temptation. One she had to overcome. Somehow.

ABBY CLUTCHED Tonya's arm the next morning as they stood outside the school waiting for the warning bell. "I thought I was gonna die!"

"I would have," Tonya said. "They'd have had to carry me outta there feet first."

"It's funny, though. You know, in a way, it was easier starting my period there than being at my dad's and having Clarice flutter around like I'd broken one of her precious pinkie nails."

"But what did you say to Mr. Logan?"

"I didn't have to say anything. He guessed. Then he was cool and talked about his dead daughter almost like I was a grown-up."

"But what about why you went there? Did you

have a chance to tell him about how your mom likes him?''

Pulling Tonya along with her, Abby moved into the shadow of the building, avoiding a group of preppy girls who loitered nearby, almost as if they were eavesdropping. "I thought everything was gonna be cool when he came over to our house afterward." She swallowed hard. "But it wasn't. Mom told me later he wouldn't be coming to see us anymore."

"Why not?"

Abby warmed slightly with her friend's empathetic indignation. "Um, he can't deal with Mom."

"Whaddya mean?"

"Her being—" Abby squirmed, hating the word "—an alcoholic."

"But she doesn't drink now."

"I guess he thinks she could, though."

"Well, could she?"

Abby clutched her book bag like an anchor. "I don't know. She was pretty upset after he left. It scared me."

"What are you gonna do?"

Feeling helpless and very alone, Abby shrugged. "I don't know."

The warning bell interrupted their conversation and they joined other students entering the building. Tonya took off down the hall toward the art room. Abby headed for social studies, wondering what, if anything, she *could* do.

Halfway through the first-period discussion of forms of government, an answer came. She dug in her purse to see if she had the right change. She could make the call at noon.

Grandma and Aunt Lily needed to know about her mother. Surely they could cheer Mom up, keep her from drinking.

Only, if she phoned them, then Aunt Lily would prob'ly talk to her, like she always did, about going to Alateen meetings.

What was the matter with adults anyway? It was hard enough being a kid and worrying about boyfriends and zits and stupid homework without having Brady and her mother screw up not only their own lives but hers as well!

NELL HAD NOT BEEN happy when her mother called at work and asked her to stop by the house on her way home. She'd hardly slept at all last night and they'd had a frantic day at the library. She looked like a walking ad for an insomniac's convention. The last thing she needed was to fall under maternal scrutiny. But there had been no putting Stella off, and truth to tell, she hadn't seen her mother lately. She couldn't even use Abby as an excuse. Before she'd left for school this morning, Abby had told her there was an after-school chorus rehearsal and that Mrs. Larkin would pick them up afterward. Nell needed to be home in time to help Abby get ready for her big date with Alan, but that wasn't for a couple of hours.

Nor did she have any excuse for missing her morning AA meeting. Yet facing all those knowing people and having them see right through her was more than she could handle on top of Brady's final words.

The carefully landscaped Victorian home sat on a deep lot near downtown. As Nell walked up the steps and onto the wrap-around porch, she remembered her dad and his teasing comments. "Your mother talked me into this drafty old barn. Lord, we could've bought three houses for what it's cost to fix up this place." And yet he'd loved the project. Nell smiled wistfully, remembering happy hours she'd spent helping him in the garage workshop, where sawdust and radio coverage of the Razorbacks kept the two of them company as they worked.

Nell gave a quick rap on the front door, then walked on in. The music system was playing a soft classical piano selection, and from the library, she heard voices. Two of them.

Lily was here, too.

All Nell wanted was to get this ordeal behind her as quickly as possible. "Anybody home?"

"In here, Nell," Stella called.

Entering the richly paneled room, Nell noticed that both her mother and sister had goblets of…surely soda or tea, not wine. She couldn't face the temptation of wine. Lily rose to her feet and spread her arms in the invitation to a hug. Nell stepped into her arms, relieved by the faint lemony scent on her sister's breath.

Stepping out of Lily's embrace, Nell dropped a kiss on her mother's head. Stella smiled, then asked, "Coffee, tea or a soda, Nell?"

She didn't want anything. At least none of what had been offered, but she needed something to hold on to. "Is the coffee made?" When her mother nodded, Nell said, "I'll get it."

In the quiet of the kitchen she leaned for a moment against the counter, summoning the strength to get her through the next few minutes. After pouring a cup of coffee, she pasted a smile on her face, returned to the library and sat in the wingback chair facing the leather couch where the other two sat.

"The yard looks nice, Mother."

Stella set down her drink. "Nathan does a good job with it. Not as good as your father did, of course, but widows can't be choosy."

"We should all be so lucky as to have a Nathan," Lily said, with a chuckle.

"How's my granddaughter these days? I haven't seen much of her lately."

"Very relieved."

Lily sat forward. "Why's that?"

"I'm sure she won't mind my telling you. Her period started yesterday. She'd been so afraid she was never going to catch up with Tonya." Nell tried a little laugh. "In hindsight, it's nothing I would have been in a hurry about."

"Bless her heart. I'll have to get her a grandmotherly present to mark the occasion."

"It's certainly a rite of passage," Lily said, picking up her iced tea and taking a sip.

"It seems like only yesterday she was a baby and tonight she has a date to the eighth-grade dance." Nell shook her head. "My how time flies," she said wincing at the truth of the old chestnut.

"Speaking of that," Lily said, "we haven't seen much of you lately. Too busy with Brady Logan?"

"That won't be a problem any longer." She took

a swallow of her coffee, black and bitter. "As the kids would say, 'He's history.'"

Stella cradled her goblet, caressing the stem with her slender, manicured fingers. "Oh, honey, what do you mean?"

"Just that. We…didn't work out."

"But you cared for him, right?" Lily's gaze was sympathetic. Both her mother and sister waited for her to say something. "Yes." Nell wanted to scream.

"You must be upset," her mother said.

"I've had better days."

"Abby said you couldn't promise you wouldn't drink."

Nell whirled on Lily. "'Abby said'? What do you mean?"

Lily blushed and ducked her head guiltily. "Abby called Mother. She's worried about you, Nell."

Great. As if she didn't know that. The last thing she needed was a triumvirate of female relatives observing her every move.

"Did you tell her you might drink?" Stella asked.

Very deliberately, Nell set down her cup. "No. I told her I wouldn't drink last night."

Stella's eyebrows peaked. "Well, that wasn't very encouraging for her."

"But it was honest. That's all I can ever promise. One day at a time."

"Maybe Abby thinks this upset over Brady Logan might make you…vulnerable." Lily glanced at her mother as if to secure concurrence. "We think you need to be especially watchful. Of course, we're both here for you whenever you need support."

Abby flushed with anger. "Do you have any idea

what it feels like to have you looking over my shoulder all the time, waiting for the next blunder, the next fall from grace?''

Lily's head snapped back. "Easy, Nell. We're only trying to help."

"I've appreciated everything you've done for me, but I need some space. And how about showing a little confidence in me?"

"You don't need to get huffy." Stella placed her goblet carefully on the coffee table. "You'll have to excuse us, but we remember those months when we were terrified for you and for Abby. When we'd call you at ten in the morning and find you still in bed, hardly coherent. When we were all on tenterhooks at family gatherings wondering if you'd make a fool of yourself. When I could hardly bear to think of what would happen if you were driving after you'd been drinking. I guess we got the answer to that one, didn't we?"

Nell stood abruptly and walked away from their accusing eyes, their long memories. The silence in the room was painful.

Lily broke the tension. "Nell, Abby was little then. She's not now. Don't put her through something like that."

Nell clenched her fingers, trying to drown out the words and the images the words evoked. Her voice came out cold, metallic. "Don't six years count for anything?"

Lily's voice was practical. "You said it yourself. Six years or six days. It's this one day that counts. We just don't want to see you mess up because you're upset about Brady."

Nell faced them then. "I love Brady, okay? It was devastating when he left last night. I'll admit it, I was tempted to drink. But, guess what? I resisted. I plan to resist tonight. And, God willing, tomorrow night. But this is *my* life, *my* decision. Not yours. And there comes a time when your solicitude is not helpful. I need to be treated like a fully functioning adult, not some morally handicapped person whose own mother, sister and daughter can't trust her."

Lily stood. "Nell, we didn't mean it like that."

Picking up her purse, Nell headed for the door. "I'm sure you didn't. I love you both, but you have to let me go. Let me be my own person. Not you, not Abby, not anybody can keep me from the next drink if I really want it. So, please, if you wish to be helpful, quit assuming weakness and start trusting me."

Just as she turned to leave the room, her mother's voice rose in concern. "But you will be careful, won't you, darling?"

Incredulous, Nell stared back at her mother for a moment, then left. She couldn't wait to get outside. She was breathing heavily when she reached the haven of her car. How dare they? Her hands shook when she tried, unsuccessfully the first time, to insert the key in the ignition. Why would they automatically assume she would take a drink just because Brady had walked out on her?

Trembling all over, she started the car and backed slowly out of the driveway. Heartache was just something you lived through. There would be no Brady in her tomorrows.

And she had to remind herself over and over that

there would also be no liquor in her tomorrows. No warm soothing of the loneliness yawning inside her. No blissful, blurred vision of reality.

And yet...

CHAPTER TWELVE

NELL STOOD behind Abby watching her in the bathroom mirror as she painstakingly applied the merest hint of blush. "Is this about right?"

"Looks perfect. Too much would make your skin look harsh and you have such a pretty complexion."

Abby shot her a skeptical look. "Mom, get a grip. I feel weird when you say things like that."

Nell fell silent. Her daughter wanted reassurance, just not too much. Figuring out the correct dosage was a maternal challenge beyond her powers at the moment. She sighed softly. That delicate line between approval and interference. The one her own mother had crossed earlier in the day. Were mothers and daughters forever doomed to get on each other's nerves? "What are you wearing tonight?" Surely that was a neutral change of topic.

"I haven't decided. Maybe my khaki skirt and that new green top I got at Old Navy or that purple flowered T-shirt and my black skirt. What do you think?" She wrinkled her brow and leaned closer, picking at a pimple on her cheek.

Nell wasn't about to involve herself in that issue. "No matter what you decide, you'll look great."

Abby turned around and leaned against the basin. "I'm so nervous."

"That's natural. I remember the first date I had. Lester Royer took me to the skating rink and all evening I was convinced he was noticing how sweaty my palms were."

"Gross. Lester?"

"Believe me, Alan Voyle is a stud, compared to poor Les. You'll have a great time."

Abby flung her arms around Nell's neck. "Thanks, Mom. I love you."

"And I love you."

After the brief hug, Abby drew back, then turned to catch one last glimpse of herself in the mirror before starting down the hall. "I'll be in my room. I've gotta call Tonya and see what she's wearing."

Watching until Abby reached her bedroom, Nell shook her head, baffled at where the years had gone and praying that Alan Voyle was as nice as he appeared to be. There was no Rick or Brady to string him up by the heels if he wasn't.

Did Abby miss having a father? In recent years, they'd never really talked about it, but she had to feel a void. Nell's father had been the hero of her life. She couldn't imagine growing up without him.

Suddenly the events of the past twenty-four hours caught up with her. Her own tardy confession about her alcoholism, Abby's coming of age and Brady's subsequent kindness to her daughter and then his angry departure. And that didn't even take into account today's sneak attack by Lily and her mother.

Then there was the other problem—the one she refused to think about. Rick. Abby's next visit to Dallas was coming up soon. What if Rick said something to Abby about living with him?

She wound her arms around her waist and hurried to the kitchen. She needed to keep busy. She pulled out a cookbook and began assembling the ingredients for devil's food cookies. Chocolate. The universal pacifier. *I'm a big girl,* she kept telling herself. *I can get through all of this.* Mother and Lily hadn't done anything they didn't normally do. Hover. Rick and Clarice wouldn't really want Abby, would they? She would certainly put a damper on their high-flying lifestyle.

Instead of getting out the mixer, Nell used a spoon to cream the butter and sugar, transferring her frustration to the batter. She could rationalize those problems all she wanted, but what about Brady? How would she ever get over him?

Damn it, I will not cry. I have no more tears. She'd been pretty rough on him last night. Had she been motivated by defensiveness or by a genuine desire to help him? What did it matter? In either case, he'd stormed out of her life. He'd had a right to be angry. But what about all those good times? The two nights they'd spent in each other's arms? For the first time in her life she had felt—in the fullest sense of the word—womanly, adored.

Dropping the spoon into the bowl with a clatter, she bent over the counter. Or had he merely been using her? She was convenient and willing. Boy, had she been willing!

No, it wasn't like that. For better or worse, she loved him.

And loving him, she couldn't help picking up on the hurt he still carried around with him. He might have come to some kind of peace about Brooke and

Nicole, but it was clear he still had demons to wrestle, and that was something he had to do alone.

So now she had no choice, none at all, except to let him go and somehow, some way go on with her life. She stared at the eggs and flour and vanilla as if she'd never seen them before. She didn't want chocolate. What good could it do? She wanted Brady. Without stopping to think, she scooped up the ball of creamed butter and sugar and threw it in the garbage, then put away the other ingredients, slamming cupboard doors as she went.

A huge sob racked her. God, she couldn't go on. Not without him. Before, she hadn't known what she was missing. Now she did.

But he had made his decision. He had walked out of her life. The sooner she reconciled herself to that fact, the better.

But even as she stood wiping her eyes with the corner of a dish towel, there remained a glimmer of hope. Maybe he would come back. When he wasn't so angry. When he'd had time to think.

When he could trust her. Forgive her.

Hope died at the same moment the doorbell rang. Nell glanced at the kitchen clock. It was too early for Alan to be arriving. She folded the towel, placed it on the counter and headed to the door. "I'll get it."

"Who is it?" Abby called, her voice panicky.

When Nell opened the door, a delivery man handed her a bouquet of rosebuds, carnations and baby's breath. "For Abby Porter," he said.

Nell thanked him and started down the hall to deliver the unexpected gift.

"Is it him?" Abby hissed from behind her door.

"No, honey. It's flowers. For you."

Nell entered the room and placed the vase on the dresser.

Abby's eyes rounded with delight. "Who are they from? Nobody's ever sent me flowers before."

"Here." Nell unpinned the small envelope attached to the pale pink bow and handed it to her daughter.

Abby pulled out the card and read it silently. When she raised her head, tears stood in her eyes.

"What?" Nell asked, concerned.

"Oh, Mom, he remembered."

"Who remembered?"

"Brady." She offered the card to her mother.

Nell hesitated. She didn't want to take it. Didn't want to read it.

"Mom?" Abby prompted.

Nell took the card and lowered her eyes to the strong masculine pen strokes. "Abby, you are a beautiful young woman. I hope tonight's dance is special for you. I'm leaving Arkansas early in the morning. Even though I won't be seeing you again, please know that you will always have a special place in my heart."

The letters of Brady's signature swam. Even though Nell had anticipated he would leave, seeing it written by his own hand had a finality that shattered her.

"Hope is a thing with feathers." From nowhere came the lines of Emily Dickinson's poem.

And things with feathers flew away.

Somehow she managed to hold herself together until Alan arrived to pick up Abby.

Then the darkness came.

And the thirst.

THE OVERCAST SKIES matched Brady's mood as he slung his bags into the back of the Escalade late Friday afternoon. He glanced back at the bland exterior of the condominium where he'd spent the past few weeks. He'd had such high hopes when he'd made the decision to sublet the unit. He shook his head. Had he been so desperate for stability in his life—for companionship and acceptance—that he'd sacrificed his reason?

In business that would have been disastrous. He mocked himself with a derisive chuckle. Just goes to show what happens when you abandon the practices and principles that resulted in success.

He headed down I-540 on his way to I-40, which would lead him west to sunny California and work—the only security in his life right now. He'd bury himself in the damn projects lined up and waiting for him.

Carl had been ecstatic, of course, when Brady had called to announce what felt like craven surrender. He hadn't had time today to do more with Buzz Valentine than tell him he'd make some decisions about the optioned property in the next few weeks. So what if he lost his earnest money? It was, after all, only money—the one thing he had plenty of.

Rain accompanied him all the way from Ft. Smith to Oklahoma City, where he planned to spend the night, but he didn't care. The swish-swish of the windshield wipers had a comforting, metronomic quality that helped soothe his churning stomach.

For the thousandth time since Tuesday night, he repeated the words. *Nell is an alcoholic.* In his mind, he'd tried to argue that she was not an alcoholic, but a *recovering* alcoholic. Tried to believe that insight made a difference. Hell, from her actions, he never would have known. She might go on for years without taking a drink, if ever. But how could he be sure?

Even if he could accept her, he couldn't accept that desperate accusation she'd flung at him, as if turning the tables on him excused her. *You're addicted.* Right. He wasn't the one drowning his sorrows in a bottle, was he? But that wasn't what she'd said. Even though he remembered her words exactly, he didn't want to consider her indictment. Addicted to anger, resentment and guilt?

Hell, yes, who wouldn't be? His old man hadn't even waited until his mother was cold in the grave before bringing Velda home and having the nerve to suggest Danny should call her "Mother." Her chipper smile and the way she clung to his dad, looking up at him as if she'd taken home the blue-ribbon hog from the county fair, were an insult to his mother's memory. Had he been the only one who'd mourned her?

He'd never forget the day he'd come home from school the week after the funeral and found all traces of his mother removed—her hairbrush no longer on the dresser, the framed photograph of her parents that had always sat on the mantel gone, her prized cut-glass serving bowl missing from the china cabinet, her closet empty of everything except the lingering scent of talcum and lavender. Even now, his jaw clenched in anger. What kind of man removes all traces of the woman he's supposedly loved, who has borne his children?

Danny had been too young, of course. What did a seven-year-old know? Especially when for most of his life their mother had been sick. He'd fallen right in with the plan, snuggling up to Velda from the beginning. It had sickened Brady, who had managed to get through most of his senior year before his father kicked him out, days short of graduation. Thank God for Coach Elbert, who'd somehow sweet-talked the superintendent into awarding him his diploma anyway. They'd mailed it to him in care of General Delivery in the town where he'd gotten work as a roofer.

He turned on the radio full blast, in the futile attempt to block out his memories and the gut-wrenching realization that Nell had nailed it, whether she knew it or not.

He hated his father.

NELL SAT on the rug cradling the wine bottle she'd pulled from the paper sack. Her frantic trip to the liquor store was a blur. All she knew was that after Abby left, the walls of the house had crushed her with their mocking silence. She'd ended up— again—abandoned and alone. The bright lights inside the store had hurt her eyes, but she was drawn instinctively to the racked bottles, lined up row after row, their ambers, crimsons and roses seductive in their appeal.

Now, running her hands up and down the smooth,

cool glass, caressing the curve leading to the slender neck and the rubbery seal over the cork, she focused on her palate, tingling in anticipation. Imagining that first euphoric swallow, the feel and taste of it coursing down her throat, warming her chest from the inside.

She closed her eyes and leaned against the sofa. It would be so simple. The corkscrew lay within easy reach on the coffee table. Her favorite rounded goblet, which nested perfectly in her palm, stood beside the corkscrew—waiting. Could she stop with one glass? Would she?

Nothing and no one else offered her the immediate comfort of the merlot resting heavy and promising in her hands.

Opening her eyes, she grabbed the corkscrew, studying it as if it represented the tempter—and the deliverer. *Remember.* The word jolted her, causing her to drop the corkscrew. *Remember your last drunk.* The words of every AA sponsor stopped her. *Before you take that first drink, relive your last drunk.*

She set the wine bottle beside her on the floor and buried her head in her hands. Did she have to? It would be ever so much easier to open the bottle and have a drink. People did it all the time.

Your last drunk! The idea grew insistently, clawing at her, refusing to let her go. Rick. The fight. The images beckoned, demanding to be revisited.

She jumped to her feet and paced to the window, remembering their spacious but homey living room, decorated with antiques she and Rick had restored, the fire crackling in the fireplace, the lambent glow of the new brass table lamp she'd purchased only that day. She'd meant only to have one little drink before Rick got home, but one had turned into three. She'd carefully rinsed her glass and put it in the dishwasher before he came in, hiding the evidence.

That evening had started out no different from every other evening in the months before, when she'd begun to dread his arrival. The cool, polite distance he kept as if she were tainted. Long gone were the welcoming kisses, the tell-me-about-your day ritual. Instead, he moved straight to the bar and fixed himself a bourbon and water. She never protested when he fixed her one, too.

Protest? She lapped it up, hoping it would inoculate her from his obvious aversion to her. That night he'd perched on the hearth, holding his drink between his knees. He looked fuzzy to her, the fire backlighting his body turning him into a fiend. She had blinked, but the image remained hazy, sinister.

His words, like a razor slice, had cut through her alcoholic haze. *I've filed for divorce. Here are the papers.* She'd sloshed her drink as she carried it to her lips and drank thirstily. He wasn't finished. *I'm moving out tonight. To Clarice's.* He set the legal-size envelope on the bar.

She could never remember if she'd flung the glass before or after he mentioned Clarice. All she knew was that suddenly she was standing in their decorator-beautiful living room, surrounded by shards of broken glass, staring at a stain created by bourbon and melting ice darkening the thick cream-colored carpet. Screaming an obscenity, she had launched herself at Rick, now standing, his face gray with dis-

gust. She had called him names she didn't even know
were in her repertoire, all the time pounding her fists
against his unyielding chest. Finally he had grabbed
her arms in a viselike grip. *You're a drunk, Nell.
What did you expect?*

Bile and phlegm had risen to her mouth, and tears,
maudlin and self-pitying, had dripped down her
cheeks, off her nose and chin. He couldn't do this to
her!

Nell laid a hand on a cool pane of glass, grounding
herself in reality. That was then. This was now. She
could stop this horror film in midreel. *You want to
stay sober? Force yourself. Remember the worst.*

Somehow, she'd staggered through the shattered
glass to the bar, where she drank directly from the
bottle of Jack Daniel's Rick had left out. She
couldn't get enough to douse the flames licking at
her psyche. She'd whirled around then. *What are we
supposed to do? Abby and I?*

*My attorney will be in touch. Meanwhile, call your
mother to come get Abby. In this condition, you're
not a fit mother.*

He'd been right, of course, Nell thought bitterly.
How could she have lost sight of Abby? No matter
how diminished Rick had made her feel, how could
she have been so irresponsible a mother?

Her reaction that night had been violent. She'd
screamed one word at him. *Bastard!*

That's when Abby had appeared, her eyes wide
with fright. *Mommy?* she'd cried, her bottom lip
trembling. Nell had scooped her up and faced Rick,
barely able to control the venom threatening to spew
out of her. *Get out,* she'd spat. He'd given her one

last look of undisguised repugnance and said, *Call your mother. Now.* And he'd left.

Nell paced to the center of the family room, staring at the wine bottle, the corkscrew, the glass. All urging her to a decision.

But memory insisted. Confront the worst. She'd stood, rooted, six-year-old Abby clutching her around the neck, asking over and over, *Mommy, who spilled the drink? Where's Daddy going?*

She remembered carrying her child to the bar, setting her on her feet and downing the remainder of the bourbon in great gulping swigs straight from the bottle. Finally Abby had nudged her. *Why did you yell at Daddy. Where is he? Why did he go?*

Nell picked up the merlot and studied it. Tempting, with its tasteful label and graceful, understated script. She nestled it to her chest, wondering why on earth she had ever answered Abby as she had. *He's left us, Abby.*

The howls had erupted then. Seeming to grow louder, more intense, as Nell drunkenly tried to explain. How could Abby ever have forgiven her?

I want my daddy. I want my daddy. I want my daddy.

Nell hadn't been able to stand Abby's screams. She'd grabbed her purse, buttoned Abby's coat around her, thrown on her own and dragged Abby to the car, her stomach revolting with every gasp of breath. After she'd buckled Abby in, she remembered fumbling on her hands and knees, searching for the ignition key she'd dropped in the snow, all the time craving another drink to calm her nerves.

Well, her prayers had been answered thanks to the

county liquor laws. On her way to confront Rick she'd pulled into a drive-thru liquor store and purchased a pint of vodka. At the next stoplight, hands shaking, she'd stripped off the seal and swallowed a third of the bottle.

Abby had become strangely quiet. Snow drifted dreamily from the sky, landing on the windshield. Headlights blurred together like a soothing watercolor wash. The combination of the car heater and the vodka warmed Nell, relaxing her as she started down one of Fayetteville's steep hills toward Clarice's. Rick needed to see what he'd done to them. To her, but especially to his daughter.

At first it had seemed like a graceful glide toward a fleecy white backdrop, but then, in a moment of sudden clarity, Nell saw the brick wall rising to meet them, her car in a sickening spin she was helpless to control. She gripped the wheel. The last thing she heard was her own voice screaming *Abby, Abby!*

That was all she could remember until she woke up in the hospital, her bandaged head full of anvils. The elongated human faces peering down at her came and went, then dissolved completely, leaving nothing but darkness and stabbing pain.

Nell turned on the lamp beside the armchair and sat down, still holding the bottle, menacingly familiar in its shape. As long as she lived, she would never forget the words of the police officer who'd visited her in the hospital. *You had a close call, Mrs. Porter. Another six inches and your daughter wouldn't have been so lucky.*

Nell's mouth soured. Who was that woman who

had so carelessly risked her child's life? Who had preferred a bottle to her own daughter?

Was she prepared to put Abby through that hell again? Worse yet, was she deliberately going to become that woman she loathed?

Still cradling the bottle of wine, slowly, deliberately, so she would never forget this moment, she stood, picked up the corkscrew and walked into the kitchen. She flipped on the light, peeled the sealant from the neck of the bottle and then, with deadly aim, impaled the center of the cork with the tip of the corkscrew. She levered the arms of the corkscrew, then heard the soft pop of the cork, smelled the faintest, tantalizing hint of grape before she lifted the bottle, upended it over the sink and watched as every last drop spiraled down the drain.

Afterward, she threw the bottle in the wastebasket, then leaned against the sink, drawing ragged breaths.

Finally she went to her purse, removed a small metallic object and clutched it in her hand, as if it possessed magical powers. Opening her fist, she placed the AA chip on the counter, rubbing her finger over the Roman numeral six etched there. Six years of sobriety. She was not willing to sacrifice that for anyone. Anything.

Picking up the chip, she bowed her head, humbled by the grace that had brought her to this moment. In the quiet kitchen, her prayer of thanksgiving, strong and healing, rose from her heart.

Never losing her grip on her six-year chip, she opened her eyes to overwhelming relief. She was back on track again.

In the morning she would call Ben, seek his counsel, but for tonight? She had triumphed over the enemy—for yet one more day.

That didn't mean she wouldn't miss Brady. Worry about Abby. Feel stifled by her mother and sister on occasion.

It simply meant she valued Nell again.

WHEN SHE HEARD Abby at the front door, Nell muted the TV. "I'm in here, honey."

"Okay."

She looked up when Abby entered the family room, her eyes sparkling. "Did you have a good time?"

Abby sank into the rocker, hitched her legs over one arm and then sighed dramatically. "Oh, Mom, I'm in love. He's *so* nice."

Nell permitted herself a concealed sigh of relief. "Tell me all about it."

And, unbelievably, Abby did, so caught up in what a good dancer Alan was, how dreamy his brown eyes were, how polite he'd been that she must've forgotten she was speaking to her mother. But then, Nell mused, Abby was like that. When she wanted to share her feelings, she could be completely up front. But when she didn't? You couldn't pry a single tidbit from her.

"Tonya was green with jealousy. Her date was a total jerk, all the time trying to make people laugh with these lame jokes and pigging out at the refreshment table."

"Tonya's day will come. We all have to kiss a few frogs in the process."

Abby twisted a strand of hair around her finger.

"I guess I was just lucky to get a prince the first time."

Nell smiled at her daughter's innocence. Yet stranger things had happened than meeting The One in eighth grade. "Alan knew a good thing when he saw you."

"Mo-om, you're prejudiced."

"Guilty."

Abby hopped up. "I'm gonna get a cola. Want one?"

"No thanks. The caffeine would keep me awake."

Nell watched the final couple of minutes of the movie while Abby was in the kitchen, then flipped off the TV.

"Mom?"

A coldness in her daughter's tone caused Nell to glance up. Ashen, Abby stood clutching the empty wine bottle. Nell cringed. Why hadn't she emptied the wastebasket before Abby got home?

"What's this?" Abby demanded. "Have you been drinking?"

Nell rose to her feet, crossed to her daughter, took the bottle from her and set it on the table. Praying for the right words, she laid her hands on her daughter's shoulders and found her troubled eyes. "No, honey, I haven't been drinking. I'll admit I was tempted, but instead, I poured all the wine down the drain."

Abby hung her head. "I should've been here."

"No. It doesn't work like that. If an alcoholic wants a drink, she'll make it happen. You don't have to keep watch over me, sweetie. I'm the one who must do that for myself. Tonight I did."

"It's Brady, isn't it?"

Nell lifted a hand and smoothed back her daughter's hair. "It's lots of things, but I'm determined never again to let alcohol become more important than the people I love. And, yes, Brady is one of those people. But how can I demonstrate that love unless I give him his freedom?" She hesitated, struck by another truth. "And honor my feelings for him by remaining sober."

Abby hugged her then, an embrace that warmed her far more than any amount of liquor could ever have done. "I'm so proud of you, Mom."

"I love you," Nell barely managed to say before her throat clogged with tears of gratitude.

The struggle would be ongoing, but what reward could be sweeter than Abby's forgiveness and love?

CHAPTER THIRTEEN

BRADY STOOD at the window of his corner office, eyes fixed on the vermillions, bronzes and sun-bright yellows of the chrysanthemums planted artfully around the L&S TechWare flagpole, imagining how the fall foliage in the Ozarks might look at its height. He cursed under his breath, wondering how long it would take before he could focus totally on the here and now. *Here* was California and his work. *Now* was not then and certainly not the tomorrows he couldn't bring himself to contemplate.

He turned around to face his desk, where a computer monitor demanded his attention. He stood for a moment, massaging the back of his neck, ropy with tension. He'd snapped at his secretary this morning, alienated a longtime client and fouled up a set of important computations. And it wasn't even ten o'clock.

He slumped into his leather desk chair and started through the letters requiring his signature. Carl and others in the front office had been great about bringing him up to date after such a long absence. He wished he could care about the new projects they'd shepherded since he'd been gone. He threw his pen down in disgust. What the hell was the matter with him? Where was the energy and excitement the company had engendered in the past?

He'd been back a month now. Why couldn't he stop thinking about Arkansas? About Nell? Picturing her in the library. At home. And tousled and sweet-smelling in a warm bed still rumpled from love-making.

On an impulse he picked up his suit jacket and headed to the outer office. "I'll be gone for a few hours," he said to his startled secretary as he breezed out the door.

He had some thinking to do in a quiet place.

And he knew Brooke and Nicole would be good listeners.

BEN HADLEY WAVED from the back booth where he sat nursing a cup of coffee. Nell threaded her way between the tables and chairs and then sat down. "Sorry I'm late. I had a frantic morning. More children than I'd counted on showed up for story hour."

Ben smiled. "Sounds like a good problem to have." He passed her his menu. "Take your time. Catch your breath. I've decided to indulge. Barbecued pork sandwich and fries. My wife would kill me."

Nell winked over the top of the menu. "My lips are sealed."

They made small talk about their Thanksgiving plans and the fate of the Razorback football team until the waitress set their food down. Nell sniffed the air. "Hmm. That barbecue smells heavenly." She appraised the salad in front of her. "Wouldn't it be nice if lettuce had a tantalizing aroma, too?"

"But don't you feel virtuous?" Ben asked, teasingly.

"I don't know that I'd go that far, but my bathroom scales will be proud of me."

Nell studied Ben as she ate. A man with a ready smile, kind, knowing eyes and years of wisdom he graciously shared. Not only with her. With anyone in need.

Yet she knew his history. It wasn't pretty. If Ben could rise from the pit of alcoholism, anyone could.

With his napkin, he wiped a trace of barbecue sauce from his lips, then looked straight at her. "How long has it been now since your Brady left?"

She flinched at the *your*. "Five weeks."

"Have you had any further episodes like the one with the wine?"

"No, and with God's help, I won't. I've done quite a bit of thinking, and I realize Brady has to live his own life. When I accused him of being addicted, I meant it as a constructive comment. But I can't change him. It's not my place even if I somehow had that power. He's the only one who can do that."

"You told me once he had a history of running away."

Nell set down her fork. "I remember."

"Do you think he ran away from you this time?"

An interesting question. Nell sat back in the booth and gathered her thoughts. "In part. I blindsided him with news that had to be an awful shock. Truth is, I wasn't who he thought I was. He was entitled to walk away from me."

Ben waited. "But?"

"In reality, I think he ran away from himself."

"Go on."

"Like all of us, he has issues to resolve, but he doesn't want to. Is maybe afraid to. After what I said about his being addicted to anger and resentment, if he'd stayed, I'd have been a constant reminder of all that he's spent years fleeing."

"Can you live with that?"

Nell reached out and touched the older man's hand. "I'll have to, won't I?"

"What is this doing to you, Nell?"

"I'll be honest, Ben. That night, before I lived through my last drunk, I thought the world had ended. That losing Brady was going to be insurmountable. But somehow I made it. And I will continue making it. I have to. For Abby, of course. But, more important, for me."

"You have a lot of people pulling for you."

"I know that. The Serenity Prayer has never been truer for me. I can't change what's happened or who I am. I've had to accept that Brady is gone. Now I'm praying for the wisdom to keep my life in balance." She patted Ben's hand before withdrawing her own. "Thanks for getting together with me outside the group. We both know I had gotten lax about regular attendance at meetings. That left me without sufficient resources when Brady couldn't deal with my alcoholism." She smiled. "I won't let it happen again."

"Good," Ben said, picking up the check and shooing her off when she attempted to pay. He fumbled with his billfold and almost as an aside, tossed out, "What would you do if Brady did come back?"

"I don't think he will. Not until and unless he deals with his past. I'm not holding my breath."

After laying down some bills, Ben found her eyes and held his gaze steady. "But if he did?"

Nell's heart raced, even as she tried to control the impulse. "Oh, Ben, I'd love him with every fiber of my being."

Ben chuckled. "Then it looks like I better start praying for miracles."

"Can't hurt," Nell murmured as she slid from the booth. But it was too much to ask. She was grateful for her sobriety. She had no right to ask for more.

CARL AND HIS WIFE Jill had invited Brady to dinner. A delicious game hen with plum sauce, risotto, fresh broccoli, chocolate mousse. Hardly bachelor fare. Now, sitting on his host's patio holding a mug of coffee, Brady should have felt comfortable, relaxed. But the sight of Carl's and Jill's easy domesticity, the silent signals they sent practically without knowing, the ways they absently touched each other filled Brady with a loneliness he was powerless to banish.

The autumn sun was setting over the hills, fiery and spectacular. Jill had left to pick up their son from soccer practice. The pungent aroma of Carl's after-dinner cigar spiced the night air. How many times had he and Brooke enjoyed the Suttons' hospitality? Sat on this very patio, laughing, telling stories, dreaming big dreams?

Carl blew a puff of smoke into the air, then stretched out his legs. Brady gently sloshed his coffee, then took a small sip, willing it to relax him. It didn't.

At first, preoccupied, he didn't take in Carl's words. Then, like a delayed broadcast, they filtered through his reminiscences. "This isn't working, is it?"

Brady wanted to pretend he didn't know what his friend was asking. But he couldn't. "No," he said quietly.

"We've been friends a long time, Logan. I've tried my damnedest to be patient. To wait for you to speak up." He rolled the cigar between his thumb and third finger. "I want what's best for you. But you're gonna have to tell me what that is and somehow I don't think it's in California. Not anymore."

Brady was choked with emotion and his head felt as if it could crack open any time now. "It's like my whole life is in limbo."

"Work?"

"I don't know, Carl. I want to care. Get revved up, you know, like I used to in the old days. And yet..." He trailed off, wishing he could see a clear path, craving normalcy.

Carl took another puff of his cigar, then turned to Brady. "You can't?"

Brady shrugged impotently. "I'm letting you down. I know that. Hell, I can't expect you and the others to put up with my whatever-you-want-to-call-it. Midlife crisis, for lack of a better term."

"You've experienced a great loss. We understand that. But at some point—"

"I need to carry my weight." He paused. "Or sell." Before, it had been only a vague idea. Now the words were out, lending a resolve that hadn't been present before.

Carl didn't seem terribly surprised. "If you sell, what then?"

What then, indeed? "I don't know."

"I think it's time you told me about Nell."

Brady drank from his mug in an effort to mask the emotions generated by Carl's unexpected question. What was there to say? "It's over."

"Bull!" The word exploded from Carl's mouth. "You can talk all you want. But I know what I see. What's the story?"

Brady sighed. What the hell, he might as well get it over with. "She's a card-carrying member of AA," he said bitterly.

"So?"

"*So?* Is that all you have to say?" Brady set down the mug, then leaped to his feet and paced to the house and back. "My wife and daughter were killed by a drunk and I'm supposed to forget that and take up with an alcoholic?"

"How long has she been in recovery?"

"Six years."

"Jeez, pal, half the people you know are either borderline alcoholics or in recovery. Are you going to condemn them, too?"

Brady stopped his pacing. "What's your point?"

Raising the cigar, Carl inhaled its bouquet, apparently considering his answer. "My point? This— you're sounding pretty damn judgmental to me. Have you never made a mistake, Logan? Give her a break. Holding grudges is exhausting work. Transferring blame is doing a disservice to a lady who just might be the lifeline you need. So what's the worst thing that could happen?"

"She could start drinking again."

"Yeah. And you could continue being a self-absorbed, rootless jerk. What's the difference?"

Brady turned his back, his teeth clenched. First, Nell. Now, Carl. They both seemed to think he thrived on resentment. Slowly he pivoted to face Carl. "Is that what you believe I am?"

Carl shrugged. "If the shoe fits…"

"What is it you think I'm supposed to do? Go ahead, let me have it."

Carl stubbed out his half-smoked cigar and rose to his feet. He approached and clamped a hand on Brady's shoulder. "I love ya, buddy. You know that. But you seem determined to self-destruct. Much as I hate to say it, Arkansas was the best thing that's happened to you since Brooke and Nicole were killed. Your Nell must've had some rough times, but it sounds to me as if she's fought back. Her sobriety record is pretty darn good. Most important, she was enough of a woman to breathe life back into you. That's rare. If I were you, I'd think twice about walking away from her."

Brady stared out beyond the patio and the pool, overcome with conflicting emotions. He didn't like the reflection of himself he'd seen in Carl's words. "How do I just ignore her alcoholism?"

"You don't. You hang in there with her, giving her every reason to find joy in life. You love her, dumb-ass. It's plain as the nose on your face. You act like being an alcoholic is all she is. Sounds as if she's much more. For starters, the woman you love."

Brady was speechless. He couldn't dispute what

Carl had said. For one simple reason. Every word he had said rang true.

Carl engulfed him in a bear hug. "Go back to Arkansas, Brady. Go home."

Jill's return prevented Brady from blubbering like a baby. He would miss Carl, he realized.

But he had things to do.

WHEN THE PHONE RANG one evening late in October, Nell muted the PBS program she'd been watching and picked up the receiver. When she heard the voice on the other end, her heart sank. Rick. She'd been laboring under the illusion that no news from him was good news. What if he'd called to talk about custody? Would it matter to him that Brady was no longer in the picture?

His tone was more unctuous than usual. "Nell, I hope this is a convenient time. There's something I need to discuss with you. About Abby."

Nell could hardly manage a response. "What's that?"

She hadn't realized how tense she'd been until she heard his answer and felt her entire body turn to rubber. "I'm afraid it's not going to work out for Abby to come here next weekend."

"Oh? Why is that?"

"Well, you see, Clarice was able to score some tickets for the big Texas game in Austin."

"Couldn't Abby go with you? I know she'd enjoy seeing the campus."

"I'm not sure that would work. We've been invited to go with some friends in their motor home, er, you know. Not exactly a child-friendly environment.''

Understatement of the year, if she knew the type of friends Rick customarily attracted. ''Abby will be disappointed,'' she said, although she wasn't at all convinced that was an accurate description of Abby's likely reaction.

''I'd appreciate it if you'd pass the news on to her. Oh, and tell her we'll be looking forward to her November visit.''

Oh, no, you don't! Nell summoned her sweetest, most neutral tone. ''You can tell her yourself.'' Before Rick could protest, she started for Abby's room. ''She's right here studying. I'm sure she'll want to hear the news from you, rather than me.''

''But—''

She didn't hear the rest of Rick's protest, because she'd handed the phone to Abby. ''Here. It's your dad.''

Then she beat a hasty retreat. It was high time Rick quit using her as the middleman, assuming she would compensate for his shortcomings. With a shock of recognition, she realized that had been the role she'd always assumed back when she'd thought their marriage was working. She'd been the peacemaker, the one who ran interference for him, smoothed over any problems. Well, she was through with that. She allowed herself a chuckle of satisfaction as she settled back into the sofa. He was on his own now.

The television program had just concluded when Abby came into the room to return the phone. When

Nell looked up, she was surprised to find a scowl on her daughter's face. "What's wrong?"

"I don't get to go," Abby said, banging the receiver into the base unit.

Something in her tone alerted Nell. She'd assumed Abby would be relieved. "Would you have enjoyed going to the Texas game with a group of your father's adult friends?"

Abby stood with one knee bent on the arm of the sofa. "No."

"Help me, honey. I don't understand what the problem is."

Abby twisted the tail of her University of Arkansas T-shirt. "They don't want me to come."

"I don't think that's it at all," Nell said, although she wasn't convinced herself. "This may be a one-time deal."

"They could've stayed home from the stupid game," Abby persisted stubbornly.

"Yes, I suppose they could." Nell felt as if she were on shaky ground. It would be all too easy to say the wrong thing.

Abby gave a dramatic shrug. "Oh, well, me and Tonya can mess around this weekend, I guess."

"Tonya and I," Nell corrected automatically, sensing there was something important that hadn't been said. She took hold of Abby's arm and dragged her down beside her. Abby slouched over, her head hanging. Nell tipped up her chin. "Your dad loves you."

"Right." Abby's eyes burned with resentment.

Out of the blue, it struck Nell. "You're disappointed."

''Duh. He's my dad. I hardly get to see him at all.''

Once that remark would've threatened Nell, but now all she could focus on was her daughter's pain. ''It's been hard for you, hasn't it? Being without a dad in your life all the time.''

''It's not your fault. Or his, I guess. But Tonya's father is so cool. Sometimes I'm really jealous of her, you know?'' Her eyes were moist with unshed tears.

''I'm sorry we haven't talked about this recently. It must be hard on you.''

''I thought for a while that it would be okay. When Brady was here, I mean. He kinda reminded me of Tonya's dad.''

Nell winced. Was it possible Abby had actually entertained the idea of Brady as a stepfather? No wonder she was upset. She'd been betrayed on every side by the adults in her life. ''It's okay to feel let down. Hurt. But sometimes things don't turn out the way we'd hoped they would. This is one of those times.''

''I know that. I'm not a kid anymore.''

Nell reached around Abby's shoulder to draw her near. ''I've got news for you, kiddo. You'll still be my child when you're sixty-five. My grown-up child. That's the way it works.'' She dropped a kiss on Abby's hair, redolent with the strawberry fragrance of the latest fad shampoo. ''But that growing-up part is hard, isn't it? When you learn that adults have feet of clay, that people don't always behave the way you'd like and that sometimes they disappoint you big time.''

"Do you think Dad loves me?" Abby asked, her voice quivering.

"Without a doubt, honey. Without a doubt."

It was only later when she was getting ready for bed that Nell realized what Rick had *not* said. Not one word about custody or visitation. Somehow, she now understood, events like football weekends with friends would play an increasingly important role in her ex-husband's life. He would love Abby, all right. When it was convenient.

BRADY HAD CLEARED his desk, packed up and was finally able to leave California at the end of the week following his conversation with Carl. Although he had contacted his attorney about the repercussions of cashing out of the business, he still had not made a decision about his future—for one simple reason. He couldn't look ahead until he confronted his past.

He'd spent the hours behind the wheel barreling across the wide-open spaces of Nevada and Utah considering Nell's and Carl's judgments of him. For much of his adulthood, he had deliberately compartmentalized his life, dealing with his immediate family and his work and keeping the past locked away behind a barrier constructed of bitterness.

Nell had breached his defenses and Carl had stormed on through. The tight control he'd always exercised over his memories and emotions had slipped away, leaving him vulnerable. And scared. The closer he came to the Colorado border, the more like a lost boy he felt. He didn't want to go back into that world where his every action had been berated, where no one had bothered to mourn his mother, where he had no place.

But his self-respect demanded it. He had to move on and this step was the key.

He spent the night in Green River, Utah, tossing fitfully, falling asleep sometime after three. He showered, shaved and had breakfast in the motel dining room, wishing all the time he could delay the inevitable.

What would he find in Colorado?

The mileposts blurred as he continued east on I-70. His thoughts turned to the two-story early twentieth-century house he'd called home. His small bedroom had overlooked the barn and the mountains beyond and shared a common wall with his parents' room. He remembered balling his fists over his ears in the futile attempt to block out the squeak of the mattress as she pushed herself higher on the pillows, followed by her relentless cough. In vain he would wait for his father to help her. On the infrequent occasions when he did, he could hear his mother say, "That's all right, Dale. There's nothing to be done." Like an echo that single word had resounded in his head. *Nothing.*

Through the years he'd kept tabs on his family through data collected via the impersonal vehicle of the internet. Both his father and Velda were still alive. Still living on the ranch. His brother Danny taught and coached at the local high school.

Brady adjusted the car heater. Danny. There was a source of shame. When Danny was born, Brady had been eleven, far more interested in sports and horses than in a demanding baby brother. Then for a

time when his mother's condition deteriorated,
Danny had been farmed out to his grandmother.
Brady had never been close to his brother. For years
after he left home, he had felt guilty. On two occasions he'd tried to contact Danny, but by then it was
too late. Danny wouldn't even talk to him. Perhaps
Velda and his father had successfully turned his
brother against him—or he'd built up his own case
of resentment. After Nicole's birth, he had made one
last attempt to contact his brother. When he'd received no answer, he'd said the hell with it.

He'd been angry for a long time. Then anger had
turned to apathy. But beneath the surface, boiling like
hot lava, lay the resentment. And, damn it, the guilt
Nell had recognized. He'd been a teenager in turmoil—cocksure, defiant, hurt. He'd bargained with
the gods, then raged at them. How could they have
done this to his mother? To him?

Then had come his father's unthinkable betrayal,
moving Velda in mere weeks after they'd laid his
mother in her grave.

Even now, as he slowed for the Grand Junction
traffic, his stomach churned with the injustice of it
all.

He gnashed his teeth. So what was he doing anyway? What could he possibly accomplish?

Yet deep inside he knew he had to go through
these next few hours if he was ever to move on with
his life.

It was noon when he pulled into Glenwood
Springs. The town had grown some and new motels
and franchise restaurants bordered the highway, but
once he reached the center of town, he noticed fa-

miliar landmarks. He pulled into a service station and filled his gas tank. As he was paying his bill, a wizened little man with a Denver Broncos ball cap punched him on the arm. "Say, aren't you Brady Logan?"

Brady flushed. "Yes. I'm sorry, but—"

"Oh, I wouldn't expect you to recognize me. I'm Buster Fowler's dad. I only recognized you because you were such a jock in high school. Buster always wanted to be just like you."

Brady covered his confusion with a laugh. "Well, I hope he turned out better than that." Then he changed the subject to Buster, whom he barely remembered. "What's Buster up to these days?"

The man visibly swelled. "He has a great job with the *Denver Post.* Selling advertising."

Brady signed the credit card receipt, hoping to put an end to the conversation. "Good to see you."

He had made it halfway to the door when the man called out, "Say, we're sure proud of that brother of yours."

Brady wheeled around. "Oh?"

"Yeah, helluva basketball coach. Took us to state last year, you know."

No, he hadn't known. It had been a while since Brady had checked out Danny on the internet. "I hope he's as lucky this year."

Only after hearing about the four returning starters and a six-foot-six sophomore did Brady manage to extricate himself from the conversation.

On a whim, he detoured past the high school before heading for the ranch. He didn't know what he expected to see. Yet Mr. Fowler's words had brought to the surface memories of his own high school days. Memories that had lain buried for years. He was tempted to go inside. Find Danny. Get that part of his visit behind him.

But it wasn't the time. Or the place.

Or was he simply procrastinating? Avoiding the worst? The ranch. Velda. His father.

Near Carbondale he turned off the highway and traveled a few miles to the familiar dirt road. The mailbox, battered by time, looked as it always had, the "Logan" painted in crooked white letters.

As a matter of course, Brady didn't consider himself a praying man, but he was conscious of forming a word in his mind—over and over again. *Help.*

He pulled around to the side of the house and parked. On the back of the house was an addition. Maybe a family room. On the sidewalk, a golden retriever lifted its head, then ambled to its feet and approached his vehicle. Brady climbed out of the SUV and leaned down to pet the dog. "Easy, pal. I'm a friend."

Straightening, he took a deep breath and walked to the kitchen door. *Help.* He knocked.

He could hear a radio playing soft music, then the sound of someone moving to the door. He hadn't known what to expect, but not what he saw when the door opened.

Before him stood a roly-poly woman with soft reddish-gray curls and beautiful brown eyes partially concealed by a pair of granny glasses. The welcoming smile on her face faded and she raised trembling fingers to her lips. When she spoke, her voice cracked. "Brady?"

Only then did he recognize faint traces of the woman he had known years before, with her well-endowed body, long auburn hair and the flirtatious dark eyes that ate his father in one gulp. The woman who had called his mother *friend*. Nursed her. Then betrayed her by marrying his father in record time. "Velda?"

She stared straight at him, sadness and shock in her gaze. "It's been a while," she said.

"Eighteen years."

"I suppose I should be killing a fatted calf or something," she murmured dryly. "Instead, I'll just ask a simple question. What do you want?"

Damn good question. What *did* he want? Then the answer came. "It's time to make peace. If that's possible."

Cocking her head, she studied him for a few seconds before standing aside. "Come in."

When he stepped over the threshold, smells and sights inundated him, carrying him back to days when he couldn't wait to get off the school bus, run up the lane to the house—and into his mother's arms. "Thank you."

Velda gestured to the kitchen table. "Have a seat. Coffee?"

"Sounds good." Neither of them said a word until she'd poured the coffee and sat down across from him. He needed to pose the question burning in his gut. To stall, he took a swallow of the coffee, thinking about what he had to ask. "Where's Dad?" he finally said.

She nodded toward the pasture. "Over there. Mending fence."

"Do you think he'll talk to me?"

She shrugged. "That's entirely between you and him."

"You're not going to give me any help here, are you?"

"Seems to me you never wanted any, if I recollect right."

"You've got me there."

Velda lifted the lid of the sugar bowl, then dipped out a teaspoonful. Stirring it into her coffee, she went on. "You never cared much for me, either."

"There were reasons."

She nodded. "Yes. There were. But there was a lot you didn't know. Didn't want to know, I imagine."

Was she trying to prepare him for something? Her tone was neither hostile nor welcoming, but she was hardly the home-wrecking siren he'd imagined her to be. "We all made some mistakes back then."

For the first time she allowed the wisp of a smile to cross her face. "Is this a new Brady Logan? One actually willing to listen?"

He had to give her credit. She wasn't backing away from painting an accurate picture of him as a teen, no matter how unflattering.

"I don't know if there's any way to deal with what happened."

"Listening's a step. The main thing is—you're here. Dale needs to know." She took hold of his hand. "Why don't you wander out to the pasture. Find your father."

Fear, oily and hot, sat in his stomach. "That's what I came to do." He stood, then paused, looking down at the small woman. Harmless. Honest. "I'll listen, Velda."

"Good," she said behind him as he walked out the kitchen door.

A cold wind blew down the valley as he made his way through the gate and across the pasture. In the distance he could see a figure in a sheepskin rancher's coat bent over a fence post. It required an effort of will to take each step that closed the distance between them. Finally, when Brady was about twenty feet from his father, the man looked up.

His body stilled and his gnarled hands closed around the fence stretcher he held. His weathered skin bore deep wrinkles and his chapped lips formed a thin line. His eyes, still steely blue, narrowed.

The man was...old. How had that happened? Somehow Brady had always pictured the father he'd known as a teenager—ageless, rock-hard, unyielding. He braced himself, awaiting his father's judgment.

But Dale Logan surprised him. He dropped the implement in his hand, then approached Brady. As if no time at all had elapsed since they'd seen each other, he simply said, "Let's go to the house, son."

The vise constricting Brady's chest loosened and he could breathe again. He'd called him *son.* That didn't erase the pain of the past, but it was a start.

Maybe that's all they needed. A start.

CHAPTER FOURTEEN

NEITHER MAN SPOKE as they walked toward the house, its white frame silhouetted against the distant mountain range now shadowed by dark clouds. Expecting to feel detachment, Brady was ill-prepared for the memories, long submerged, which rose to his consciousness or for his sense of connection to this place.

And certainly not for the impulse of something akin to affection he felt for his father.

He plunged his hands into his pockets, fighting his weakness. Or would Nell call it forgiveness? He'd been wronged, damn it. He couldn't afford that luxury.

He *would* think of Nell at a time like this, her gaze tender even as she accused him of addiction. Resentment and anger had fueled many of his actions, but, by now, they were familiar companions. Could he give them up? Was she asking too much?

Inside the house, his father took off his coat and slung it across the back of a kitchen chair, then hung his Stetson on a peg near the door. Brady, likewise, draped his coat over a chair while Velda filled his coffee cup and another for his father. Then she looked inquiringly at Dale, sending one of those messages that pass between a man and a woman that requires no words.

His father sat down in the place across the table from Brady. "Stay, Velda. You're part of this, too." Without a word, Velda slipped into the chair beside her husband.

Dale lifted his cup and blew on the steaming liquid. Finally he fixed his eyes on Brady. "Why now?" was all he said.

Brady considered his answer. "Because someone I care about accused me of being addicted to the anger and pain of my past. She suggested it would be therapeutic for me to face my demons."

His father's eyes were cold. "Is that how you think of us?"

Brady felt defensiveness kick in. "I never understood. I still don't."

"What? Spill it, son."

Brady fingered the distressed wood of the kitchen table, remembering the long-ago times he'd gripped the edge of this same table as an anchor in the sea of his rage. "Didn't you care about Mom at all?" He was surprised to hear the crack in his voice.

"Is that what you think? That I didn't care?"

"You tell me." He nodded at his stepmother. "Sorry, Velda, but, Dad, you certainly didn't waste any time moving on, did you? Did you ever stop for one minute to think how that made me feel? It was as if you didn't care. You planted Mom in the ground and then, within two months, remarried. You expected me to just accept that. To forget all about my mother." The coffee in his stomach soured.

Velda's eyes darkened with concern. "We didn't let you grieve, did we, Brady?"

"I've grieved for years." He stared at his father. "You're the one who never grieved."

His father slumped in his chair. "You couldn't be more wrong."

"Well, excuse me, if I fail to see it."

"You're still angry." His father made the words a statement.

"Damn right."

"I tried to talk to you back then. So did your mother. You wouldn't listen."

"To what?"

"The plans we made for what would happen when—" his father stumbled over the words "—when she died. You refused ever to hear us out. You'd stomp out of the room."

"What plans? What are you talking about?" It was all Brady could do to remain seated.

Velda covered Brady's hand with her own. "Your mother picked me."

"Picked you for what?"

Dale raked a hand through his thinning hair. "Let me start at the beginning. Your mother knew about Velda."

Surely he wasn't hearing correctly. "Knew what?"

"That she was a godsend during the last weeks of her illness. That she was a kind woman and a good friend. Your mother had been sick for so long, but she was always loving. Always thinking of others. She didn't want me to be alone. Didn't want you boys to be motherless. She'd known Velda for years.

Liked her. I was torn up with grief and, well—'' he patted his wife's arm ''—Velda was there for me.''

''But you married so quickly.''

''I'd grieved for years before your mother died. I couldn't do it any more. It was either lose myself or start a new life. I had your mother's blessing. I didn't see any reason to wait.''

Brady leaped to his feet. ''What about me? Wasn't I reason enough to wait? Danny?''

''Like I said, there was no talking to you. You were determined not to hear.''

Brady paced the floor, finally bracing himself against the counter, his back to his father. ''Hear what exactly?''

From behind him came the explanation, told in a labored voice by the man he'd spent years hating. The shock of his mother's diagnosis, her long illness, his parents' agonizing over the future, over what would become of their sons. Even as her health declined, his mother's insistence that her husband get his rest, her refusal to let him do for her what she could still do for herself.

Brady closed his eyes. That explained those awful nights when his mother's relentless coughing spells went unattended by his father.

''I begged her to let me help,'' his father continued, ''but she knew I needed my strength for the ranch.'' There was a long silence broken only by the furnace blower and icy raindrops flicking at the kitchen window. ''Toward the end, she began talking about what would happen to us—you, me, Danny. She understood how heavily I had come to depend on Velda, the one friend I knew I could count on day or night.''

Stirring in Brady was a vague recollection of coming home from school to find Velda reading to his mother.

"It was your mother who first suggested that I take another wife. Quickly." He cleared his throat. "She wanted it to be Velda."

Brady turned to face them. "Still, you didn't waste any time."

"I had loved your father and mother for a long time," Velda murmured. "We would never have proceeded without your mother's blessing."

"I hated you," Brady said, addressing his father.

"I know. And in a way I hated you. You wouldn't listen to us when we tried to explain, not to me and not to your mother. It was as if you didn't want to hear the truth—that your mother was terminal. Then, afterward, you took all your grief and anger out on me."

"If you understood that, why did you treat me so badly?"

He raised his eyes and expelled a deep sigh. "I was wild with the pain of losing your mother. Worried sick about the future. Anger was my outlet, I guess, and you gave me plenty of cause to unleash it."

"You were like two wounded bears," Velda said.

"You'd grown physically big and strong, Brady. I thought you could take it. You were my whipping post. I forgot you were still just a kid."

"You made some pretty unreasonable demands."

"I did some things I'm not proud of. I couldn't

deal with my emotions where you were concerned. Maybe I was afraid of letting you get too close. Afraid what it would do to me if something happened to you or Danny.'' He snorted at the irony. ''Pretty screwed-up thinking when you consider what I did was drive you away.''

Brady saw himself at eighteen, standing in the doorway, his backpack slung over his shoulder, facing his father. *I hate you for forgetting about Mom. For marrying that slut. If I never see you again, it'll be too soon.* And his father's cutting reply. *Get out!*

''Why didn't you ever look for me?''

''I could ask you the same thing.''

Brady sat back down, studying his coffee cup.

Velda smiled sadly. ''You're two of the stubbornest men I know.''

Brady quirked his lips. ''Must run in the family.'' His father seemed lost in thought. Brady took a swallow of the tepid coffee, then set the cup down before continuing. ''What now?''

''Are you still so angry?'' his father asked.

Brady looked up, aware of an inner calmness he hadn't felt…maybe ever. ''No,'' he said with wonderment.

''Could you…would you tell us about these missing eighteen years?'' The hardness in his father's eyes had disappeared.

Brady sat back in his chair. ''Yeah,'' he said, ''I think I can. But first, Velda, I owe you an apology.''

She smiled. ''Accepted.''

He nodded, breathed deeply and then began speaking. Neither his father nor Velda said a word during his recitation—the odd jobs that had led to a junior college computer course, losing himself in the world of cyber-technology, meeting Carl, moving to California, setting up the company.

But then, a huge lump formed in his throat. He struggled to talk about Brooke, then Nicole and, ultimately, the accident. At that point his father reached across the table and grasped his hand in an iron grip. Brady fell silent after telling about the collision.

"I understand that kind of grief," his father said.

When Brady looked into his father's eyes, he knew he was hearing the truth.

"And after that?" Velda prompted.

It was almost six when Brady finally finished. Unbelievably, he'd found himself telling them about Nell and Abby, about the chance for a new life he'd walked away from.

"You have a history of turning your back, son. Any idea why?"

His brain buzzed and his chest went hollow. "No," he said. But he *did* know. It wasn't something he felt like sharing now with others. He reviewed his boyhood, his youth, the recent months. The answer lay before him. Clear. Uncompromising. He hadn't felt worthy of love. Not after his mother died—and then Brooke and Nicole. He had convinced himself he deserved punishment.

Velda stood. "I better get us some supper. But before I do, I want to tell you something, Brady. I remember you as a teenager. You always felt things deeply and not always temperately. Your emotions were intense. I don't imagine you've changed much. Take that intensity and turn it to good. Love your Nell and Abby."

Brady pondered her advice. After leaving here all those years ago, he'd thought he could insulate himself from hurt. He'd let down his barricades with Brooke and Nicole. And then had come the accident followed by his self-inflicted emotional imprisonment. Until Nell. If he were to go back to Arkansas, it would have to be with openness and trust, and he didn't know if that was possible.

His father, too, rose to his feet. When Brady looked into his eyes, he saw something astonishing. Approval. "Reckon we better phone Danny and get him over here," he said.

"Yeah," Brady said, clenching his hands. "I guess I have some explaining to do. I abandoned him."

"He idolized you," his father said quietly.

"I, uh, tried a coupla times to get in touch with him. He never responded."

Velda arched an eyebrow. "Any wonder? He inherited that stubborn gene, too."

Dale laid a hand on Brady's shoulder. "Lucky thing, I guess, that it's not too late. Right, son?"

Brady swallowed hard, then nodded, his voice lost somewhere in the vicinity of his heart.

NELL WAS LATE getting to her mother's house for Lily's birthday party. She'd had to stop at the store, then pick up Abby at Tonya's.

Abby sat beside her in the front seat, cradling Lily's wrapped gift. "How old is Aunt Lily anyway?"

"Thirty-six."

"Yikes. I didn't think she was that old."

That old. Nell managed a bitter smile. At thirty-four, she, too, must be totally over the hill in her daughter's estimation. "Next thing you know we'll both be using walkers."

Abby glanced up at her. "I didn't mean it like that."

"I know, honey. We must seem ancient to you."

"I guess you can't be too old if you and Brady could fall in love."

What was it with the girl? She wouldn't leave it alone. Almost daily she found a way to insinuate Brady's name into the conversation. "Why do you keep talking about him?"

"I miss him, I guess."

Nell pulled to the curb in front of her mother's house and parked the car. "It's unrealistic to think like that. Brady is gone."

"But I just keep hoping—"

"What? That he'll mysteriously reappear? That we'll get back together?"

Head down, Abby studied the package in her lap.

"We have to move on, honey. I'll be fine. I *am* fine."

"Grandma doesn't think so."

Nell rolled her eyes. When would her family quit second-guessing her? "Could we please just get out of the car and go to the party?"

Abby shrugged. "I guess."

All the way up the walk, Nell concentrated on reducing her pulse rate. This was supposed to be a festive occasion, she reminded herself.

"Darlings!" Her mother threw open the door and

held out her arms in greeting. "We were worried when you were late."

Nell grimaced. Worried about what? That she'd started drinking? That she'd been in an accident? "The grocery store was crowded. My shopping took longer than I thought."

"Nell, is that you? At last?" Lily, dressed in a stunning mauve pantsuit, joined them in the hall. "I kept telling Mother you'd be right along."

"Happy birthday," Nell said, kissing her sister on the cheek.

Lily beamed, then dropped an arm around Abby's shoulder. "And how's my favorite niece? I understand you have a boyfriend. I want to hear *all* about him."

They made their way into the living room, where Evan was sprawled on the carpet playing trucks with Chase. He looked up with a smile. "Hi, Nell, Abby."

Abby added their gift to those stacked on the coffee table, then joined Chase and Evan on the floor.

"So what exciting things have you been doing on your birthday?" Nell inquired.

"Let's see. The florist delivered roses from Evan about ten, then I met my book club for lunch and this afternoon I had the most divine massage."

"Sounds heavenly."

Narrowing her eyes, Stella studied Nell. "You could use a massage. You look tense. Stressed."

"Now that you mention it," Lily leaned closer, "you do look a bit pinched."

A bit pinched? A line straight out of Jane Austen. "I'm fine," Nell said.

"You haven't heard from that Brady person?"

"No, Mother. I didn't expect to."

Lily intervened. "Mother, Nell doesn't need this."

Ignoring Lily, Stella laid a hand on Nell's leg. "And you're sure you're all right with that?"

Nell tried to be fair. Her mother had every right to be concerned, just as she would be if Alan Voyle broke up with Abby. "No, but that's the reality, like it or not. Aren't you actually asking something else?"

"What, dear?"

Lily's eyes rounded in sudden understanding.

"Whether I've been drowning my sorrows, so to speak."

"Nell!" Stella covered her bosom with the flat of her hand. "Why, we never—"

"Yes, you have. But I'm beginning to understand what you've been telling me. It's because you love me and want the best for me. I can't argue with that." She leaned forward and went on more calmly. "I need you to trust that I will persevere and remain sober because *I* want to. This is *my* problem and I'm the only one who can address it.

"We all know there will be difficult times. But, look. I made it through this episode with Brady without a drink. I don't intend to let anybody down. Especially myself."

"Oh, honey," Stella whispered, her eyes shiny with tears.

"I simply have to take each day as it comes."

Abby, who had clearly been eavesdropping, scooted across the floor and rested her head in Nell's lap. "I'm proud of you, Mom."

Lily looked fondly at Nell. "Me, too."

Stella hesitated, then added her endorsement. "And Mother makes three."

Nell ran her hand over Abby's silky hair, the ball in her stomach dissolving. "Thank you. I feel better already."

"We all do," Lily said.

Stella stood and waved her arm at the birthday presents. "Well, for heaven's sake, ladies, let's get this celebration underway. Lily's birthday and Nell's new tomorrows."

Then her mother winked at her, a gesture that included only her. Not Lily. Not Abby. A gesture that made Nell believe she'd finally gotten her point across—and was still, and always, loved.

BRADY HAD STAYED three days in Colorado before hitting the road. Now, headed toward Arkansas, he had the leisure to reflect on his visit. It had not been an easy time. There had been too many years and too much history to overcome in one brief visit. Too many misunderstandings. Especially with Danny, who had seemed unable to give Brady the same benefit of the doubt his father had.

How could he have been so oblivious at the time to his brother's sensitivity and grief? Had Brady thought he had a corner on the market?

Sure, Danny had been living with their grandparents during that last year, but why hadn't he kept in better touch? Gone to see him? The kid had to have been scared shitless.

So how could he blame his brother for his lack of enthusiasm when he learned Brady had returned?

Danny hadn't been rude, exactly. Just indifferent. As if he didn't trust Brady to maintain the relationship they'd started.

Hell, why should Danny trust him? Much as Brady hated to admit it, Nell had been right. He'd fed on his own bitterness and let far too many years pass without confronting himself and what had happened during that awful senior year. When Brooke had challenged him to face the past, he'd shut her out, just as he had anyone who'd ever questioned him. Until now.

The highway climbed steadily toward Vail Pass, and Brady idly wondered how far he could get today. How long before he reached Arkansas? The intervening miles stretched painfully in front of him. Miles he needed for some deep thinking.

What awaited him when he arrived? He had to be sure about his intentions before he approached Nell. This time he couldn't question her.

Look what had happened because he'd failed to listen to his parents. But trusting Nell was different. It meant forgiving her and giving up his unfair association of her with the man responsible for the deaths of his wife and daughter. It meant living in the present, not the past.

He'd never seen her drunk and he didn't want to. Ever. But he needed to be prepared for that eventuality—and for his role in supporting her sobriety. If he made a commitment to her, he would be in it for the long haul, warts and all.

By her honesty, she'd given him back his life. Was he willing to help do the same for her?

"C'MON, ABBY, just once around his block."

Abby, astraddle her bicycle, threw Tonya a disgusted look. "What're you gonna do if we see him?"

"Swoon." Tonya sped off down the street.

Reluctantly, Abby followed, knowing she'd die of embarrassment if Mr. Sanders, their English teacher, spotted them. She had to admit he was adorable and way cool, but she didn't understand why Tonya was wasting her time on somebody that old. Why didn't she find someone her own age, like one of Alan's friends?

Besides feeling geeky about Mr. Sanders, it was kinda sad being in this neighborhood. She couldn't help remembering that day she'd come down this same street on her way to Brady's condo. How nice he'd been. Kinda like a father.

Her mom had really, really liked him. She was trying to act brave now, but Abby could tell she was sad. Sorta like the light in her eyes was set on dim.

Ahead of her, Tonya pumped her fist and pointed toward a small house wedged between two three-story apartment buildings. It had all these cars in the front yard and looked like a hangout for college guys. But she guessed that's sorta what Mr. Sanders was. He was a first-year teacher, just out of the U of A.

Loud stereo music boomed from an open window, but even going past slowly, they couldn't see anyone. Tonya stopped at the corner, then shrugged when Abby drew alongside. "Crap. No stud spotting today."

Abby gazed beyond her friend and saw in the distance the entrance to Brady's condominium complex. It was getting dark, but surely it wouldn't hurt to ride by. She could show Tonya where Brady had lived.

"Follow me," she said, pulling into the intersection ahead of Tonya.

"Where're we going?" Tonya called, but Abby just kept pedaling toward the condominium, all the time feeling queasy with regret. He was never coming back.

She stopped at the edge of the lot, where Tonya caught up with her. "What're you looking at, Abby?"

"There." She pointed toward Brady's unit. "That's where my mother's boyfriend lived."

"He's gone, though, right?"

Abby's toes curled inside her sneakers. "Yeah," she said quietly. Why was she about to cry? This was stupid. She hardly knew the man. It wasn't like he had ever planned on being part of their family or anything. But she was convinced he'd really cared about her. She loved her dad, of course, but sometimes she felt like he didn't know much about daughters. Not like Brady did. You could tell how much he'd loved Nicole.

"Hey, dorkess, what are we standin' here for? I gotta get home."

"Okay," Abby said. She straddled her bike, then paused for one last look at the condo.

What she saw caused her to grip the handlebars so tightly her knuckles whitened. *Oh, please, oh, please* she found herself imploring, her breath coming in tiny gasps. *Let it be him.*

An Escalade had turned into the far entrance to the parking lot. Abby motioned Tonya to follow as she concealed herself behind a hedge.

"What are you doing?" Tonya demanded.

"Shh." Abby narrowed her eyes, waiting to see if it could possibly be. The Escalade parked, then a man wearing a ball cap climbed out—a tall man with broad shoulders. Abby crossed her fingers, continuing her mantra, afraid to trust her eyes. What if she was wrong? He opened the tailgate, gathered some luggage and, unbelievably, made straight for the right condo unit.

"Omigod," Abby breathed.

"What?"

"It's him. Brady. He's back."

Tonya moved closer, squinting through the branches. "Wow," she breathed. "For an old guy, he's a hunk."

They watched until he closed the front door and then slowly pedaled back the way they had come. Tonya tried to talk to her, ask her all these nosy questions, but Abby didn't have anything to say.

Was he back for good? Or just coming to pick up some stuff he'd left?

Maybe it didn't matter. The important thing was that he *was* back and that gave her mother a chance.

And a chance was better than nothing.

All the way home Abby plotted her strategy. She was just a kid, but this time she wasn't going to mind her own business. Or was she? Maybe this was her business, too.

NELL SHOOK OUT the towels as she moved them from the washer to the dryer. Tearing off a sheet of fabric softener, she passed it under her nose before adding it to the load. The manufacturer had come darn close to the scent of fresh spring air.

Spring. Her favorite time of year. With fortitude and patience, in April she would get her seven-year chip. Few outside of AA had any understanding of the significance of these milestones. She was proud of each of her chips and, after her recent close call, had made a vow to relive those high points, which could be equally as motivating as the low moments.

Humming to herself as she turned on the dryer, Nell reflected on the change in her mother since the night of Lily's party. She no longer prefaced comments with "Lily and I think..." and her recent phone calls had been chatty rather than thinly veiled inquisitions.

Nell turned to the laundry table and began folding the underwear she'd taken out of the dryer earlier, acknowledging the relief she felt now that things were back to normal, or whatever passed for normal. After Brady had left, she'd settled back into the routine of work, meetings and family. Maybe she'd only imagined that brief window of opportunity when she'd glimpsed a future that had included Brady. Even then, though, she had understood he wasn't ready for commitment—not until he made some kind of peace with what had happened to his wife and daughter. And with his early years in Colorado about which he refused to speak. However, she'd been hopeful that with time...

Nell smoothed a half slip, then folded it in thirds. Part of what she'd loved about him was the very fact that he cared so deeply. There was nothing superficial or contrived about his emotions. He was a man capable of loving passionately.

Damn. She wished she hadn't used that word with

its painful reminders of warm, soft lips, exploring fingers and eager, aching flesh. She ran her hands over the slip, wondering if she ever would've dared to wear something exotic, tantalizing…maybe one of those see-through teddies or….

"Mom! You'll never guess what!"

Nell started. She hadn't even heard the front door. She grinned, wondering what late-breaking development in Abby's life led to the mega-decibel volume of her voice.

"Where are you?" Abby's exasperated tone was hard to miss.

"In the utility room." Nell gathered the folded clothes to her chest and stepped into the kitchen.

Breathless, Abby stopped in the doorway, her face red from exertion, her eyes snapping with excitement. "I rode home as fast as I could. I couldn't wait to tell you the news."

"What news, honey?"

"He's back!"

Had she missed something? Had Alan Voyle been on a trip? "Who? Alan?"

Abby spread her arms in triumph. "Duh, Mother. Brady!"

She clutched the laundry more tightly. "What do you mean?"

"I saw him, Mom. He didn't see me, but I know it was him. He drove that same kind of car and went into that same building."

Nell felt sick. She made it to the table, laid the clothes down and sank into a chair. He was here. In Fayetteville. But he hadn't called. Hadn't come by.

"Are you all right?" she could hear Abby asking.

"Yes," she said, aware she was flat-out lying to her daughter.

Abby pulled a chair from the table and, drawing one foot up under her, sat down. "Don't you see? Everything's going to be all right."

"Abby, calm down, it's—"

"All you have to do is go see him. It's simple."

Nell wished with all her heart that she could view the world from such an idealized perspective. "No, I can't. If he wants to see me, he'll call."

Abby blew the hair off her face. "Mo-ther. That's so retro. It's the twenty-first century. You don't have to sit around waiting for a man."

"If he'd been interested, he'd have called by now."

Abby glanced at her watch. "Give him time. He only just got to town."

Nell's heart shifted into triphammer speed. "How do you know?"

"When Tonya and I spied on him, he was unloading bags from his car."

Nell wouldn't, couldn't get her hopes up. He'd just come to town to finalize his move back to California. Nell reached over and patted her daughter's hand. "You have to get used to it, honey, as I have. Brady is a wonderful man, but he won't be part of our lives."

"Bull!" Abby leaped from her chair. "He loves you. You love him. All you have to do is march over there and tell him. I betcha he feels the same way."

"It wouldn't be proper."

"Adults!" Abby rolled her eyes before putting her hands on Nell's shoulders. "You're the one always talking to me about taking risks. About how you have to be willing to stick up for what you believe. To go after what you want.''

If the subject hadn't been so serious, Nell would've been tempted to smile. Abby was right. She had preached all those lessons—and now they were coming back to haunt her. ''I can't.''

Her daughter shook her gently and gave her a skeptical look. ''Don't turn chicken on me, Mom. If you don't go for it now, you'll look back and always wish you had.''

Nell shrugged in defeat. When the kid was right, she was right!

CHAPTER FIFTEEN

BRADY PULLED OFF the rutted road at the edge of the resort property and sat in the Escalade, amazed at the way the view had opened up now that many of the trees had shed their leaves. In the early morning cold, condensation off the lake created clouds of mist that moved, specterlike, across the blue surface of the water. On the far hillside a few trees still displayed vivid colors.

His option was nearly up. It was decision time. Good sense dictated he should abandon his foolish dream, but, then, good sense had nothing to do with the excitement he'd been helpless to prevent when he crossed the state line into Arkansas. Nor with the sense of well-being generated by the scene before him.

He stepped out of his vehicle, shouldered a day pack and started off through the woods, awed by the scent of pine and the chatter of birds darting from limb to limb. He didn't want to think about the power this land exerted over him. It was either a major weakness or a sign. And he didn't believe in signs.

Or did he? What else to call his stumbling across Nell's message at the Edgewater Inn?

Nell had called the bed-and-breakfast a sanctuary. Was that what he had been seeking? He halted, his

attention arrested by several buzzards wheeling overhead. Nature. Predator. Prey. Cyclical. Ever the
same, ever different. A far cry from Silicon Valley.

As he tramped on, he was able to name what this
place meant to him. Freedom from the past. New
beginnings. Serenity. Yes, even a sanctuary.

But part of that sense of connection and belonging
rested with Nell. More of her words came back to
him. *I have to believe that somewhere out there is
someone for me. Someone I can trust. Someone I can
love.*

He had hurt her with his condemnation of her
drinking. With his self-righteous judgment, his leap
to make her the scapegoat for his own anger. Before
going to Colorado, he had never thought of himself
as a black-and-white thinker. Yet he had painted his
father and Velda with the monochrome of rancor,
when, in fact, the situation had been far more complex.

Reaching a large limestone outcropping, he
dropped his pack and sat on the edge, his feet dan-
gling. A squirrel skittered past, intent on gathering
his store of winter acorns.

He had been unfair to Nell. He'd put off calling
her or going to see her. This time he had to be sure.
She was deserving of the best a man could give her—
and for her that meant trust and love. No matter what.

If he was truthful, it was the ''no matter what''
that scared him. Yet no one knew better than he that
life doesn't come with guarantees. Certainly he'd
never imagined Brooke and Nicole's accident.
Maybe it was the things you didn't worry about that

caused the gravest problems, so what was the point of borrowing trouble?

Some things were in his control. Facing his fears. Loving Nell for the wonderful woman she was, not the desperate one he'd never known. Trusting her.

He leaned back on the cool rock, pillowing his head in his linked hands. A sudden thought came to him—powerful and affirming. His personal storm had passed, and in its aftermath, he now realized, was his rainbow—Nell.

He laughed aloud, a sound joyous and free. He, too, was a believer in rainbows.

NELL SAT at her office desk trying to read book reviews in the *Library Journal*. Yet her concentration was shot and she found herself rereading every three or four lines.

Two days had passed since Abby's announcement, and Nell still hadn't heard from Brady. She'd thought a lot about Abby's suggestion that she go to him, but ultimately it had to be his choice whether he could live with an alcoholic.

Yet even as that thought surfaced, her inner demon—or angel?—accused her. *So you're willing to leave it all up to him? You've lived "safe" a long time. What about taking a chance? How else will you know what might have been? Why settle for "safe" when you might have "fulfilling?"*

She threw down the magazine and plunged her hands through her hair. She didn't need voices like that haunting her, eroding her carefully constructed world, exposing her loneliness.

What about Abby? Oh, yes, her guardian spirit had

to bring that up. Somehow, in a very short time, Brady had become important to her daughter. Could she overlook that? Especially when the girl's own father found parenting difficult?

Get off it, Nell. Give up the rationalizations. You love the man. You think that comes without risk? But there's no prize without risk. You want rainbows? Okay. They come at a cost.

Nell stood up and looked around her office, where she'd accomplished absolutely zilch in the past two days. This state of affairs simply couldn't go on.

All right, she would do it. She would see him. She would go prepared for anything—even rejection.

And with her heart in her hands.

NELL SHRUGGED INTO her red all-weather coat, waved goodbye to Reggie Pettigrew who was manning the checkout desk and slipped out of the library. A hard freeze was predicted for tonight and the air was already sharp with cold. Head down against the strong north wind, she hurried toward her car. She would get this over with this afternoon. Abby had a late basketball practice and it was the Larkins' turn to pick the girls up. If Brady was at home, she would have the ordeal behind her before dinner. Then she could settle things with Abby once and for all.

Tripping over a crack in the sidewalk, she nearly fell, saved only by a strong arm around her waist. "Careful."

When she looked up, her breath stopped. "Brady?" His serious expression put her on guard.

"I've been waiting for you."

"Oh?" She could think of nothing further to say,

the awkwardness between them an impediment to rational thought.

"We need to talk."

When she stepped back and raised her head, the wind whipped strands of hair into her face. "You're right. Abby told me you were back."

"How did she know?"

"She saw you."

Putting his hands in his pockets, he studied her, his expression difficult to read. "I should've called."

"I wasn't expecting it."

He nodded, as if she'd confirmed something he already knew.

It was now or never. "I agree that we need to talk. In fact, I was just on my way to see you."

"I said some awful things to you."

"And I withheld the truth."

He moved closer and it required all her self-control not to reach up and brush her fingers over his cheek. Her breath came raggedly. She was even more attracted to him than she'd remembered. More than anything, she craved the comfort of his embrace.

Then his gaze caught hers and in it she saw a flicker of yearning. He lifted his hand and smoothed the hair out of her eyes. "Do you have time now?"

Not trusting herself to speak, she nodded.

"Could you come to my place? I want to show you something."

"I'll follow you," she said.

He walked her to her car. Once she was behind the wheel, he held the door just long enough to murmur, "Be careful. I don't want to lose you now."

Nell's hand shook as she turned the ignition key.

She couldn't read too much into those words. He was just being polite. Or maybe he was talking about losing her in traffic.

But what if he meant he didn't want to lose *her?* What if she could permit herself hope?

Nell discovered something as she followed Brady to his condominium. Time passes more easily when you're praying.

HEEDLESS OF THE strong wind, Brady waited outside for Nell, knowing that the next hour or so would determine his entire future. He'd been unprepared for his reaction when he'd first seen her outside the library. All other considerations had evaporated in the rush of love that had swept over him—followed by fear, empty and cold. What if he was too late?

Yet when she'd said she had been on her way here, he'd relaxed. Maybe there was a chance. He'd already lost so much. He couldn't lose her.

She turned into the parking space next to his and he hurried to meet her. "Come along inside. I'll brew us a hot cup of coffee."

She smiled and his heart thawed. "I'd like that."

He took her by the arm and, once inside, took her coat, then ushered her to the ugly oversize sofa. "Make yourself at home, or as much at home as possible in this mausoleum. I'll be right back."

He carefully measured the coffee, added water and flipped on the switch, rehearsing in his mind what he would say to her, how he could convince her of his change of heart. From the pass-through he could see her head bent over a magazine she'd picked up from the coffee table. His throat thickened. He didn't want to talk. He wanted to pull her into his arms and carry her down the hall to his room, where the one redeeming feature of this furnished condo waited—a feather-soft, king-size bed.

She looked up expectantly when he entered the room. "This ought to warm you up," he said, handing her a mug, then taking a seat at the opposite end of the sofa.

"Thank you." When she carried the cup to her lips, her downcast eyelashes reminded him of the morning she'd covered his bare chest with butterfly kisses that drove him wild. "It's very tasty."

He smiled. "My specialty."

She looked at him. He looked at her. It was a silence suspended between hope and fear. Finally she said, "What now?"

He couldn't stand the waiting a second longer. "Why were you coming here this afternoon?"

Leaning forward, she set down her coffee before turning toward him. Her eyes glittered and when she spoke, her voice was raspy. "To see if there was a chance." She hesitated. "And to tell you I love you."

Dizzying waves of relief washed over him. In a flash he had moved beside her and pulled her into his arms. "Nell, sweetheart, I love you, too." He buried his mouth in her hair, smelling of sunshine, wind and green, growing things. He framed her face between his hands and looked into those deep eyes he'd dreamed about every single night they'd been apart.

Her hands tightened on his shoulders. "I haven't changed. I...I'll always be an alcoholic."

"You're much more than that." He kissed each eyelid, then her nose. "You will always and forever be the woman I love."

"I've been so afraid."

"Of what?"

"That you wouldn't come back." She seemed to struggle to go on. "Or that you'd reject me."

He chuckled. "Funny. I was afraid of the same thing. After the ugly things I said, I knew I'd blown it with you."

"So why did you come back?"

"I had to take the chance it wasn't too late."

"But I said some pretty awful things to you, too."

"All of which were right on target." He leaned back against the sofa, pulling her with him. "I *was* addicted."

She lifted her head. *"Was?"*

"How much time do you have?"

She shrugged. "I don't know. How much do you need? I should leave before six-thirty. Abby gets home from basketball then."

Two hours. It had to be enough. "That should do it. I need to tell you some things."

Somehow unburdening himself was easier with her by his side, the warmth of her body soothing years of pain. He started with his childhood, the mother he'd adored, her lingering illness and death, then the abrupt change when his father had married Velda. His unwillingness to listen. His anger and rebellion. His abandonment of Danny. The decision to put the first eighteen years of his life behind him. She already knew about Brooke and Nicole, but he found he needed to go through it all again. Even the accident. He ended with his recent visit with his father and the beginning they'd made. It was nearly six when he finished. "I can't live any longer with anger, resentment and grief."

"Acceptance," she whispered. "It isn't easy."

"No," he agreed. "It isn't."

"You loved your mother very much. Perhaps it's only lately that you've mourned her, along with Brooke and Nicole."

He looked at her. "I'd never considered that, but I think you're right."

"No wonder you were in such pain."

"Until I met you." He traced her hairline with a finger.

"You're sure?" The question in her eyes revealed fragility and vulnerability and conveyed far more than the words suggested.

He knew this was the defining moment. He had to be certain. Anything less would be a disservice to her and a betrayal of himself. This meant commitment. Unconditional love. Still clasping her, he stood up, drawing her with him. He held her, then, at arm's length, studying her beloved face. "Dearest Nell, I am absolutely, positively certain."

"Oh, Brady." She sagged against him and before he knew what he was doing, he found her lips, his body fiery with need. She met his tongue thrust for thrust, her mouth warm and sweet. "I've missed you so much," she whimpered.

"I'm not leaving," he said. Then, pulling back and taking her by the hand, he led her into the spare bedroom, which he'd converted to a makeshift office.

"Remember, I told you I have something to show you." He ushered her through the door, then stood behind her, his arms circling her waist. "What do you think?"

He heard her tiny gasp, before she pivoted in his arms. "Brady, is that what I think it is?" Her eyes were shining.

"It's the architect's initial rendering for the Vista Inn and Resort." Before he'd left for California he'd commissioned this preliminary step. He could have canceled out. He could have let his option lapse. But he hadn't. Deep down, he'd always known why. He was destined to come home. To Arkansas. To Nell.

"It's beautiful," she breathed, the admiration in her eyes humbling.

"No," he corrected. "It's nice. You're beautiful." He held her lightly, sliding his hands down her back, over her rounded hips. "What time did you say you had to be home?" He nuzzled her neck.

"Soon," she murmured langorously. "Too soon."

He bent his head and began unbuttoning her blouse, rimming the top of her bra with his forefinger. "Sure you couldn't stay a little longer?"

She thrust her hands inside the back of his trousers, the pressure on his buttocks increasing the urgency threatening to send him over the edge. "Maybe I could call the Larkins."

"Sounds like an inspired idea," he said, easing her blouse over her shoulders and partway down her arms.

"I need to use the phone," she managed to say between kisses.

"No problem," he said, propelling her down the hall. "There's one in the bedroom."

An hour later, sated and spent, he cuddled Nell's satin-smooth body into his, thanking his lucky stars for the Larkins' flexibility and his landlord's bed that had more than lived up to its promise. Way more.

"OMIGOD, OHMIGOD." Abby burst through the front door mere minutes after Nell arrived home. She had just stepped out of the shower, having cleansed from her body the traces of lovemaking that made her weak in the knees just thinking about it. She'd even decided maybe she would dare to buy that sheer teddy she'd fantasized about.

Gathering her terry-cloth robe around her, she knotted the sash and stepped into the hall. "What's the matter? Did something happen at practice?"

Abby was practically jumping up and down with excitement. "You'll never believe it."

What now? "I'm all ears."

"I've gotta show you. Come into my room." Abby dumped the contents of her backpack on the floor, then rifled through books, pens and notebooks until she came up with a rumpled piece of computer paper. "In computer class today we had an assignment to look up someone we knew on the internet to see what information was there."

"So?"

"I picked Brady." She thrust the paper into Nell's hands. "Go ahead. Read."

She looked down at a print-out of an article from the *Wall Street Journal*. The title meant nothing to her. "Silicon Valley Creates Instant Millionaires." She let her eyes scan the sheet until she found Brady's name, followed by the words, *entrepreneurial genius, estimated worth $50,000,000*. Nell collapsed into Abby's desk chair. For a minute, she was afraid she was going to pass out.

Abby bounced from one foot to the other. "Isn't that exciting?"

Nell thought about it. No wonder he could afford to hit the road for months following the accident, take an option on the Beaver Lake land, drive an expensive vehicle. Why hadn't he told her? This sounded like some crazy imitation of a reality TV show. She couldn't help herself—she erupted in shaky, manic laughter.

Abby did a double take. "Mom, are you all right?"

"I think maybe your news changes everything. No way is he going to stay in Fayetteville, Arkansas."

"Mom, don't you get it? It's like he's Prince Charming."

Nell hiccupped, caught between laughter and tears. "Be that as it may, but I have a feeling this Cinderella is back to scrubbing pots and pans and cleaning the fireplace."

"I don't believe you."

"Why on earth not?"

"Because you've seen him, haven't you? You've told him how you feel."

Abby was way too sharp. "How on earth would you know that?"

"Well, duh, Mother." She pointed to the collar of Nell's robe. "Look at your neck. You've got a hickey the size of a headlight!"

NELL WENT AROUND the next day at work adjusting the silky scarf wrapped around her neck, hoping no one besides Abby would detect the all-too-visible signs of an enchanted hour of lovemaking. The smug grin had not left Abby's face since. This morning before she'd left for school, she'd shot Nell a knowing look, then said, "Lookin' good, Mom."

But the hickey blooming at the base of her throat was the least of her worries. Fifty million dollars! An unthinkable amount, almost obscene. She couldn't begin to wrap her mind around that information. How could Brady have withheld such a vital part of himself? There was no way he would turn his back on his lucrative business. And no matter how much she loved him, she couldn't uproot Abby and leave her family. California was glitzy and foreign. This was her home, the place where she'd wrestled with addiction, where she felt safe, secure.

She stood at the copy machine, lost in thought. The truth was, his wealth scared her to death. Just like her alcoholism had to scare him.

She gathered up the flyers and returned to her office, eyeing the clock. Half an hour to go. Then home. To Brady. Before she'd left him yesterday afternoon, she'd invited him to dinner tonight. Knowing Abby would be at the high school football game, Nell had originally envisioned an intimate evening— soft, romantic music, flickering candles, good food.

And, just in case, she'd thought about putting fresh sheets on the bed.

But Abby's bombshell had changed all that. Now instead of a flirtatious smile, she'd greet Brady with a huge question and butterflies in her stomach.

BRADY HAD BEEN euphoric all day. Everywhere he looked was something to like—the smogless blue skies, the hometown-friendly store clerks, the harvest decorations bedecking most front porches. Yet the hours until he could be with Nell again had passed too slowly. His heart warmed every time he thought about her sweet, spontaneous responses to his love-making. She had no idea what a sexy, desirable woman she was. Rick must've been an idiot.

Or the wrong man. The next thought brought a grin to his face. Heck, maybe all along she'd been waiting for him. Well, her waiting days were over. Now that he'd come back to her, he would never let her go. Life, he'd learned, was too short to be eaten up by grudges and pain.

Yet sitting here at the dining room table after her delicious pork roast dinner, with the light from two tapers the only illumination in the room, he sensed something was out of kilter. Nell had been abnormally quiet, the silences filled by the mellow strains of dinner music. When she had talked, it had been about work, Abby and AA. Especially AA. As if she was trying to warn him off. She'd confessed to her bout with temptation when he'd left to return to California. He recognized that she needed to tell him the worst, so he let her relate each detail of the night of her accident and of her recent struggle.

As she talked his stomach churned, both with memories of Brooke and Nicole and the all-too-real eventuality she painted for him. No more kidding himself. Her sobriety was hard-earned. Always there would be the fragile balance between will and temptation. Yet he'd told her he was certain about his feelings and about his commitment.

He studied her across the table. Her skin was pale above the soft robin's-egg blue sweater she wore. Her serious gray eyes spoke volumes about her struggles—and her fears.

Yet in that moment he loved her more than he could ever have thought possible. Whatever the future held, they would face it together. He waited until she finished talking. She sat, hands folded in her lap, head bowed.

"Okay," he said. "That's out of the way."

She looked up. "What do you mean?"

"The attempt to run me off. It didn't work, Nell. So now, how about the truth?"

"The truth?"

"Yes. Why are you so hell-bent to put obstacles in our path?"

"Obstacles?" Her mouth flattened to a thin line. "Since you're so into the truth, why don't you come clean, too?"

What was she talking about? "I don't know what you mean."

"The little detail about yourself you forgot to mention."

He hadn't a clue. "Detail?"

She reached into the pocket of her skirt and drew out a folded piece of paper. She handed it to him. "Were you ever going to tell me?"

He unfolded the sheet of paper and scanned the contents. That damn *Wall Street Journal* article. Why was she looking at him with such resignation? Such sadness? "What about it?"

"Brady, my God, you're a millionaire."

"So?" What in hell was the problem?

"You didn't tell me."

"No, I didn't. You know why? Because it isn't important. It's just money, most of it on paper. I hardly ever think about it. Yes, I can live well and that's nice, but the money itself is meaningless."

"How can you say that?"

"Because my success was never about money. It was about proving to my old man that I'd amount to something after all."

"Oh."

"Does it matter?"

"I can't live in California, Brady. I'm a home-body."

Now he understood. She thought he was going back to California, that he expected her to adapt to his lifestyle, when in fact it was just the other way around.

He circled the table and knelt beside her chair. "You're too late, Nell."

She bit her lip, then spoke. "When do you go?"

If she hadn't looked so forlorn, he'd have chuckled. Instead, he rose to his feet, took her by the hand, then pulled her into his arms. "I'm not going any-where, especially not without you."

Her voice quavered. "What do you mean?"

"I bought the land today."

"You did?"

"And that's not all. I've rented office space, hired a project architect and am in the process of setting up an Arkansas corporation. I like Arkansas—the land, the people, everything. Above all, I love you. Money and success mean nothing if you don't have someone with whom to share them. You and Abby are my 'someones' and you'll have one heckuva time getting rid of me."

She trembled in his arms and he wrapped her even closer. "So you're an alcoholic and I'm a million-aire. Big deal. I can put up with you if you can put up with me." He tilted her chin and smiled down at her. Her face was alight with hope, a flame he wanted to tend for as long as he lived. "Marry me, Nell."

No sooner were the words out of his mouth than the front door banged and Abby came barreling into the room. Talk about timing.

"Oops, sorry," she said, doing a theatrical about-face.

"No, wait, Abby," Brady said, still holding Nell in his arms. "Help me out here."

Abby turned around, cocked her head and studied him. "Sure. Whaddya need?"

He nodded down at Nell. "Convince the woman to marry me."

"Mo-om—" Abby sprinted across the room and

joined the hug. "Are you crazy?" Then Abby grinned at him. "Of course she'll marry you."

The two of them stepped back and looked at Nell, who turned from one to the other, her eyes glistening, her cheeks pink. "Are you ganging up on me?"

"If that's what it takes," Brady said.

Nell seemed about to speak, but hesitated. Brady's heart was in his throat. She moved to put an arm around Abby. "Are you sure, honey? You know what this means?"

Abby stood up tall. "Yes. It means you'll have a husband who loves you and I will have a way cool stepfather."

Nell gazed at her daughter for a long moment. The love in her eyes almost hurt Brady to watch. Then she turned those same eyes on him. "I would be honored, Brady."

He enclosed his new family in his arms, home at last. A chuckle rose from deep in his belly. "It's not every day a fella gets two lovely females for the price of one."

NELL DETAINED Ben Hadley after her Saturday morning meeting the next day. "Walk me to my car?" she asked.

"It would be my pleasure," he said gallantly taking her by the elbow.

It was a gorgeous November day, sunny and cloudless with the kind of chill that brings roses to the cheeks. "I have news," Nell said as they exited the church.

Ben kept walking. "And what would that be?"

"I'm getting married."

He dropped her arm, took off his hat and, with wild abandon, threw it into the air. "Hallelujah and amen!" After he retrieved his hat, he faced her, beaming with unadulterated joy. "How did that come about?"

Her eyes danced. "Let's put it this way. I accepted some things I couldn't change, had the courage to change some things about myself and finally had the wisdom to know the difference."

Throwing her arms around the older man who had always been there for her, she whispered, "Oh, Ben, my name is Nell and I am loved."

EPILOGUE

NELL STEPPED OUT of the bathroom, pulling her satin peignoir closer around her. Brady, in plaid flannel pajama bottoms, lounged on the striped love seat in one corner of their cozy bedroom in the Edgewater Inn. A floor lamp cast soft light across the room. She could feel the pulse in her neck quickening as her eyes fixed on his bare chest. Despite having been married before, this felt like her first honeymoon. Like a real honeymoon.

He held out an arm, beckoning her to join him. She snuggled against him, reveling in the sea-fresh aphrodisiac of his cologne. "It was a great wedding, wasn't it?" he said, fondling her shoulder.

"It couldn't have been better. I hadn't realized how moved I would be by having our family and friends all together." She smiled, remembering her mother beaming from her first-row pew; Lily, radiant in a deep purple dress; Chase prancing up the aisle as ringbearer; her co-workers and many of her AA friends gathered to wish her well. She would never forget the moment when the organ swelled and she took Ben's arm as he led her toward her handsome groom.

She continued, "How special it was that your dad and Velda could be here." Although the situation had been somewhat awkward, Stella had taken the matter in hand and made his parents welcome. "Did you mind about Danny?"

A shadow fell across his face. "I would've liked him to be my best man. But I guess our relationship will take time. At least he answered my last e-mail."

"Well, Carl filled in beautifully. I enjoyed meeting him and Jill."

"They're great people." He sat quietly for a moment, then went on, "Abby was a gorgeous maid of honor. If you hadn't been such a beautiful bride, I'd have had a hard time keeping my eyes off my new daughter."

"I was so proud of her."

"Do you think she'll be all right in Dallas while we're gone?"

"Now that she's accepted you as part of her family, I think she's realized she has to make more of an effort with her father and Clarice. She told me the other day that maybe there were some things she hadn't understood. That maybe she hadn't given them much of a chance."

Brady chuckled as he played with her hair. "Sounds like she's growing up."

Nell sighed. "Too fast."

"But just think," he said, moving his hand to part the collar of her peignoir, "that'll leave all the more time for us."

Nell nestled her head into his neck and rubbed gentle little circles over his chest with her fingertips. "That could be good," she agreed.

"Say, before you get me too hot and bothered to think straight, I have a confession to make."

Her hand stilled. Not another one. She had had it with surprises. She lifted her head. "What?"

"You think I brought you here to the Edgewater Inn because you told me about it in the library that time, right?"

"Of course."

"That's not why."

"It isn't?"

"Nope." He leaned across her to retrieve a small journal from the lamp table. "You've stayed in this very room before."

The inn wasn't that big. She'd thought it mere coincidence. "How did you know?"

He thumbed through the book, flattened it to one page and handed it to her. "Recognize this?"

Nell read her entry in disbelief. *I've been so alone. When you've loved and lost, doubt replaces hope, insecurity replaces confidence and you wonder who you are. Whether you can go on. Or even want to.* She had actually been that woman, sent off to the restful bed-and-breakfast by her mother and sister following her final divorce hearing. She read on, her eyes filling with tears as she remembered that Nell. *This time of quiet and contemplation has been a great gift, restoring my belief that no matter how severe the storm, rainbows can happen. Regardless of how desolate I feel right now, I have to believe that somewhere out there is someone for me. Someone I can trust. Someone I can love. When I find him, the two of us will come to the Edgewater Inn. Together.*

When she glanced up, Brady was studying her, his

eyes bathing her with love. "I came looking for you."

"I...I don't understand."

"I didn't care about anything. I'd lost hope. And then I read your entry. You understood how I felt, but with one difference. You believed in rainbows."

"And?"

"I decided I wanted to meet the rainbow woman." He picked up her hand, urging her understanding. "That's why I came to Fayetteville."

"Brady, that's wild. I can hardly believe it."

"Believe it." He took the book from her and flipped through more pages, then settling on one, handed it back to her. "Read."

He moved closer, putting his arm back around her, his warm breath stirring the hair at the back of her neck. Whispering the words aloud, she began to read the firm, clear handwriting. *For most, this place is a sanctuary. I would like to believe it could be. I read in these pages of celebration, new beginnings, old joys revisited. Only in one entry have I found another who understands pain. Nell, whoever you are, if there are such things as rainbows, help me find them. Then maybe, just maybe, we* will *come back here together.*

She drew a stuttering breath. If it was possible to feel more love for another, to be more loved by another, she couldn't imagine it. "I never knew," she murmured.

"The only thing that matters is that I found you, my beautiful Nell."

When he pulled her against him and lowered his

lips to hers, she didn't even realize her robe had fallen open revealing the lacy see-through teddy she'd bought especially for him. For her rainbow man.

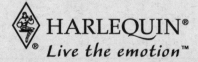

An offer you can't afford to refuse!

High-valued coupons for upcoming books

**A sneak peek at Harlequin's newest line—
Harlequin Flipside™**

**Send away for a hardcover by *New York Times*
bestselling author Debbie Macomber**

How can you get all this?

Buy four Harlequin or Silhouette books during
October–December 2003, fill out the form below and send
the form and four proofs of purchase (cash register receipts)
to the address below.

I accept this amazing offer!
Send me a coupon booklet:

Name (PLEASE PRINT)

Address   Apt. #

City   State/Prov.   Zip/Postal Code
                                                          098 KIN DXHT

Please send this form, along with your cash register receipts
as proofs of purchase, to:

In the U.S.:
Harlequin Coupon Booklet Offer, P.O. Box 9071, Buffalo, NY 14269-9071

In Canada:
Harlequin Coupon Booklet Offer, P.O. Box 609, Fort Erie, Ontario L2A 5X3

Allow 4–6 weeks for delivery. Offer expires December 31, 2003.
Offer good only while quantities last.

HARLEQUIN®
Live the emotion™

Silhouette®
Where love comes alive™

Visit us at www.eHarlequin.com

Q42003

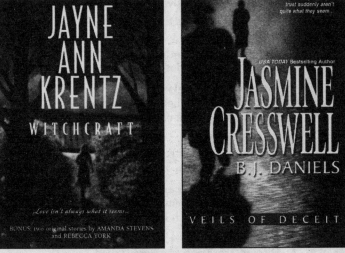

If you enjoyed what you just read,
then we've got an offer you can't resist!

Take 2 bestselling love stories FREE!

Plus get a FREE surprise gift!

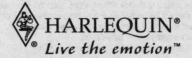